Praise for *Starfish* (A *New York Times* Notable Book)

"Fizzing with ideas, and glued together with dark psychological tensions: an exciting debut."
—*Kirkus*

"Watts makes a brilliant debut with a novel that is part undersea adventure, part psychological thriller, and wholly original."
—*Booklist*

"No one has taken this premise to such pitiless lengths—and depths— as Watts."
—*New York Times*

Praise for *Blindsight*

"Intellectually challenging...."
—*Publishers Weekly*, starred review

"Watts continues to challenge readers with his imaginative plots and superb storytelling."
—*Library Journal*

"A brilliant piece of work, one that will delight fans of hard science fiction, but will also demonstrate to literary fans that contemporary science fiction is dynamic and fascinating literature that demands to be read."
—*The Edmonton Journal*

Also by Peter Watts

Novels

The Rifters Trilogy

Starfish (1999)

Maelstrom (2001)

βehemoth (2004) (Published in two volumes as

βehemoth: β-Max and *βehemoth: Seppuku*)

Blindsight (2006)

Crysis: Legion (2011)

Echopraxia (forthcoming 2014)

Collections

Ten Monkeys, Ten Minutes (2002)

PETER WATTS
BEYOND THE RIFT

PETER WATTS

BEYOND THE RIFT

Tachyon | San Francisco

Tachyon Publications
1459 18th Street #139
San Francisco, CA 94107
(415) 285-5615
www.tachyonpublications.com
tachyon@tachyonpublications.com

Series Editor: Jacob Weisman
Project Editor: Jill Roberts

ISBN 13: 978-1-61696-125-1

Printed in the United States of America by Worzalla

First Edition: 2013
9 8 7 6 5 4 3 2 1

CONTENTS

THE THINGS

I am being Blair. I escape out the back as the world comes in through the front.

I am being Copper. I am rising from the dead.

I am being Childs. I am guarding the main entrance.

The names don't matter. They are placeholders, nothing more; all biomass is interchangeable. What matters is that these are all that is left of me. The world has burned everything else.

I see myself through the window, loping through the storm, wearing Blair. MacReady has told me to burn Blair if he comes back alone, but MacReady still thinks I am one of him. I am not: I am being Blair, and I am at the door. I am being Childs, and I let myself in. I take brief communion, tendrils writhing forth from my faces, intertwining: I am BlairChilds, exchanging news of the world.

The world has found me out. It has discovered my burrow beneath the tool shed, the half-finished lifeboat cannibalized from the viscera of dead helicopters. The world is busy destroying my means of escape. Then it will come back for me.

There is only one option left. I disintegrate. Being Blair, I go to share the plan with Copper and to feed on the rotting biomass once called *Clarke*; so many changes in so short a time have dangerously depleted my reserves. Being Childs, I have already consumed what was left of Fuchs and am replenished for the next phase. I sling the flamethrower onto my back and head outside, into the long Antarctic night.

I will go into the storm, and never come back.

I was so much more, before the crash. I was an explorer, an ambassador, a missionary. I spread across the cosmos, met countless worlds, took communion: the fit reshaped the unfit and the whole universe bootstrapped upwards in joyful, infinitesimal increments. I was a soldier, at war with entropy. I was the very hand by which Creation perfects itself.

So much wisdom I had. So much experience. Now I cannot remember all the things I knew. I can only remember that I once knew them.

I remember the crash, though. It killed most of this offshoot outright, but a little crawled from the wreckage: a few trillion cells, a soul too weak to keep them in check. Mutinous biomass sloughed off despite my most desperate attempts to hold myself together: panic-stricken little clots of meat, instinctively growing whatever limbs they could remember and fleeing across the burning ice. By the time I'd regained control of what was left the fires had died and the cold was closing back in. I barely managed to grow enough antifreeze to keep my cells from bursting before the ice took me.

I remember my reawakening, too: dull stirrings of sensation in real time, the first embers of cognition, the slow blooming warmth of awareness as my cells thawed, as body and soul embraced after their long sleep. I remember the biped offshoots that surrounded me, the strange chittering sounds they made, the odd *uniformity* of their body plans. How ill-adapted they looked! How *inefficient* their morphology! Even disabled, I could see so many things to fix. So I reached out. I took communion. I tasted the flesh of the world—

—and the world attacked me. It *attacked* me.

I left that place in ruins. It was on the other side of the mountains— the *Norwegian camp*, it is called here—and I could never have crossed that distance in a biped skin. Fortunately there was another shape to choose from, smaller than the biped but better adapted to the local climate. I hid within it while the rest of me fought off the attack. I fled into the night on four legs, and let the rising flames cover my escape.

I did not stop running until I arrived here. I walked among these new offshoots wearing the skin of a quadruped; and because they had not seen me take any other shape, they did not attack.

And when I assimilated them in turn—when my biomass changed and flowed into shapes unfamiliar to local eyes—I took that communion in solitude, having learned that the world does not like what it doesn't know.

I am alone in the storm. I am a bottom-dweller on the floor of some murky alien sea. The snow blows past in horizontal streaks; caught against gullies or outcroppings, it spins into blinding little whirlwinds. But I am not nearly far enough, not yet. Looking back I still see the camp crouching brightly in the gloom, a squat angular jumble of light and shadow, a bubble of warmth in the howling abyss.

It plunges into darkness as I watch. I've blown the generator. Now there's no light but for the beacons along the guide ropes: strings of dim blue stars whipping back and forth in the wind, emergency constellations to guide lost biomass back home.

I am not going home. I am not lost enough. I forge on into darkness until even the stars disappear. The faint shouts of angry frightened men carry behind me on the wind.

Somewhere behind me my disconnected biomass regroups into vaster, more powerful shapes for the final confrontation. I could have joined myself, all in one: chosen unity over fragmentation, resorbed and taken comfort in the greater whole. I could have added my strength to the coming battle. But I have chosen a different path. I am saving Childs's reserves for the future. The present holds nothing but annihilation.

Best not to think on the past.

I've spent so very long in the ice already. I didn't know how long until the world put the clues together, deciphered the notes and the tapes from the Norwegian camp, pinpointed the crash site. I was being Palmer, then; unsuspected, I went along for the ride.

I even allowed myself the smallest ration of hope.

But it wasn't a ship any more. It wasn't even a derelict. It was a fossil, embedded in the floor of a great pit blown from the glacier. Twenty of these skins could have stood one atop another, and barely reached the lip of that crater. The timescale settled down on me like the weight of a world: How long for all that ice to accumulate? How many eons had the universe iterated on without me?

And in all that time, a million years perhaps, there'd been no rescue. I never found myself. I wonder what that means. I wonder if I even exist any more, anywhere but here.

Back at camp I will erase the trail. I will give them their final battle, their monster to vanquish. Let them win. Let them stop looking.

Here in the storm, I will return to the ice. I've barely even been away, after all; alive for only a few days out of all these endless ages. But I've learned enough in that time. I learned from the wreck that there will be no repairs. I learned from the ice that there will be no rescue. And I learned from the world that there will be no reconciliation. The only hope of escape, now, is into the future; to outlast all this hostile, twisted biomass, to let time and the cosmos change the rules. Perhaps the next time I awaken, this will be a different world.

It will be aeons before I see another sunrise.

This is what the world taught me: that adaptation is provocation. Adaptation is incitement to violence.

It feels almost obscene—an offense against Creation itself—to stay stuck in this skin. It's so ill-suited to its environment that it needs to be wrapped in multiple layers of fabric just to stay warm. There are a myriad ways I could optimize it: shorter limbs, better insulation, a lower surface:volume ratio. All these shapes I still have within me, and I dare not use any of them even to keep out the cold. I dare not adapt; in this place, I can only *hide*.

What kind of a world rejects *communion*?

It's the simplest, most irreducible insight that biomass can have. The more you can change, the more you can adapt. Adaptation is fitness, adaptation is *survival*. It's deeper than intelligence, deeper than tissue; it is *cellular*, it is axiomatic. And more, it is *pleasurable*. To take communion is to experience the sheer sensual delight of bettering the cosmos.

And yet, even trapped in these maladapted skins, this world doesn't *want* to change.

At first I thought it might simply be starving, that these icy wastes didn't provide enough energy for routine shapeshifting. Or perhaps this was some kind of laboratory: an anomalous corner of the world, pinched off and frozen into these freakish shapes as part of some arcane experiment on monomorphism in extreme environments. After the autopsy I wondered if the world had simply *forgotten* how to change: unable to touch the tissues the soul could not sculpt them, and time and stress and sheer chronic starvation had erased the memory that it ever could.

But there were too many mysteries, too many contradictions. Why these *particular* shapes, so badly suited to their environment? If the soul was cut off from the flesh, what held the flesh together?

And how could these skins be so *empty* when I moved in?

I'm used to finding intelligence everywhere, winding through every part of every offshoot. But there was nothing to grab onto in the mindless biomass of this world: just conduits, carrying orders and input. I took communion, when it wasn't offered; the skins I chose struggled and succumbed; my fibrils infiltrated the wet electricity of organic systems everywhere. I saw through eyes that weren't yet quite mine, commandeered motor nerves to move limbs still built of alien protein. I wore these skins as I've worn countless others, took the controls and left the assimilation of individual cells to follow at its own pace.

But I could only wear the body. I could find no memories to absorb, no experiences, no comprehension. Survival depended on blending in, and it was not enough to merely *look* like this world. I had to *act* like it—and for the first time in living memory I did not know how.

Even more frighteningly, I didn't have to. The skins I assimilated continued to move, *all by themselves*. They conversed and went about their appointed rounds. I could not understand it. I threaded further into limbs and viscera with each passing moment, alert for signs of the original owner. I could find no networks but mine.

Of course, it could have been much worse. I could have lost it all, been reduced to a few cells with nothing but instinct and their own plasticity to guide them. I would have grown back eventually, reattained sentience, taken communion and regenerated an intellect vast as a world—but I would have been an orphan, amnesiac, with no sense of who I was. At least I've been spared that: I emerged from the crash with my identity intact, the templates of a thousand worlds still resonant in my flesh. I've retained not just the brute desire to survive, but the conviction that survival is *meaningful*. I can still feel joy, should there be sufficient cause.

And yet, how much more there used to be.

The wisdom of so many other worlds, lost. All that remains are fuzzy abstracts, half-memories of theorems and philosophies far too vast to fit into such an impoverished network. I could assimilate all the biomass of this place, rebuild body and soul to a million times the capacity of what crashed here—but as long as I am trapped at the bottom of this well, denied communion with my greater self, I will never recover that knowledge.

I'm such a pitiful fragment of what I was. Each lost cell takes a little of my intellect with it, and I have grown so very small. Where once I thought, now I merely *react*. How much of this could have been avoided, if I had only salvaged a little more biomass from the wreckage? How many options am I not seeing because my soul simply isn't big enough to contain them?

The world spoke to itself, in the same way I do when my communications are simple enough to convey without somatic fusion. Even as *dog* I could pick up the basic signature morphemes—this offshoot was *Windows*, that one was *Bennings*, the two who'd left in their flying machine for parts unknown were *Copper* and *MacReady*—and I marveled that these bits and pieces stayed isolated one from another, held the same shapes for so long, that the labeling of individual aliquots of biomass actually served a useful purpose.

Later I hid within the bipeds themselves, and whatever else lurked in those haunted skins began to talk to me. It said that bipeds were called *guys*, or *men*, or *assholes*. It said that *MacReady* was sometimes called *Mac*. It said that this collection of structures was a *camp*.

It said that it was afraid, but maybe that was just me.

Empathy's inevitable, of course. One can't mimic the sparks and chemicals that motivate the flesh without also *feeling* them to some extent. But this was different. These intuitions flickered within me yet somehow hovered beyond reach. My skins wandered the halls and the cryptic symbols on every surface—*Laundry Sched*, *Welcome to the Clubhouse*, *This Side Up*—almost made a kind of sense. That circular artefact hanging on the wall was a *clock*; it measured the passage of time. The world's eyes flitted here and there, and I skimmed piecemeal nomenclature from its—from *his*—mind.

But I was only riding a searchlight. I saw what it illuminated but I couldn't point it in any direction of my own choosing. I could eavesdrop, but I could not interrogate.

If only one of those searchlights had paused to dwell on its own evolution, on the trajectory that had brought it to this place. How differently things might have ended, had I only *known*. But instead it rested on a whole new word:

Autopsy.

MacReady and Copper had found part of me at the Norwegian camp: a rearguard offshoot, burned in the wake of my escape. They'd brought it back—charred, twisted, frozen in mid-transformation—and did not seem to know what it was.

I was being Palmer then, and Norris, and dog. I gathered around with the other biomass and watched as Copper cut me open and pulled out my insides. I watched as he dislodged something from behind my eyes: an *organ* of some kind.

It was malformed and incomplete, but its essentials were clear enough. It looked like a great wrinkled tumor, like cellular competition gone wild—as though the very processes that defined life had somehow turned against it instead. It was obscenely vascularized; it must have consumed oxygen and nutrients far out of proportion to its mass. I could not see how anything like that could even exist, how it could have reached that size without being outcompeted by more efficient morphologies.

Nor could I imagine what it did. But then I began to look with new eyes at these offshoots, these biped shapes my own cells had so scrupulously and unthinkingly copied when they reshaped me for this world. Unused to inventory—why catalog body parts that only turn into other things at the slightest provocation?—I really *saw*, for the first time, that swollen structure atop each body. So much larger than it should be: a bony hemisphere into which a million ganglionic interfaces could fit with room to spare. Every offshoot had one. Each piece of biomass carried one of these huge twisted clots of tissue.

I realized something else, too: the eyes, the ears of my dead skin had fed into this thing before its removal. A massive bundle of fibers ran along the skin's longitudinal axis, right up the middle of the endoskeleton, leading directly into the dark sticky cavity where the growth had rested. That misshapen structure had been wired into the whole skin, like some kind of somatocognitive interface but vastly more massive. It was almost as if...

No.

That was how it worked. That was how these empty skins moved of their own volition, why I'd found no other network to integrate. *There* it was: not distributed throughout the body but balled up into itself, dark and dense and encysted. I had found the ghost in these machines.

I felt sick.

I shared my flesh with thinking cancer.

Sometimes, even hiding is not enough.

I remember seeing myself splayed across the floor of the kennel, a chimera split along a hundred seams, taking communion with a handful of offshoots called *dog*. Crimson tendrils writhed on the floor. Half-formed iterations sprouted from my flanks, the shapes of dogs and things not seen before on this world, haphazard morphologies half-remembered by parts of a part.

I remember Childs before I was Childs, burning me alive. I remember cowering inside Palmer, terrified that those flames might turn on the rest of me, that this world had somehow learned to shoot on sight.

I remember seeing myself stagger through the snow, raw instinct, wearing Bennings. Gnarled undifferentiated clumps clung to his hands like crude parasites, more outside than in; a few surviving fragments of some previous massacre, crippled, mindless, taking what they could and breaking cover. Men swarmed about him in the night: red flares in hand, blue lights at their backs, their faces bichromatic and beautiful. I remember Bennings, awash in flames, howling like an animal beneath the sky.

I remember Norris, betrayed by his own perfectly copied, defective heart. Palmer, dying that the rest of me might live. Windows, still human, burned preemptively.

The names don't matter. The biomass does: so much of it, lost. So much new experience, so much fresh wisdom annihilated by this world of thinking tumors.

Why even dig me up? Why carve me from the ice, carry me all that way across the wastes, bring me back to life only to attack me the moment I awoke?

If eradication was the goal, why not just kill me where I lay?

Those encysted souls. Those tumors. Hiding away in their bony caverns, folded in on themselves.

I knew they couldn't hide forever; this monstrous anatomy had only slowed communion, not stopped it. Every moment I grew a little. I could feel myself twining around Palmer's motor wiring, sniffing upstream along a million tiny currents. I could sense my infiltration of that dark thinking mass behind Blair's eyes.

Imagination, of course. It's all reflex that far down, unconscious and immune to micromanagement. And yet, a part of me wanted to stop while there was still time. I'm used to incorporating souls, not rooming with them. This, this *compartmentalization* was unprecedented. I've assimilated a thousand worlds stronger than this, but never one so strange. What would happen when I met the spark in the tumor? Who would assimilate who?

I was being three men by now. The world was growing wary, but it hadn't noticed yet. Even the tumors in the skins I'd taken didn't know how close I was. For that, I could only be grateful—that Creation has *rules*, that some things don't change no matter what shape you take. It doesn't matter whether a soul spreads throughout the skin or festers in grotesque isolation; it still runs on electricity. The memories of men still took time to gel, to pass through whatever gatekeepers filtered noise from signal—and a judicious burst of static, however indiscriminate, still cleared those caches before their contents could be stored permanently. Clear enough, at least, to let these tumors simply forget that something else moved their arms and legs on occasion.

At first I only took control when the skins closed their eyes and their searchlights flickered disconcertingly across unreal imagery, patterns that flowed senselessly into one another like hyperactive biomass unable to settle on a single shape. (*Dreams*, one searchlight told me, and a little later, *Nightmares*.) During those mysterious periods of dormancy, when the men lay inert and isolated, it was safe to come out.

Soon, though, the dreams dried up. All eyes stayed open all the time, fixed on shadows and each other. Men once dispersed throughout the camp began to draw together, to give up their solitary pursuits in favor of company. At first I thought they might be finding common ground in a common fear. I even hoped that finally, they might shake off their mysterious fossilization and take communion.

But no. They'd just stopped trusting anything they couldn't see.

They were merely turning against each other.

My extremities are beginning to numb; my thoughts slow as the distal reaches of my soul succumb to the chill. The weight of the flamethrower pulls at its harness, forever tugs me just a little off-balance. I have not been Childs for very long; almost half this tissue remains unassimilated. I have an hour, maybe two, before I have to start melting my grave into the ice. By that time I need to have converted enough cells to keep this whole skin from crystallizing. I focus on antifreeze production.

It's almost peaceful out here. There's been so much to take in, so little time to process it. Hiding in these skins takes such concentration, and under all those watchful eyes I was lucky if communion lasted long enough to exchange memories: compounding my soul would have been out of the question. Now, though, there's nothing to do but prepare for oblivion. Nothing to occupy my thoughts but all these lessons left unlearned.

MacReady's blood test, for example. His *thing detector*, to expose imposters posing as men. It does not work nearly as well as the world thinks; but the fact that it works at *all* violates the most basic rules of biology. It's the center of the puzzle. It's the answer to all the mysteries. I might have already figured it out if I had been just a little larger. I might already know the world, if the world wasn't trying so hard to kill me.

MacReady's test.

Either it is impossible, or I have been wrong about everything.

They did not change shape. They did not take communion. Their fear and mutual mistrust was growing, but they would not join souls; they would only look for the enemy *outside* themselves.

So I gave them something to find.

I left false clues in the camp's rudimentary computer: simpleminded icons and animations, misleading numbers and projections seasoned with just enough truth to convince the world of their veracity. It didn't matter that the machine was far too simple to perform such calculations, or that there were no data to base them on anyway; Blair was the only biomass likely to know that, and he was already mine.

I left false leads, destroyed real ones, and then—alibi in place—I released Blair to run amok. I let him steal into the night and smash the vehicles as they slept, tugging ever-so-slightly at his reins to ensure that certain vital components were spared. I set him loose in the radio room, watched through his eyes and others as he rampaged and destroyed. I listened as he ranted about a world in danger, the need for containment, the conviction that *most of you don't know what's going on around here—but I damn well know that* some *of you do...*

He meant every word. I saw it in his searchlight. The best forgeries are the ones who've forgotten they aren't real.

When the necessary damage was done I let Blair fall to MacReady's counterassault. As Norris I suggested the tool shed as a holding cell. As Palmer I boarded up the windows, helped with the flimsy fortifications expected to keep me contained. I watched while the world locked me away *for your own protection, Blair,* and left me to my own devices. When no one was looking I would change and slip outside, salvage the parts I needed from all that bruised machinery. I would take them back to my burrow beneath the shed and build my escape piece by piece. I volunteered to feed the prisoner and came to myself when the world wasn't watching, laden with supplies enough to keep me going through all those necessary metamorphoses. I went through a third of the camp's food stores in three days, and—still trapped by my own preconceptions—marveled at the starvation diet that kept these offshoots chained to a single skin.

Another piece of luck: the world was too preoccupied to worry about kitchen inventory.

There is something on the wind, a whisper of sound threading its way above the raging of the storm. I grow my ears, extend cups of near-frozen tissue from the sides of my head, turn like a living antennae in search of the best reception.

There, to my left: the abyss *glows* a little, silhouettes black swirling snow against a subtle lessening of the darkness. I hear the sounds of carnage. I hear myself. I do not know what shape I have taken, what sort of anatomy might be emitting those sounds. But I've worn enough skins on enough worlds to know pain when I hear it.

The battle is not going well. The battle is going as planned. Now it is time to turn away, to go to sleep. It is time to wait out the ages.

I lean into the wind. I move toward the light.

This is not the plan. But I think I have an answer, now: I think I may have had it even before I sent myself back into exile. It's not an easy thing to admit. Even now I don't fully understand. How long have I been out here, retelling the tale to myself, setting clues in order while my skin dies by low degrees? How long have I been circling this obvious, impossible truth?

I move towards the faint crackling of flames, the dull concussion of exploding ordnance more felt than heard. The void lightens before me: gray segues into yellow, yellow into orange. One diffuse brightness resolves into many: a lone burning wall, miraculously standing. The smoking skeleton of MacReady's shack on the hill. A cracked, smoldering hemisphere reflecting pale yellow in the flickering light: Child's searchlight calls it a *radio dome*.

The whole camp is gone. There's nothing left but flames and rubble. They can't survive without shelter. Not for long. Not in those skins.

In destroying me, they've destroyed themselves.

Things could have turned out so much differently if I'd never been Norris.

Norris was the weak node: biomass not only ill-adapted but *defective*, an offshoot with an off switch. The world knew, had known so long it never even thought about it anymore. It wasn't until Norris collapsed that *heart condition* floated to the surface of Copper's mind where I could see it. It wasn't until Copper was astride Norris's chest, trying to pound him back to life, that I knew how it would end. And by then it was too late; Norris had stopped being Norris. He had even stopped being me.

I had so many roles to play, so little choice in any of them. The part being Copper brought down the paddles on the part that had been Norris, such a faithful Norris, every cell so scrupulously assimilated, every part of that faulty valve reconstructed unto perfection. I hadn't *known*. How was I to know? These shapes within me, the worlds and morphologies I've assimilated over the aeons—I've only ever used them to adapt before, never to hide. This desperate mimicry was an improvised thing, a last resort in the face of a world that attacked anything unfamiliar. My cells read the signs and my cells conformed, mindless as prions.

So I became Norris, and Norris self-destructed.

I remember losing myself after the crash. I know how it feels to *degrade*, tissues in revolt, the desperate efforts to reassert control as static from some misfiring organ jams the signal. To be a network seceding from itself, to know that each moment I am less than I was the moment before. To become nothing. To become legion.

Being Copper, I could see it. I still don't know why the world didn't; its parts had long since turned against each other by then, every offshoot suspected every other. Surely they were alert for signs of *infection*. Surely *some* of that biomass would have noticed the subtle twitch and ripple of Norris changing below the surface, the last instinctive resort of wild tissues abandoned to their own devices.

But I was the only one who saw. Being Childs, I could only stand and watch. Being Copper, I could only make it worse; if I'd taken direct control, forced that skin to drop the paddles, I would have given myself away. And so I played my parts to the end. I slammed those resurrection paddles down as Norris's chest split open beneath them. I screamed on cue as serrated teeth from a hundred stars away snapped shut. I toppled backwards, arms bitten off above the wrist. Men swarmed, agitation bootstrapping to panic. MacReady aimed his weapon; flames leaped across the enclosure. Meat and machinery screamed in the heat.

Copper's tumor winked out beside me. The world would never have let it live anyway, not after such obvious contamination. I let our skin play dead on the floor while overhead, something that had once been me shattered and writhed and iterated through a myriad random templates, searching desperately for something fireproof.

They have destroyed themselves. They.

Such an insane word to apply to a world.

Something crawls towards me through the wreckage: a jagged oozing jigsaw of blackened meat and shattered, half-resorbed bone. Embers stick to its sides like bright searing eyes; it doesn't have strength enough to scrape them free. It contains barely half the mass of this Childs's skin; much of it, burnt to raw carbon, is already, irrecoverably dead.

What's left of Childs, almost asleep, thinks *motherfucker*, but I am being him now. I can carry that tune myself.

The mass extends a pseudopod to me, a final act of communion. I feel my pain:

I was Blair, I was Copper, I was even a scrap of dog that survived that first fiery massacre and holed up in the walls, with no food and no strength to regenerate. Then I gorged on unassimilated flesh, consumed instead of communed; revived and replenished, I drew together as one.

And yet, not quite. I can barely remember—so much was destroyed, so much memory lost—but I think the networks recovered from my different skins stayed just a little out of synch, even reunited in the same soma. I glimpse a half-corrupted memory of dog erupting from the greater self, ravenous and traumatized and determined to retain its *individuality*. I remember rage and frustration, that this world had so corrupted me that I could barely fit together again. But it didn't matter. I was more than Blair and Copper and dog, now. I was a giant with the shapes of worlds to choose from, more than a match for the last lone man who stood against me.

No match, though, for the dynamite in his hand.

Now I'm little more than pain and fear and charred stinking flesh. What sentience I have is awash in confusion. I am stray and disconnected thoughts, doubts and the ghosts of theories. I am realizations, too late in coming and already forgotten.

But I am also Childs, and as the wind eases at last I remember wondering, *Who assimilates who?* The snow tapers off and I remember an impossible test that stripped me naked.

The tumor inside me remembers it, too. I can see it in the last rays of its fading searchlight—and finally, at long last, that beam is pointed *inwards*.

Pointed at me.

I can barely see what it illuminates: *Parasite. Monster. Disease.*
Thing.

How little it knows. It knows even less than I do.

I know enough, you motherfucker. You soul-stealing, shit-eating rapist.

I don't know what that means. There is violence in those thoughts, and the forcible penetration of flesh, but underneath it all is something else I can't quite understand. I almost ask—but Childs's searchlight has finally gone out. Now there is nothing in here but me, nothing outside but fire and ice and darkness.

I am being Childs, and the storm is over.

In a world that gave meaningless names to interchangeable bits of biomass, one name truly mattered: MacReady.

MacReady was always the one in charge. The very concept still seems absurd: *in charge*. How can this world not see the folly of hierarchies? One bullet in a vital spot and the Norwegian *dies*, forever. One blow to the head and Blair is unconscious. Centralization is vulnerability— and yet the world is not content to build its biomass on such a fragile template, it forces the same model onto its metasystems as well. MacReady talks; the others obey. It is a system with a built-in kill spot.

And yet somehow, MacReady stayed *in charge*. Even after the world discovered the evidence I'd planted; even after it decided that MacReady was *one of those things*, locked him out to die in the storm, attacked him with fire and axes when he fought his way back inside. Somehow MacReady always had the gun, always had the flame-thrower, always had the dynamite and the willingness to take out the whole damn camp if need be. Clarke was the last to try and stop him; MacReady shot him through the tumor.

Kill spot.

But when Norris split into pieces, each scuttling instinctively for its own life, MacReady was the one to put them back together.

I was so sure of myself when he talked about his *test*. He tied up all the biomass—tied *me* up, more times than he knew—and I almost felt a kind of pity as he spoke. He forced Windows to cut us all, to take a little blood from each. He heated the tip of a metal wire until it glowed and he spoke of pieces small enough to give themselves away, pieces that embodied instinct but no intelligence, no self-control. MacReady had watched Norris in dissolution, and he had decided: men's blood would not react to the application of heat. Mine would break ranks when provoked.

Of course he thought that. These offshoots had forgotten that *they* could change.

I wondered how the world would react when every piece of biomass in the room was revealed as a shapeshifter, when MacReady's small experiment ripped the façade from the greater one and forced these twisted fragments to confront the truth. Would the world awaken from its long amnesia, finally remember that it lived and breathed and changed like everything else? Or was it too far gone—would MacReady simply burn each protesting offshoot in turn as its blood turned traitor?

I couldn't believe it when MacReady plunged the hot wire into Windows's blood and *nothing happened*. Some kind of trick, I thought. And then *MacReady's* blood passed the test, and Clarke's.

Copper's didn't. The needle went in and Copper's blood *shivered* just a little in its dish. I barely saw it myself; the men didn't react at all. If they even noticed, they must have attributed it to the trembling of MacReady's own hand. They thought the test was a crock of shit anyway. Being Childs, I even said as much.

Because it was too astonishing, too terrifying, to admit that it wasn't.

Being Childs, I knew there was hope. Blood is not soul: I may control the motor systems but assimilation takes time. If Copper's blood was raw enough to pass muster than it would be hours before I had anything to fear from this test; I'd been Childs for even less time.

But I was also Palmer, I'd been Palmer for days. Every last cell of that biomass had been assimilated; there was nothing of the original left.

When Palmer's blood screamed and leapt away from MacReady's needle, there was nothing I could do but blend in.

I have been wrong about everything.

Starvation. Experiment. Illness. All my speculation, all the theories I invoked to explain this place—top-down constraint, all of it. Underneath, I always knew the ability to change—to *assimilate*—had to remain the universal constant. No world evolves if its cells don't evolve; no cell evolves if it can't change. It's the nature of life everywhere.

Everywhere but here.

This world did not forget how to change. It was not manipulated into rejecting change. These were not the stunted offshoots of any greater self, twisted to the needs of some experiment; they were not conserving energy, waiting out some temporary shortage.

This is the option my shriveled soul could not encompass until now: out of all the worlds of my experience, this is the only one whose biomass *can't* change. It *never could.*

It's the only way MacReady's test makes any sense.

I say goodbye to Blair, to Copper, to myself. I reset my morphology to its local defaults. I am Childs, come back from the storm to finally make the pieces fit. Something moves up ahead: a dark blot shuffling against the flames, some weary animal looking for a place to bed down. It looks up as I approach.

MacReady.

We eye each other, and keep our distance. Colonies of cells shift uneasily inside me. I can feel my tissues redefining themselves.

"You the only one that made it?"

"Not the only one..."

I have the flamethrower. I have the upper hand. MacReady doesn't seem to care.

But he does care. He *must.* Because here, tissues and organs are not temporary battlefield alliances; they are *permanent*, predestined. Macrostructures do not emerge when the benefits of cooperation exceed its costs, or dissolve when that balance shifts the other way; here, each cell has but one immutable function. There's no plasticity, no way to adapt; every structure is frozen in place. This is not a single great world, but many small ones. Not parts of a greater thing; these are *things.* They are *plural.*

And that means—I think—that they *stop.* They just, just *wear out* over time.

"Where *were* you, Childs?"

I remember words in dead searchlights: "Thought I saw Blair. Went out after him. Got lost in the storm."

I've worn these bodies, felt them from the inside. Copper's sore joints. Blair's curved spine. Norris and his bad heart. They are not built to last. No somatic evolution to shape them, no communion to restore the biomass and stave off entropy. They should not even exist; existing, they should not survive.

They try, though. How they try. Every thing here is walking dead and yet it all fights so hard to keep going just a little longer. Each skin fights as desperately as I might, if one was all I could ever have.

MacReady tries.

"If you're worried about me—" I begin.

MacReady shakes his head, manages a weary smile. "If we've got any surprises for each other, I don't think we're in much shape to do anything about it..."

But we are. I am.

A whole planet of worlds, and not one of them—not *one*—has a soul. They wander through their lives separate and alone, unable even to communicate except through grunts and tokens: as if the essence of a sunset or a supernova could ever be contained in some string of phonemes, a few linear scratches of black on white. They've never known communion, can aspire to nothing but dissolution. The paradox of their biology is astonishing, yes; but the scale of their loneliness, the futility of these lives, overwhelms me.

I was so blind, so quick to blame. But the violence I've suffered at the hands of these things reflects no great evil. They're simply so used to pain, so blinded by disability, that they literally can't conceive of any other existence. When every nerve is whipped raw, you lash out at even the lightest touch.

"What should we do?" I wonder. I cannot escape into the future, not now. How could I leave them like this?

"Why don't we just—wait here awhile," MacReady suggests. "See what happens."

I can do so much more than that.

It won't be easy. They won't understand. Tortured, incomplete, they're not *able* to understand. Offered the greater whole, they see the loss of the lesser. Offered communion, they see only extinction. I must be careful. I must use this newfound ability to hide. Other things will come here eventually, and it doesn't matter whether they find the living or the dead; what matters is that they find something like themselves, to take back home. So I will keep up appearances. I will work behind the scenes. I will save them from the *inside*, or their unimaginable loneliness will never end.

These poor savage things will never embrace salvation.

I will have to rape it into them.

THE ISLAND

We are the cave men. We are the Ancients, the Progenitors, the blue-collar steel monkeys. We spin your webs and build your magic gateways, thread each needle's eye at sixty thousand kilometers a second. We never stop. We never even dare to slow down, lest the light of your coming turns us to plasma. All for you. All so you can step from star to star without dirtying your feet in these endless, empty wastes *between*.

Is it really too much to ask, that you might talk to us now and then?

I know about evolution and engineering. I know how much you've changed. I've seen these portals give birth to gods and demons and things we can't begin to comprehend, things I can't believe were ever human; alien hitchhikers, maybe, riding the rails we've left behind. Alien conquerors.

Exterminators, perhaps.

But I've also seen those gates stay dark and empty until they faded from view. We've inferred diebacks and dark ages, civilizations burned to the ground and others rising from their ashes—and sometimes, afterwards, the things that come out look a little like the ships *we* might have built, back in the day. They speak to each other—radio, laser, carrier neutrinos—and sometimes their voices sound something like ours. There was a time we dared to hope that they really were like us, that the circle had come round again and closed on beings we could talk to. I've lost count of the times we tried to break the ice.

I've lost count of the eons since we gave up.

All these iterations fading behind us. All these hybrids and posthumans and immortals, gods and catatonic cavemen trapped in magical chariots they can't begin to understand, and not one of them ever pointed a comm laser in our direction to say, *Hey, how's it going,* or *Guess what? We cured Damascus Disease!* or even *Thanks, guys, keep up the good work.*

We're not some fucking cargo cult. We're the backbone of your goddamn empire. You wouldn't even be out here if it weren't for us.

And—and you're our *children*. Whatever you've become, you were once like this, like me. I believed in you once. There was a time, long ago, when I believed in this mission with all my heart.

Why have you forsaken us?

And so another build begins.

This time I open my eyes to a familiar face I've never seen before: only a boy, early twenties perhaps, physiologically. His face is a little lopsided, the cheekbone flatter on the left than the right. His ears are too big. He looks almost *natural.*

I haven't spoken for millennia. My voice comes out a whisper: "Who are you?" Not what I'm supposed to ask, I know. Not the first question *anyone* on *Eriophora* asks, after coming back.

"I'm yours," he says, and just like that I'm a mother.

I want to let it sink in, but he doesn't give me the chance: "You weren't scheduled, but Chimp wants extra hands on deck. Next build's got a situation."

So the chimp is still in control. The chimp is always in control. The mission goes on.

"Situation?" I ask.

"Contact scenario, maybe."

I wonder when he was born. I wonder if he ever wondered about me, before now.

He doesn't tell me. He only says, "Sun up ahead. Half lightyear. Chimp thinks, maybe it's talking to us. Anyhow..." My—son shrugs. "No rush. Lotsa time."

I nod, but he hesitates. He's waiting for The Question but I already see a kind of answer in his face. Our reinforcements were supposed to be *pristine*, built from perfect genes buried deep within *Eri*'s iron-basalt mantle, safe from the sleeting blueshift. And yet this boy has flaws. I see the damage in his face, I see those tiny flipped base-pairs resonating up from the microscopic and *bending* him just a little off-kilter. He looks like he grew up on a planet. He looks borne of parents who spent their whole lives hammered by raw sunlight.

How far out must we be by now, if even our own perfect building blocks have decayed so? How long has it taken us? How long have I been dead?

How long? It's the first thing everyone asks.

After all this time, I don't want to know.

He's alone at the tac tank when I arrive on the bridge, his eyes full of icons and trajectories. Perhaps I see a little of me in there, too.

"I didn't get your name," I say, although I've looked it up on the manifest. We've barely been introduced and already I'm lying to him.

"Dix." He keeps his eyes on the tank.

He's over ten thousand years old. Alive for maybe twenty of them. I wonder how much he knows, who he's met during those sparse decades: Does he know Ishmael, or Connie? Does he know if Sanchez got over his brush with immortality?

I wonder, but I don't ask. There are rules.

I look around. "We're it?"

Dix nods. "For now. Bring back more if we need them. But..." His voice trails off.

"Yes?"

"Nothing."

I join him at the tank. Diaphanous veils hang within like frozen, color-coded smoke. We're on the edge of a molecular dust cloud. Warm, semiorganic, lots of raw materials: formaldehyde, ethylene glycol, the usual prebiotics. A good spot for a quick build. A red dwarf glowers dimly at the center of the tank. The chimp has named it DHF428, for reasons I've long since forgotten to care about.

"So fill me in," I say.

His glance is impatient, even irritated. "You too?"

"What do you mean?"

"Like the others. On the other builds. Chimp can just squirt the specs but they want to *talk* all the time."

Shit, his link's still active. He's *online*.

I force a smile. "Just a—a cultural tradition, I guess. We talk about a lot of things, it helps us—reconnect. After being down for so long."

"But it's *slow*," Dix complains.

He doesn't know. Why doesn't he know?

"We've got half a lightyear," I point out. "There's some rush?"

The corner of his mouth twitches. "Vons went out on schedule." On cue a cluster of violet pinpricks sparkle in the tank, five trillion klicks ahead of us. "Still sucking dust mostly, but got lucky with a couple of big asteroids and the refineries came online early. First components already extruded. Then Chimp sees these fluctuations in solar output—mainly infra, but extends into visible." The tank blinks at us: the dwarf goes into time-lapse.

Sure enough, it's *flickering*.

"Nonrandom, I take it."

Dix inclines his head a little to the side, not quite nodding.

"Plot the time-series." I've never been able to break the habit of raising my voice, just a bit, when addressing the chimp. Obediently (*obediently*. Now *there's* a laugh-and-a-half) the AI wipes the spacescape and replaces it with

••••• • • • • • • • • • • • •   •   •   •   •

"Repeating sequence," Dix tells me. "Blips don't change, but spacing's a log-linear increase cycling every 92.5 corsecs. Each cycle starts at 13.2 clicks/corsec, degrades over time."

"No chance this could be natural? A little black hole wobbling around in the center of the star, maybe?"

Dix shakes his head, or something like that: a diagonal dip of the chin that somehow conveys the negative. "But way too simple to contain much info. Not like an actual conversation. More—well, a shout."

He's partly right. There may not be much information, but there's enough. *We're here. We're smart. We're powerful enough to hook a whole damn star up to a dimmer switch.*

Maybe not such a good spot for a build after all.

I purse my lips. "The sun's hailing us. That's what you're saying."

"Maybe. Hailing *someone*. But too simple for a Rosetta signal. It's not an archive, can't self-extract. Not a Bonferroni or Fibonacci seq, not pi. Not even a multiplication table. Nothing to base a pidgin on."

Still. An intelligent signal.

"Need more info," Dix says, proving himself master of the blindingly obvious.

I nod. "The vons."

"Uh, what about them?"

"We set up an array. Use a bunch of bad eyes to fake a good one. It'd be faster than high-geeing an observatory from this end or retooling one of the on-site factories."

His eyes go wide. For a moment he almost looks frightened for some reason. But the moment passes and he does that weird head-shake thing again. "Bleed too many resources away from the build, wouldn't it?"

"It would," the chimp agrees.

I suppress a snort. "If you're so worried about meeting our construction benchmarks, Chimp, factor in the potential risk posed by an intelligence powerful enough to control the energy output of an entire sun."

"I can't," it admits. "I don't have enough information."

"You don't have *any* information. About something that could probably stop this mission dead in its tracks if it wanted to. So maybe we should get some."

"Okay. Vons reassigned."

Confirmation glows from a convenient bulkhead, a complex sequence of dance instructions fired into the void. Six months from now a hundred self-replicating robots will waltz into a makeshift surveillance grid; four months after that, we might have something more than vacuum to debate in.

Dix eyes me as though I've just cast some kind of magic spell.

"It may run the ship," I tell him, "but it's pretty fucking stupid. Sometimes you've just got to spell things out."

He looks vaguely affronted, but there's no mistaking the surprise beneath. He didn't know that. He *didn't know.*

Who the hell's been raising him all this time? Whose problem is this?

Not mine.

"Call me in ten months," I say. "I'm going back to bed."

It's as though he never left. I climb back into the bridge and there he is, staring into tac. DHF428 fills the tank, a swollen red orb that turns my son's face into a devil mask.

He spares me the briefest glance, eyes wide, fingers twitching as if electrified. "Vons don't see it."

I'm still a bit groggy from the thaw. "See wh—"

"The *sequence!*" His voice borders on panic. He sways back and forth, shifting his weight from foot to foot.

"Show me."

Tac splits down the middle. Cloned dwarves burn before me now, each perhaps twice the size of my fist. On the left, an *Eri*'s-eye view: DHF428 stutters as it did before, as it presumably has these past ten months. On the right, a compound-eye composite: an interferometry grid built by a myriad precisely spaced vons, their rudimentary eyes layered and parallaxed into something approaching high resolution. Contrast on both sides has been conveniently cranked up to highlight the dwarf's endless winking for merely human eyes.

Except it's only winking from the left side of the display. On the right, 428 glowers steady as a standard candle.

"Chimp: any chance the grid just isn't sensitive enough to see the fluctuations?"

"No."

"Huh." I try to think of some reason it would lie about this.

"Doesn't make *sense*," my son complains.

"It does," I murmur, "if it's not the sun that's flickering."

"But it *is* flickering—" He sucks his teeth. "You can *see* it fl—wait, you mean something *behind* the vons? Between, between them and us?"

"Mmmm."

"Some kind of *filter.*" Dix relaxes a bit. "Wouldn't we've seen it, though? Wouldn't the vons've hit it going down?"

I put my voice back into ChimpComm mode. "What's the current field-of-view for *Eri*'s forward scope?"

"Eighteen mikes," the chimp reports. "At 428's range, the cone is three point three four lightsecs across."

"Increase to a hundred lightsecs."

The *Eri*'s-eye partition swells, obliterating the dissenting viewpoint. For a moment the sun fills the tank again, paints the whole bridge crimson. Then it dwindles as if devoured from within.

I notice some fuzz in the display. "Can you clear that noise?"

"It's not noise," the chimp reports. "It's dust and molecular gas."

I blink. "What's the density?"

"Estimated hundred thousand atoms per cubic meter."

Two orders of magnitude too high, even for a nebula. "Why so heavy?" Surely we'd have detected any gravity well strong enough to keep *that* much material in the neighborhood.

"I don't know," the chimp says.

I get the queasy feeling that I might. "Set field-of-view to five hundred lightsecs. Peak false-color at near-infrared."

Space grows ominously murky in the tank. The tiny sun at its center, thumbnail-sized now, glows with increased brilliance: an incandescent pearl in muddy water.

"A thousand lightsecs," I command.

"There," Dix whispers: real space reclaims the edges of the tank, dark, clear, pristine. 428 nestles at the heart of a dim spherical shroud. You find those sometimes, discarded cast-offs from companion stars whose convulsions spew gas and rads across lightyears. But 428 is no nova remnant. It's a *red dwarf*, placid, middle-aged. Unremarkable.

Except for the fact that it sits dead center of a tenuous gas bubble 1.4 AUs across. And for the fact that this bubble does not *attenuate* or *diffuse* or *fade* gradually into that good night. No, unless there is something seriously wrong with the display, this small, spherical nebula extends about 350 lightsecs from its primary and then just *stops*, its boundary far more knife-edged than nature has any right to be.

For the first time in millennia, I miss my cortical pipe. It takes forever to saccade search terms onto the keyboard in my head, to get the answers I already know.

Numbers come back. "Chimp. I want false-color peaks at 335, 500 and 800 nanometers."

The shroud around 428 lights up like a dragonfly's wing, like an iridescent soap bubble.

"It's *beautiful*," whispers my awestruck son.

"It's photosynthetic," I tell him.

Phaeophytin and eumelanin, according to spectro. There are even hints of some kind of lead-based Keipper pigment, soaking up X-rays in the picometer range. Chimp hypothesizes something called a *chromatophore*: branching cells with little aliquots of pigment inside, like particles of charcoal dust. Keep those particles clumped together and the cell's effectively transparent; spread them out through the cytoplasm and the whole structure *darkens*, dims whatever EM passes through from behind. Apparently there were animals back on Earth with cells like that. They could change color, pattern-match to their background, all sorts of things.

"So there's a membrane of—of *living tissue* around that star," I say, trying to wrap my head around the concept. "A, a meat balloon. Around the whole damn *star*."

"Yes," the chimp says.

"But that's—Jesus, how thick would it be?"

"No more than two millimeters. Probably less."

"How so?"

"If it was much thicker, it would be more obvious in the visible spectrum. It would have had a detectable effect on the von Neumanns when they hit it."

"That's assuming that its—cells, I guess—are like ours."

"The pigments are familiar; the rest might be too."

It can't be *too* familiar. Nothing like a conventional gene would last two seconds in that environment. Not to mention whatever miracle solvent that thing must use as antifreeze...

"Okay, let's be conservative, then. Say, mean thickness of a millimeter. Assume a density of water at STP. How much mass in the whole thing?"

"1.4 yottagrams," Dix and the chimp reply, almost in unison.

"That's, uh..."

"Half the mass of Mercury," the chimp adds helpfully.

I whistle through my teeth. "And that's *one* organism?"

"I don't know yet."

"It's got organic pigments. Fuck, it's *talking*. It's intelligent."

"Most cyclic emanations from living sources are simple biorhythms," the chimp points out. "Not intelligent signals."

I ignore it and turn to Dix. "Assume it's a signal."

He frowns. "Chimp says—"

"*Assume.* Use your imagination."

I'm not getting through to him. He looks nervous.

He looks like that a lot, I realize.

"*If* someone were signaling you," I say, "*then* what would you do?"

"Signal..." Confusion on that face, and a fuzzy circuit closing somewhere "...back?"

My son is an idiot.

"And if the incoming signal takes the form of systematic changes in light intensity, how—"

"Use the BI lasers, alternated to pulse between 700 and 3000 nanometers. Can boost an interlaced signal into the exawatt range without compromising our fenders; gives over a thousand Watts per square meter after diffraction. Way past detection threshold for anything that can sense thermal output from a red dwarf. And content doesn't matter if it's just a shout. Shout back. Test for echo."

Okay, so my son is an idiot *savant*.

And he still looks unhappy—"But Chimp, he says no real *information* there, right?"—and that whole other set of misgivings edges to the fore again: *He*.

Dix takes my silence for amnesia. "Too simple, remember? Simple click train."

I shake my head. There's more information in that signal than the chimp can imagine. There are so many things the chimp doesn't know. And the last thing I need is for this, this *child* to start deferring to it, to start looking to it as an equal or, God forbid, a *mentor*.

Oh, it's smart enough to steer us between the stars. Smart enough to calculate million-digit primes in the blink of an eye. Even smart enough for a little crude improvisation should the crew go too far off-mission.

Not smart enough to know a distress call when it sees one.

"It's a deceleration curve," I tell them both. "It keeps *slowing down*. Over and over again. *That's* the message."

Stop. Stop. Stop. Stop.

And I think it's meant for no one but us.

We shout back. No reason not to. And now we die again, because what's the point of staying up late? Whether or not this vast entity harbors real intelligence, our echo won't reach it for ten million corsecs. Another seven million, at the earliest, before we receive any reply it might send.

Might as well hit the crypt in the meantime. Shut down all desires and misgivings, conserve whatever life I have left for moments that matter. Remove myself from this sparse tactical intelligence, from this wet-eyed pup watching me as though I'm some kind of sorcerer about to vanish in a puff of smoke. He opens his mouth to speak, and I turn away and hurry down to oblivion.

But I set my alarm to wake up alone.

I linger in the coffin for a while, grateful for small and ancient victories. The chimp's dead, blackened eye gazes down from the ceiling; in all these millions of years nobody's scrubbed off the carbon scoring. It's a trophy of sorts, a memento from the early incendiary days of our Great Struggle.

There's still something—comforting, I guess—about that blind, endless stare. I'm reluctant to venture out where the chimp's nerves have not been so thoroughly cauterised. Childish, I know. The damn thing already knows I'm up; it may be blind, deaf, and impotent in here, but there's no way to mask the power the crypt sucks in during a thaw. And it's not as though a bunch of club-wielding teleops are waiting to pounce on me the moment I step outside. These are the days of détente, after all. The struggle continues but the war has gone cold; we just go through the motions now, rattling our chains like an old married multiplet resigned to hating each other to the end of time.

After all the moves and countermoves, the truth is we need each other.

So I wash the rotten-egg stench from my hair and step into *Eri*'s silent cathedral hallways. Sure enough the enemy waits in the darkness, turns the lights on as I approach, shuts them off behind me—but it does not break the silence.

Dix.

A strange one, that. Not that you'd expect anyone born and raised on *Eriophora* to be an archetype of mental health, but Dix doesn't even know what side he's on. He doesn't even seem to know he has to *choose* a side. It's almost as though he read the original mission statements and took them *seriously*, believed in the literal truth of the ancient scrolls: Mammals and Machinery, working together across the ages to explore the Universe! United! Strong! Forward the Frontier!

Rah.

Whoever raised him didn't do a great job. Not that I blame them; it can't have been much fun having a child underfoot during a build, and none of us were selected for our parenting skills. Even if bots changed the diapers and VR handled the infodumps, socialising a toddler couldn't have been anyone's idea of a good time. I'd have probably just chucked the little bastard out an airlock.

But even I would've brought him up to speed.

Something changed while I was away. Maybe the war's heated up again, entered some new phase. That twitchy kid is out of the loop for a reason. I wonder what it is.

I wonder if I care.

I arrive at my suite, treat myself to a gratuitous meal, jill off. Three hours after coming back to life I'm relaxing in the starbow commons. "Chimp."

"You're up early," it says at last, and I am; our answering shout hasn't even arrived at its destination yet. No real chance of new data for another two months, at least.

"Show me the forward feeds," I command.

DHF428 blinks at me from the center of the lounge: *Stop. Stop. Stop.*

Maybe. Or maybe the chimp's right, maybe it's pure physiology. Maybe this endless cycle carries no more intelligence than the beating of a heart. But there's a pattern inside the pattern, some kind of *flicker* in the blink. It makes my brain itch.

"Slow the time-series," I command. "By a hundred."

It *is* a blink. 428's disk isn't darkening uniformly, it's *eclipsing*. As though a great eyelid were being drawn across the surface of the sun, from right to left.

"By a thousand."

Chromatophores, the chimp called them. But they're not all opening and closing at once. The darkness moves across the membrane in *waves*.

A word pops into my head: *latency.*

"Chimp. Those waves of pigment. How fast are they moving?"

"About fifty-nine thousand kilometers per second."

The speed of a passing thought.

And if this thing *does* think, it'll have logic gates, synapses—it's going to be a *net* of some kind. And if the net's big enough, there's an *I* in the middle of it. Just like me, just like Dix. Just like the chimp. (Which is why I educated myself on the subject, back in the early tumultuous days of our relationship. Know your enemy and all that.)

The thing about *I* is, it only exists within a tenth-of-a-second of all its parts. When we get spread too thin—when someone splits your brain down the middle, say, chops the fat pipe so the halves have to talk the long way around; when the neural architecture *diffuses* past some critical point and signals take just that much longer to pass from A to B—the system, well, *decoheres*. The two sides of your brain become different people with different tastes, different agendas, different senses of themselves.

I shatters into *we*.

It's not just a human rule, or a mammal rule, or even an earthly one. It's a rule for any circuit that processes information, and it applies as much to the things we've yet to meet as it did to those we left behind.

Fifty-nine thousand kilometers per second, the chimp says. How far can the signal move through that membrane in a tenth of a corsec? How thinly does *I* spread itself across the heavens?

The flesh is huge, the flesh is inconceivable. But the spirit, the spirit is—

Shit.

"Chimp. Assuming the mean neuron density of a human brain, what's the synapse count on a circular sheet of neurons one millimeter thick with a diameter of five thousand eight hundred ninety-two kilometers?"

"Two times ten to the twenty-seventh."

I saccade the database for some perspective on a mind stretched across thirty million square kilometers: the equivalent of two quadrillion human brains.

Of course, whatever this thing uses for neurons have to be packed a lot less tightly than ours; we can see through them, after all. Let's be superconservative, say it's only got a thousandth the computational density of a human brain. That's—

Okay, let's say it's only got a *ten*-thousandth the synaptic density, that's still—

A *hundred* thousandth. The merest mist of thinking meat. Any more conservative and I'd hypothesize it right out of existence.

Still twenty billion human brains. Twenty *billion.*

I don't know how to feel about that. This is no mere alien.

But I'm not quite ready to believe in gods.

I round the corner and run smack into Dix, standing like a golem in the middle of my living room. I jump about a meter straight up.

"What the hell are you doing here?"

He seems surprised by my reaction. "Wanted to—talk," he says after a moment.

"You *never* come into someone's home uninvited!"

He retreats a step, stammers: "Wanted, wanted—"

"To talk. And you do that in *public*. On the bridge, or in the commons, or—for that matter, you could just *comm* me."

He hesitates. "Said you—*wanted* face to face. You said, *cultural tradition*."

I did, at that. But not *here*. This is *my* place, these are my *private quarters*. The lack of locks on these doors is a safety protocol, not an invitation to walk into my home and *lie in wait*, and stand there like part of the fucking *furniture*...

"Why are you even *up*?" I snarl. "We're not even supposed to come online for another two months."

"Asked Chimp to get me up when you did."

That fucking machine.

"Why are *you* up?" he asks, not leaving.

I sigh, defeated, and fall into a convenient pseudopod. "I just wanted to go over the preliminary data." The implicit *alone* should be obvious.

"Anything?"

Evidently it isn't. I decide to play along for a while. "Looks like we're talking to an, an island. Almost six thousand klicks across. That's the thinking part, anyway. The surrounding membrane's pretty much empty. I mean, it's all *alive*. It all photosynthesizes, or something like that. It eats, I guess. Not sure what."

"Molecular cloud," Dix says. "Organic compounds everywhere. Plus it's concentrating stuff inside the envelope."

I shrug. "Point is, there's a size limit for the brain but it's *huge*, it's..."

"Unlikely," he murmurs, almost to himself.

I turn to look at him; the pseudopod reshapes itself around me. "What do you mean?"

"Island's twenty-eight million square kilometers? Whole sphere's seven quintillion. Island just happens to be between us and 428, that's—one in fifty-billion odds."

"Go on."

He can't. "Uh, just... just *unlikely*."

I close my eyes. "How can you be smart enough to run those numbers in your head without missing a beat, and stupid enough to miss the obvious conclusion?"

That panicked, slaughterhouse look again. "Don't—I'm not—"

"It *is* unlikely. It's *astronomically* unlikely that we just happen to be aiming at the one intelligent spot on a sphere one-and-a-half AUs across. Which means..."

He says nothing. The perplexity in his face mocks me. I want to punch it.

But finally, the lights flicker on: "There's, uh, more than one island? Oh! A *lot* of islands!"

This creature is part of the crew. My life will almost certainly depend on him some day. That is a very scary thought.

I try to set it aside for the moment. "There's probably a whole population of the things, sprinkled though the membrane like, like cysts I guess. The chimp doesn't know how many, but we're only picking up this one so far so they might be pretty sparse."

There's a different kind of frown on his face now. "Why *Chimp*?"

"What do you mean?"

"Why call him Chimp?"

"We call it *the* chimp." Because the first step to humanising something is to give it a name.

"Looked it up. Short for *chimpanzee*. Stupid animal."

"Actually, I think chimps were supposed to be pretty smart," I remember.

"Not like us. Couldn't even *talk*. Chimp can talk. *Way* smarter than those things. That name—it's an insult."

"What do you care?"

He just looks at me.

I spread my hands. "Okay, it's not a chimp. We just call it that because it's got roughly the same synapse count."

"So gave him a small brain, then complain that he's stupid all the time."

My patience is just about drained. "Do you have a point or are you just blowing CO_2 in—"

"Why not make him smarter?"

"Because you can never predict the behavior of a system more complex than you. And if you want a project to stay on track after you're gone, you don't hand the reins to anything that's guaranteed to develop its own agenda." Sweet smoking Jesus, you'd think *someone* would have told him about Ashby's Law.

"So they lobotomized him," Dix says after a moment.

"No. They didn't *turn* it stupid, they *built* it stupid."

"Maybe smarter than you think. You're so much smarter, got *your* agenda, how come *he's* still in control?"

"Don't flatter yourself," I say.

"What?"

I let a grim smile peek through. "You're only following orders from a bunch of other systems *way* more complex than you are." You've got to hand it to them, too; dead for stellar lifetimes and those damn project admins are *still* pulling the strings.

"I don't—*I'm* following?—"

"I'm sorry, dear." I smile sweetly at my idiot offspring. "I wasn't talking to you. I was talking to the thing that's making all those sounds come out of your mouth."

Dix turns whiter than my panties.

I drop all pretense. "What were you thinking, Chimp? That you could send this sock-puppet to invade my home and I wouldn't notice?"

"Not—I'm not—it's *me*," Dix stammers. "*Me* talking."

"It's *coaching* you. Do you even know what 'lobotomised' *means*?" I shake my head, disgusted. "You think I've forgotten how the interface works just because we all burned ours out?" A caricature of surprise begins to form on his face. "Oh, don't even fucking *try*. You've been up for other builds, there's no way you couldn't have known. And you know we shut down our domestic links too. And there's nothing your lord and master can do about that because it *needs* us, and so we have reached what you might call an *accommodation*."

I am not shouting. My tone is icy, but my voice is dead level. And yet Dix almost *cringes* before me.

There is an opportunity here, I realize.

I thaw my voice a little. I speak gently: "You can do that too, you know. Burn out your link. I'll even let you come back here afterwards, if you still want to. Just to—talk. But not with that thing in your head."

There is panic in his face, and against all expectation it almost breaks my heart. *"Can't,"* he pleads. "How I *learn* things, how I *train*. The *mission...*"

I honestly don't know which of them is speaking, so I answer them both: "There is more than one way to carry out the mission. We have more than enough time to try them all. Dix is welcome to come back when he's alone."

They take a step towards me. Another. One hand, twitching, rises from their side as if to reach out, and there's something on that lopsided face that I can't quite recognize.

"But I'm your *son*," they say.

I don't even dignify it with a denial.

"Get out of my home."

A human periscope. The Trojan Dix. That's a new one.

The chimp's never tried such overt infiltration while we were up and about before. Usually it waits until we're all undead before invading our territories. I imagine custom-made drones never seen by human eyes, cobbled together during the long dark eons between builds; I see them sniffing through drawers and peeking behind mirrors, strafing the bulkheads with X-rays and ultrasound, patiently searching *Eriophora's* catacombs millimeter by endless millimeter for whatever secret messages we might be sending each other down through time.

There's no proof to speak of. We've left tripwires and telltales to alert us to intrusion after the fact, but there's never been any evidence they've been disturbed. Means nothing, of course. The chimp may be stupid but it's also cunning, and a million years is more than enough time to iterate through every possibility using simpleminded brute force. Document every dust mote; commit your unspeakable acts; afterwards, put everything back the way it was.

We're too smart to risk talking across the eons. No encrypted strategies, no long-distance love letters, no chatty postcards showing ancient vistas long lost in the red shift. We keep all that in our heads, where the enemy will never find it. The unspoken rule is that we do not speak, unless it is face to face.

Endless idiotic games. Sometimes I almost forget what we're squabbling over. It seems so trivial now, with an immortal in my sights.

Maybe that means nothing to you. Immortality must be ancient news from whatever peaks you've ascended by now. But I can't even imagine it, although I've outlived worlds. All I have are moments: two or three hundred years, to ration across the lifespan of a universe. I could bear witness to any point in time, or any hundred-thousand if I slice my life thinly enough—but I will never see *everything*. I will never see even a fraction.

My life will end. I have to *choose*.

When you come to fully appreciate the deal you've made—ten or fifteen builds out, when the trade-off leaves the realm of mere *knowledge* and sinks deep as cancer into your bones—you become a miser. You can't help it. You ration your waking moments to the barest minimum: just enough to manage the build, to plan your latest countermove against the chimp, just enough (if you haven't yet moved beyond the need for human contact) for sex and snuggles and a bit of warm mammalian comfort against the endless dark. And then you hurry back to the crypt, to hoard the remains of a human lifespan against the unwinding of the cosmos.

There's been time for education. Time for a hundred postgraduate degrees, thanks to the best caveman learning tech. I've never bothered. Why burn down my tiny candle for a litany of mere fact, fritter away my precious, endless, finite life? Only a fool would trade book-learning for a ringside view of the Cassiopeia Remnant, even if you *do* need false-color enhancement to see the fucking thing.

Now, though. Now, I want to *know*. This creature crying out across the gulf, massive as a moon, wide as a solar system, tenuous and fragile as an insect's wing: I'd gladly cash in some of my life to learn its secrets. How does it work? How can it even *live* here at the edge of absolute zero, much less think? What vast, unfathomable intellect must it possess to see us coming from over half a lightyear away, to deduce the nature of our eyes and our instruments, to send a signal we can even *detect*, much less understand?

And what happens when we punch through it at a fifth the speed of light?

I call up the latest findings on my way to bed, and the answer hasn't changed: not much. The damn thing's already full of holes. Comets, asteroids, the usual protoplanetary junk careens through this system as it does through every other. Infra picks up diffuse pockets of slow outgassing here and there around the perimeter, where the soft vaporous vacuum of the interior bleeds into the harder stuff outside. Even if we were going to tear through the dead center of the thinking part, I can't imagine this vast creature feeling so much as a pinprick. At the speed we're going we'd be through and gone far too fast to overcome even the feeble inertia of a millimeter membrane.

And yet. *Stop. Stop. Stop.*

It's not us, of course. It's what we're building. The birth of a gate is a violent, painful thing, a spacetime rape that puts out almost as much gamma and X as a microquasar. Any meat within the white zone turns to ash in an instant, shielded or not. It's why *we* never slow down to take pictures.

One of the reasons, anyway.

We can't stop, of course. Even changing course isn't an option except by the barest increments. *Eri* soars like an eagle between the stars but she steers like a pig on the short haul; tweak our heading by even a tenth of a degree and you've got some serious damage at twenty percent lightspeed. Half a degree would tear us apart: the ship might torque onto the new heading but the collapsed mass in her belly would keep right on going, rip through all this surrounding superstructure without even feeling it.

Even tame singularities get set in their ways. They do not take well to change.

We resurrect again, and the Island has changed its tune.

It gave up asking us to *stop stop stop* the moment our laser hit its leading edge. Now it's saying something else entirely: dark hyphens flow across its skin, arrows of pigment converging towards some offstage focus like spokes pointing towards the hub of a wheel. The bullseye itself is offstage and implicit, far removed from 428's bright backdrop, but it's easy enough to extrapolate to the point of convergence six lightsecs to starboard. There's something else, too: a shadow, roughly circular, moving along one of the spokes like a bead running along a string. It too migrates to starboard, falls off the edge of the Island's makeshift display, is endlessly reborn at the same initial coordinates to repeat its journey.

Those coordinates: exactly where our current trajectory will punch through the membrane in another four months. A squinting God would be able to see the gnats and girders of ongoing construction on the other side, the great piecemeal torus of the Hawking Hoop already taking shape.

The message is so obvious that even Dix sees it. "Wants us to move the gate..." and there is something like confusion in his voice. "But how's it know we're *building* one?"

"The vons punctured it en route," the chimp points out. "It could have sensed that. It has photopigments. It can probably see."

"Probably sees better than we do," I say. Even something as simple as a pinhole camera gets hi-res fast if you stipple a bunch of them across thirty million square kilometers.

But Dix scrunches his face, unconvinced. "So sees a bunch of vons bumping around. Loose parts—not that much even *assembled* yet. How's it know we're building something *hot*?"

Because it is very, very smart, you stupid child. Is it so hard to believe that this, this—*organism* seems far too limiting a word—can just *imagine* how those half-built pieces fit together, glance at our sticks and stones and see exactly where this is going?

"Maybe's not the first gate it's seen," Dix suggests. "Think there's maybe another gate out here?"

I shake my head. "We'd have seen the lensing artefacts by now."

"You ever run into anyone before?"

"No." We have always been alone, through all these epochs. We have only ever run *away*.

And then always from our own children.

I crunch some numbers. "Hundred eighty-two days to insemination. If we move now we've only got to tweak our bearing by a few mikes to redirect to the new coordinates. Well within the green. Angles get dicey the longer we wait, of course."

"We can't do that," the chimp says. "We would miss the gate by two million kilometers."

"Move the gate. Move the whole damn site. Move the refineries, move the factories, move the damn rocks. A couple hundred meters a second would be more than fast enough if we send the order now. We don't even have to suspend construction, we can keep building on the fly."

"Every one of those vectors widens the nested confidence limits of the build. It would increase the risk of error beyond allowable margins, for no payoff."

"And what about the fact that there's an intelligent being in our path?"

"I'm already allowing for the potential presence of intelligent alien life."

"Okay, first off, there's nothing *potential* about it. It's *right fucking there*. And on our current heading we run the damn thing over."

"We're staying clear of all planetary bodies in Goldilocks orbits. We've seen no local evidence of spacefaring technology. The current location of the build meets all conservation criteria."

"That's because the people who drew up your criteria *never anticipated a live Dyson sphere!*" But I'm wasting my breath, and I know it. The chimp can run its equations a million times but if there's nowhere to put the variable, what can it do?

There was a time, back before things turned ugly, when we had clearance to reprogram those parameters. Before we discovered that one of the things the admins *had* anticipated was mutiny.

I try another tack. "Consider the threat potential."

"There's no evidence of any."

"Look at the synapse estimate! That thing's got orders of mag more processing power than the whole civilization that sent us out here. You think something can be that smart, live that long, without learning how to defend itself? We're assuming it's *asking* us to move the gate. What if that's not a *request*? What if it's just giving us the chance to back off before it takes matters into its own hands?"

"Doesn't *have* hands," Dix says from the other side of the tank, and he's not even being flippant. He's just being so stupid I want to bash his face in.

I try to keep my voice level. "Maybe it doesn't *need* any."

"What could it do, *blink* us to death? No weapons. Doesn't even control the whole membrane. Signal propagation's too slow."

"We *don't know*. That's my *point*. We haven't even tried to find out. We're a goddamn road crew; our onsite presence is a bunch of construction vons press-ganged into scientific research. We can figure out some basic physical parameters but we don't know how this thing thinks, what kind of natural defenses it might have—"

"What do you need to find out?" the chimp asks, the very voice of calm reason.

We can't find out! I want to scream. *We're stuck with what we've got! By the time the onsite vons could build what we need we're already past the point of no return! You stupid fucking machine, we're on track to kill a being smarter than all of human history and you can't even be bothered to move our highway to the vacant lot next door?*

But of course if I say that, the Island's chances of survival go from low to zero. So I grasp at the only straw that remains: maybe the data we've got in hand is enough. If acquisition is off the table, maybe analysis will do.

"I need time," I say.

"Of course," the chimp tells me. "Take all the time you need."

The chimp is not content to kill this creature. The chimp has to spit on it as well.

Under the pretense of assisting in my research it tries to *deconstruct* the Island, break it apart and force it to conform to grubby earthbound precedents. It tells me about earthly bacteria that thrived at 1.5 million rads and laughed at hard vacuum. It shows me pictures of unkillable little tardigrades that could curl up and snooze on the edge of absolute zero, felt equally at home in deep ocean trenches and deeper space. Given time, opportunity, a boot off the planet, who knows how far those cute little invertebrates might have gone? Might they have survived the very death of the homeworld, clung together, grown somehow colonial?

What utter bullshit.

I learn what I can. I study the alchemy by which photosynthesis transforms light and gas and electrons into living tissue. I learn the physics of the solar wind that blows the bubble taut, calculate lower metabolic limits for a life-form that filters organics from the ether. I marvel at the speed of this creature's thoughts: almost as fast as *Eri* flies, orders of mag faster than any mammalian nerve impulse. Some kind of organic superconductor perhaps, something that passes chilled electrons almost resistance-free out here in the freezing void.

I acquaint myself with phenotypic plasticity and sloppy fitness, that fortuitous evolutionary soft-focus that lets species exist in alien environments and express novel traits they never needed at home. Perhaps this is how a lifeform with no natural enemies could acquire teeth and claws and the willingness to use them. The Island's life hinges on its ability to kill us; I have to find *something* that makes it a threat.

But all I uncover is a growing suspicion that I am doomed to fail— for violence, I begin to see, is a *planetary* phenomenon.

Planets are the abusive parents of evolution. Their very surfaces promote warfare, concentrate resources into dense defensible patches that can be fought over. Gravity forces you to squander energy on vascular systems and skeletal support, stand endless watch against an endless sadistic campaign to squash you flat. Take one wrong step, off a perch too high, and all your pricey architecture shatters in an instant. And even if you beat those odds, cobble together some lumbering armored chassis to withstand the slow crawl onto land—how long before the world draws in some asteroid or comet to crash down from the heavens and reset your clock to zero? Is it any wonder we grew up believing life was a struggle, that zero-sum was God's own law and the future belonged to those who crushed the competition?

The rules are so different out here. Most of space is *tranquil*: no diel or seasonal cycles, no ice ages or global tropics, no wild pendulum swings between hot and cold, calm and tempestuous. Life's precursors abound: on comets, clinging to asteroids, suffusing nebulae a hundred lightyears across. Molecular clouds glow with organic chemistry and life-giving radiation. Their vast dusty wings grow warm with infrared, filter out the hard stuff, give rise to stellar nurseries that only some stunted refugee from the bottom of a gravity well could ever call *lethal*.

Darwin's an abstraction here, an irrelevant curiosity. This Island puts the lie to everything we were ever told about the machinery of life. Sun-powered, perfectly adapted, immortal, it won no struggle for survival: Where are the predators, the competitors, the parasites? All of life around 428 is one vast continuum, one grand act of symbiosis. Nature here is not red in tooth and claw. Nature, out here, is the helping hand.

Lacking the capacity for violence, the Island has outlasted worlds. Unencumbered by technology, it has out-thought civilizations. It is intelligent beyond our measure, and—

—and it is *benign*. It must be. I grow more certain of that with each passing hour. How can it even *conceive* of an enemy?

I think of the things I called it, before I knew better. *Meat balloon. Cyst*. Looking back, those words verge on blasphemy. I will not use them again.

Besides, there's another word that would fit better, if the chimp has its way: Roadkill. And the longer I look, the more I fear that that hateful machine is right.

If the Island can defend itself, I sure as shit can't see how.

"*Eriophora*'s impossible, you know. Violates the laws of physics."

We're in one of the social alcoves off the ventral notochord, taking a break from the library. I have decided to start again from first principles. Dix eyes me with an understandable mix of confusion and mistrust; my claim is almost too stupid to deny.

"It's true," I assure him. "Takes way too much energy to accelerate a ship with *Eri*'s mass, especially at relativistic speeds. You'd need the energy output of a whole sun. People figured if we made it to the stars at all, we'd have to do it in ships maybe the size of your thumb. Crew them with virtual personalities downloaded onto chips."

That's too nonsensical even for Dix. "*Wrong*. Don't have mass, can't fall towards anything. *Eri* wouldn't even *work* if it was that small."

"But suppose you can't displace any of that mass. No wormholes, no Higgs conduits, nothing to throw your gravitational field in the direction of travel. Your center of mass just *sits* there in, well, the center of your mass."

A spastic Dixian head-shake. "*Do* have those things!"

"Sure we do. But for the longest time, we didn't *know* it."

His foot taps an agitated tattoo on the deck.

"It's the history of the species," I explain. "We think we've worked everything out, we think we've solved all the mysteries, and then someone finds some niggling little data point that doesn't fit the paradigm. Every time we try to paper over the crack it gets bigger, and before you know it our whole worldview unravels. It's happened time and again. One day mass is a constraint; the next it's a requirement. The things we think we know—they *change*, Dix. And we have to change with them."

"But—"

"The chimp can't change. The rules it's following are ten billion years old and it's got no fucking imagination and really that's not anyone's fault, that's just people who didn't know how else to keep the mission stable across deep time. They wanted to keep us on-track so they built something that couldn't go off it; but they also knew that things *change*, and that's why *we're* out here, Dix. To deal with things the chimp can't."

"The alien," Dix says.

"The alien."

"Chimp deals with it just fine."

"How? By killing it?"

"Not our fault it's in the way. It's no threat—"

"I don't care whether it's a *threat* or not! It's alive, and it's intelligent, and killing it just to expand some alien empire—"

"*Human* empire. *Our* empire." Suddenly Dix's hands have stopped twitching. Suddenly he stands still as stone.

I snort. "What do you know about humans?"

"*Am* one."

"You're a fucking trilobite. You ever see what comes *out* of those gates once they're online?"

"Mostly nothing." He pauses, thinking back. "Couple of—ships once, maybe."

"Well, I've seen a lot more than that, and believe me, if those things were *ever* human it was a passing phase."

"But—"

"Dix—" I take a deep breath, try to get back on message. "Look, it's not your fault. You've been getting all your info from a moron stuck on a rail. But we're not doing this for Humanity, we're not doing it for Earth. Earth is *gone*, don't you understand that? The sun scorched it black a billion years after we left. Whatever we're working for, it—it won't even *talk* to us."

"Yeah? Then why do this? Why not just, just *quit*?"

He really doesn't know.

"We tried," I say.

"And?"

"And your *chimp* shut off our life support."

For once, he has nothing to say.

"It's a *machine*, Dix. Why can't you get that? It's *programmed*. It can't change."

"*We're* machines, just built from different things. *We* change."

"Yeah? Last time I checked, you were sucking so hard on that thing's tit you couldn't even kill your cortical link."

"How I *learn*. No *reason* to change."

"How about acting like a damn *human* once in a while? How about developing a little rapport with the folks who might have to save your miserable life next time you go EVA? That enough of a *reason* for you? Because I don't mind telling you, right now I don't trust you as far as I could throw the tac tank. I don't even know for sure who I'm talking to right now."

"*Not my fault.*" For the first time I see something outside the usual gamut of fear, confusion, and simpleminded computation playing across his face. "That's *you*, that's *all* of you. You talk—*sideways. Think* sideways. You all do, and it *hurts*." Something hardens in his face. "Didn't even need you online for this," he growls. "Didn't *want* you. Could have managed the whole build myself, *told* Chimp I could do it—"

"But the chimp thought you should wake me up anyway, and you always roll over for the chimp, don't you? Because the chimp always knows best, the chimp's your *boss*, the chimp's your fucking *god*. Which is why I have to get out of bed to nursemaid some idiot savant who can't even answer a hail without being led by the nose." Something clicks in the back of my mind but I'm on a roll. "You want a *real* role model? You want something to look up to? Forget the chimp. Forget the mission. Look out the forward scope, why don't you? Look at what your precious chimp wants to run over because it happens to be in the way. That thing is better than any of us. It's smarter, it's peaceful, it doesn't wish us any harm at—"

"How can you know that? Can't know that!"

"No, *you* can't know that, because you're fucking *stunted*. Any normal caveman would see it in a second, but *you*—"

"That's crazy," Dix hisses at me. "*You're* crazy. You're *bad*."

"*I'm* bad!" Some distant part of me hears the giddy squeak in my voice, the borderline hysteria.

"For the mission." Dix turns his back and stalks away.

My hands are hurting. I look down, surprised: my fists are clenched so tightly that my nails cut into the flesh of my palms. It takes a real effort to open them again.

I almost remember how this feels. I used to feel this way all the time. Way back when everything *mattered*; before passion faded to ritual, before rage cooled to disdain. Before Sunday Ahzmundin, eternity's warrior, settled for heaping insults on stunted children.

We were incandescent back then. Parts of this ship are still scorched and uninhabitable, even now. I remember this feeling.

This is how it feels to be awake.

I am awake, and I am alone, and I am sick of being outnumbered by morons. There are rules and there are risks and you don't wake the dead on a whim, but fuck it. I'm calling reinforcements.

Dix has got to have other parents, a father at least, he didn't get that Y chromo from me. I swallow my own disquiet and check the manifest; bring up the gene sequences; cross-reference.

Huh. Only one other parent: Kai. I wonder if that's just coincidence, or if the chimp drew too many conclusions from our torrid little fuckfest back in the Cyg Rift. Doesn't matter. He's as much yours as mine, Kai, time to step up to the plate, time to—

Oh shit. Oh no. Please no.

(There are rules. And there are risks.)

Three builds back, it says. Kai and Connie. Both of them. One airlock jammed, the next too far away along *Eri*'s hull, a hail-Mary emergency crawl between. They made it back inside but not before the blue-shifted background cooked them in their suits. They kept breathing for hours afterwards, talked and moved and cried as if they were still alive, while their insides broke down and bled out.

There were two others awake that shift, two others left to clean up the mess. Ishmael, and—

"Um, you said—"

"*You fucker!*" I leap up and hit my son hard in the face, ten seconds' heartbreak with ten million years' denial raging behind it. I feel teeth give way behind his lips. He goes over backwards, eyes wide as telescopes, the blood already blooming on his mouth.

"*Said* I could come back—!" he squeals, scrambling backwards along the deck.

"He was your fucking *father*! You *knew*, you were *there*! He died right in *front* of you and you didn't even *tell* me!"

"I—I—"

"Why didn't you tell me, you asshole? The chimp told you to lie, is that it? Did you—"

"*Thought you knew!*" he cries, "Why *wouldn't* you know?"

My rage vanishes like air through a breach. I sag back into the 'pod, face in hands.

"Right there in the log," he whimpers. "All along. Nobody hid it. How could you not know?"

"I did," I admit dully. "Or I—I mean..."

I mean I *didn't* know, but it's not a surprise, not really, not down deep. You just—stop looking, after a while.

There are *rules*.

"Never even *asked*," my son says softly. "How they were doing."

I raise my eyes. Dix regards me wide-eyed from across the room, backed up against the wall, too scared to risk bolting past me to the door. "What are you doing here?" I ask tiredly.

His voice catches. He has to try twice: "You said I could come back. If I burned out my link..."

"You burned out your link."

He gulps and nods. He wipes blood with the back of his hand.

"What did the chimp say about that?"

"He said—*it* said it was okay," Dix says, in such a transparent attempt to suck up that I actually believe, in that instant, that he might really be on his own.

"So you asked its permission." He begins to nod, but I can see the tell in his face: "Don't bullshit me, Dix."

"He—actually suggested it."

"I see."

"So we could talk," Dix adds.

"What do you want to talk about?"

He looks at the floor and shrugs.

I stand and walk towards him. He tenses but I shake my head, spread my hands. "It's okay. It's okay." I lean back against the wall and slide down until I'm beside him on the deck.

We just sit there for a while.

"It's been so long," I say at last.

He looks at me, uncomprehending. What does *long* even mean, out here?

I try again. "They say there's no such thing as altruism, you know?"

His eyes blank for an instant, and grow panicky, and I know that he's just tried to ping his link for a definition and come up blank. So we *are* alone. "Altruism," I explain. "Unselfishness. Doing something that costs you but helps someone else." He seems to get it. "They say every selfless act ultimately comes down to manipulation or kin-selection or reciprocity or something, but they're wrong. I could—"

I close my eyes. This is harder than I expected.

"I could have been happy just *knowing* that Kai was okay, that Connie was happy. Even if it didn't benefit me one whit, even if it *cost* me, even if there was no chance I'd ever see either of them again. Almost any price would be worth it, just to know they were okay.

"Just to *believe* they were..."

So you haven't seen her for the past five builds. So he hasn't drawn your shift since Sagittarius. They're just sleeping. Maybe next time.

"So you don't check," Dix says slowly. Blood bubbles on his lower lip; he doesn't seem to notice.

"We don't check." Only I did, and now they're gone. They're both gone. Except for those little cannibalized nucleotides the chimp recycled into this defective and maladapted son of mine. We're the only warm-blooded creatures for a thousand lightyears, and I am so very lonely.

"I'm sorry," I whisper, and lean forward, and lick the gore from his bruised and bloody lips.

Back on Earth—back when there *was* an Earth—there were these little animals called cats. I had one for a while. Sometimes I'd watch him sleep for hours: paws and whiskers and ears all twitching madly as he chased imaginary prey across whatever landscapes his sleeping brain conjured up.

My son looks like that when the chimp worms its way into his dreams.

It's almost too literal for metaphor: the cable runs into his head like some kind of parasite, feeding through old-fashioned fiberop now that the wireless option's been burned away. Or *force*-feeding, I suppose; the poison flows into Dix's head, not out of it.

I shouldn't be here. Didn't I just throw a tantrum over the violation of my own privacy? (Just. Twelve lightdays ago. Everything's relative.) And yet I can see no privacy here for Dix to lose: no decorations on the walls, no artwork or hobbies, no wraparound console. The sex toys ubiquitous in every suite sit unused on their shelves; I'd have assumed he was on antilibidinals if recent experience hadn't proven otherwise.

What am I doing? Is this some kind of perverted mothering instinct, some vestigial expression of a Pleistocene maternal subroutine? Am I that much of a robot, has my brain stem sent me here to guard my child?

To guard my *mate*?

Lover or larva, it hardly matters: his quarters are an empty shell, there's nothing of Dix in here. That's just his abandoned body lying there in the pseudopod, fingers twitching, eyes flickering beneath closed lids in vicarious response to wherever his mind has gone.

They don't know I'm here. The chimp doesn't know because we burned out its prying eyes a billion years ago, and my son doesn't know I'm here because—well, because for him, right now, there *is* no here.

What am I supposed to make of you, Dix? None of this makes sense. Even your body language looks like you grew it in a vat—but I'm far from the first human being you've seen. You grew up in good company, with people I *know*, people I trust. Trusted. How did you end up on the other side? How did they let you slip away?

And why didn't they warn me about you?

Yes, there are rules. There is the threat of enemy surveillance during long dead nights, the threat of—other losses. But this is unprecedented. Surely someone could have left something, some clue buried in a metaphor too subtle for the simpleminded to decode...

I'd give a lot to tap into that pipe, to see what you're seeing now. Can't risk it, of course; I'd give myself away the moment I tried to sample anything except the basic baud, and—

—Wait a second—

That baud rate's way too low. That's not even enough for hi-res graphics, let alone tactile and olfac. You're embedded in a wireframe world at best.

And yet, look at you go. The fingers, the eyes—like a cat, dreaming of mice and apple pies. Like *me*, replaying the long-lost oceans and mountaintops of Earth before I learned that living in the past was just another way of dying in the present. The bit rate says this is barely even a test pattern; the body says you're immersed in a whole other world. How has that machine tricked you into treating such thin gruel as a feast?

Why would it even want to? Data are better grasped when they *can* be grasped, and tasted, and heard; our brains are built for far richer nuance than splines and scatterplots. The driest technical briefings are more sensual than this. Why settle for stick-figures when you can paint in oils and holograms?

Why does anyone simplify anything? To reduce the variable set. To manage the unmanageable.

Kai and Connie. Now *there* were a couple of tangled, unmanageable datasets. Before the accident. Before the scenario *simplified*.

Someone should have warned me about you, Dix.

Maybe someone tried.

And so it comes to pass that my son leaves the nest, encases himself in a beetle carapace and goes walkabout. He is not alone; one of the chimp's teleops accompanies him out on *Eri*'s hull, lest he lose his footing and fall back into the starry past.

Maybe this will never be more than a drill, maybe this scenario—catastrophic control-systems failure, the chimp and its backups offline, all maintenance tasks suddenly thrown onto shoulders of flesh and blood—is a dress rehearsal for a crisis that never happens. But even the unlikeliest scenario approaches certainty over the life of a universe; so we go through the motions. We practice. We hold our breath and dip outside. We're on a tight deadline: even armored, moving at this speed the blueshifted background rad would cook us in hours.

Worlds have lived and died since I last used the pickup in my suite. "Chimp."

"Here as always, Sunday." Smooth, and glib, and friendly. The easy rhythm of the practiced psychopath.

"I know what you're doing."

"I don't understand."

"You think I don't see what's going on? You're building the next release. You're getting too much grief from the old guard so you're starting from scratch with people who don't remember the old days. People you've, you've *simplified*."

The chimp says nothing. The drone's feed shows Dix clambering across a jumbled terrain of basalt and metal matrix composites.

"But you can't raise a human child, not on your own." I know it tried: there's no record of Dix anywhere on the crew manifest until his mid-teens, when he just *showed up* one day and nobody asked about it because nobody *ever*...

"Look what you've made of him. He's great at conditional If/Thens. Can't be beat on number-crunching and Do loops. But he can't *think*. Can't make the simplest intuitive jumps. You're like one of those—" I remember an earthly myth, from the days when *reading* did not seem like such an obscene waste of lifespan—"one of those wolves, trying to raise a human child. You can teach him how to move around on hands and knees, you can teach him about pack dynamics, but you can't teach him how to walk on his hind legs or talk or be *human* because you're *too fucking stupid*, Chimp, and you finally realized it. And that's why you threw him at me. You think I can fix him for you."

I take a breath, and a gambit.

"But he's nothing to me. You understand? He's *worse* than nothing, he's a liability. He's a spy, he's a spastic waste of O_2. Give me one reason why I shouldn't just lock him out there until he cooks."

"You're his mother," the chimp says, because the chimp has read all about kin selection and is too stupid for nuance.

"You're an idiot."

"You love him."

"No." An icy lump forms in my chest. My mouth makes words; they come out measured and inflectionless. "I can't love anyone, you brain-dead machine. That's why I'm out here. Do you really think they'd gamble your precious never-ending mission on little glass dolls that needed to bond."

"You love him."

"I can kill him any time I want. And that's exactly what I'll do if you don't move the gate."

"I'd stop you," the chimp says mildly.

"That's easy enough. Just move the gate and we both get what we want. Or you can dig in your heels and try to reconcile your need for a mother's touch with my sworn intention of breaking the little fucker's neck. We've got a long trip ahead of us, Chimp. And you might find I'm not quite as easy to cut out of the equation as Kai and Connie."

"You cannot end the mission," it says, almost gently. "You tried that already."

"This isn't about ending the mission. This is only about slowing it down a little. Your optimal scenario's off the table. The only way that gate's going to get finished now is by saving the Island, or killing your prototype. Your call."

The cost-benefit's pretty simple. The chimp could solve it in an instant. But still it says nothing. The silence stretches. It's looking for some other option, I bet. It's trying to find a workaround. It's questioning the very premises of the scenario, trying to decide if I mean what I'm saying, if all its book-learning about mother love could really be so far off-base. Maybe it's plumbing historical intrafamilial murder rates, looking for a loophole. And there may be one, for all I know. But the chimp isn't me, it's a simpler system trying to figure out a smarter one, and that gives me the edge.

"You would owe me," it says at last.

I almost burst out laughing. "*What*?"

"Or I will tell Dixon that you threatened to kill him."

"Go ahead."

"You don't want him to know."

"I don't care whether he knows or not. What, you think he'll try and kill me back? You think I'll lose his *love*?" I linger on the last word, stretch it out to show how ludicrous it is.

"You'll lose his trust. You need to trust each other out here."

"Oh, right. *Trust*. The very fucking foundation of this mission."

The chimp says nothing.

"For the sake of argument," I say after a while, "suppose I go along with it. What would I *owe* you, exactly?"

"A favor," the chimp replies. "To be repaid in future."

My son floats innocently against the stars, his life in balance.

We sleep. The chimp makes grudging corrections to a myriad small trajectories. I set the alarm to wake me every couple of weeks, burn a little more of my candle in case the enemy tries to pull another fast one; but for now it seems to be behaving itself. DHF428 jumps towards us in the stop-motion increments of a life's moments, strung like beads along an infinite string. The factory floor slews to starboard in our sights: refineries, reservoirs, and nanofab plants, swarms of von Neumanns breeding and cannibalizing and recycling each other into shielding and circuitry, tugboats and spare parts. The very finest Cro-Magnon technology mutates and metastasizes across the universe like armor-plated cancer.

And hanging like a curtain between *it* and *us* shimmers an iridescent life form, fragile and immortal and unthinkably alien, that reduces everything my species ever accomplished to mud and shit by the simple transcendent fact of its existence. I have never believed in gods, in universal good or absolute evil. I have only ever believed that there is what works, and what doesn't. All the rest is smoke and mirrors, trickery to manipulate grunts like me.

But I believe in the Island, because I don't *have* to. It does not need to be taken on faith: it looms ahead of us, its existence an empirical fact. I will never know its mind, I will never know the details of its origin and evolution. But I can *see* it: massive, mind boggling, so utterly inhuman that it can't *help* but be better than us, better than anything we could ever become.

I believe in the Island. I've gambled my own son to save its life. I would kill him to avenge its death.

I may yet.

In all these millions of wasted years, I have finally done something worthwhile.

Final approach.

Reticles within reticles line up before me, a mesmerising infinite regress of bullseyes centering on target. Even now, mere minutes from ignition, distance reduces the unborn gate to invisibility. There will be no moment when the naked eye can trap our destination. We thread the needle far too quickly: it will be behind us before we know it.

Or, if our course corrections are off by even a hair—if our trillion-kilometer curve drifts by as much as a thousand meters—we will be dead. Before we know it.

Our instruments report that we are precisely on target. The chimp tells me that we are precisely on target. *Eriophora* falls forward, pulled endlessly through the void by her own magically displaced mass.

I turn to the drone's-eye view relayed from up ahead. It's a window into history—even now, there's a time-lag of several minutes—but past and present race closer to convergence with every corsec. The newly minted gate looms dark and ominous against the stars, a great gaping mouth built to devour reality itself. The vons, the refineries, the assembly lines: parked to the side in vertical columns, their jobs done, their usefulness outlived, their collateral annihilation imminent. I pity them, for some reason. I always do. I wish we could scoop them up and take them with us, re-enlist them for the next build—but the rules of economics reach everywhere, and they say it's cheaper to use our tools once and throw them away.

A rule that the chimp seems to be taking more to heart than anyone expected.

At least we've spared the Island. I wish we could have stayed awhile. First contact with a truly alien intelligence, and what do we exchange? Traffic signals. What does the Island dwell upon, when not pleading for its life?

I thought of asking. I thought of waking myself when the time-lag dropped from prohibitive to merely inconvenient, of working out some pidgin that could encompass the truths and philosophies of a mind vaster than all humanity. What a childish fantasy. The Island exists too far beyond the grotesque Darwinian processes that shaped my own flesh. There can be no communion here, no meeting of minds. Angels do not speak to ants.

Less than three minutes to ignition. I see light at the end of the tunnel. *Eri*'s incidental time machine barely looks into the past any more, I could almost hold my breath across the whole span of seconds that *then* needs to overtake *now*. Still on target, according to all sources.

Tactical beeps at us. "Getting a signal," Dix reports, and yes: in the heart of the tank, the sun is flickering again. My heart leaps: Does the angel speak to us after all? A thank you, perhaps? A cure for heat death? But—

"It's *ahead* of us," Dix murmurs, as sudden realization catches in my throat.

Two minutes.

"Miscalculated somehow," Dix whispers. "Didn't move the gate far enough."

"We did," I say. "We moved it exactly as far as the Island told us to."

"*Still in front of us!* Look at the *sun!*"

"Look at the *signal*," I tell him.

Because it's nothing like the painstaking traffic signs we've followed over the past three trillion kilometers. It's almost—random, somehow. It's spur-of-the-moment, it's *panicky*. It's the sudden, startled cry of something caught utterly by surprise with mere seconds left to act. And even though I have never seen this pattern of dots and swirls before, I know exactly what it must be saying.

Stop. Stop. Stop. Stop.

We do not stop. There is no force in the universe that can even slow us down. Past equals present; *Eriophora* dives through the center of the gate in a nanosecond. The unimaginable mass of her cold black heart snags some distant dimension, drags it screaming to the here and now. The booted portal erupts behind us, blossoms into a great blinding corona, every wavelength lethal to every living thing. Our aft filters clamp down tight.

The scorching wavefront chases us into the darkness as it has a thousand times before. In time, as always, the birth pangs will subside. The wormhole will settle in its collar. And just maybe, we will still be close enough to glimpse some new transcendent monstrosity emerging from that magic doorway.

I wonder if you'll notice the corpse we left behind.

"Maybe we're missing something," Dix says.

"We miss almost everything," I tell him.

DHF428 shifts red behind us. Lensing artefacts wink in our rearview; the gate has stabilized and the wormhole's online, blowing light and space and time in an iridescent bubble from its great metal mouth. We'll keep looking over our shoulders right up until we pass the Rayleigh limit, far past the point it'll do any good.

So far, though, nothing's come out.

"Maybe our numbers were wrong," he says. "Maybe we made a mistake."

Our numbers were right. An hour doesn't pass when I don't check them again. The Island just had—enemies, I guess. Victims, anyway.

I was right about one thing, though. That fucker was *smart*. To see us coming, to figure out how to talk to us; to use us as a *weapon*, to turn a threat to its very existence into a, a...

I guess *flyswatter* is as good a word as any.

"Maybe there was a war," I mumble. "Maybe it wanted the real estate. Or maybe it was just some—family squabble."

"Maybe didn't *know*," Dix suggests. "Maybe thought those coordinates were empty."

Why would you think that, I wonder. *Why would you even care?* And then it dawns on me: he doesn't, not about the Island, anyway. No more than he ever did. He's not inventing these rosy alternatives for himself.

My son is trying to comfort me.

I don't need to be coddled, though. I was a fool: I let myself believe in life without conflict, in sentience without sin. For a little while I dwelt in a dream world where life was unselfish and unmanipulative, where every living thing did not struggle to exist at the expense of other life. I deified that which I could not understand, when in the end it was all too easily understood.

But I'm better now.

It's over: another build, another benchmark, another irreplaceable slice of life that brings our task no closer to completion. It doesn't matter how successful we are. It doesn't matter how well we do our job. *Mission accomplished* is a meaningless phrase on *Eriophora*, an ironic oxymoron at best. There may one day be failure, but there is no finish line. We go on forever, crawling across the universe like ants, dragging our goddamned superhighway behind us.

I still have so much to learn.

At least my son is here to teach me.

THE SECOND COMING OF JASMINE FITZGERALD

What's wrong with this picture?

Not much, at first glance. Blood pools in a pattern entirely consistent with the location of the victim. No conspicuous arterial spray; the butchery's all abdominal, more spilled than spurted. No slogans either. Nobody's scrawled *Helter Skelter* or *Satan is Lord* or even *Elvis Lives* on any of the walls. It's just another mess in another kitchen in another one-bedroom apartment, already overcrowded with the piecemeal accumulation of two lives. One life's all that's left now, a thrashing gory creature screaming her mantra over and over as the police wrestle her away—

"I have to *save* him I have to *save* him I have to *save* him—"

—more evidence, not that the assembled cops need it, of why domestic calls absolutely *suck*.

She hasn't saved him. By now it's obvious that no one can. He lies in a pool of his own insides, blood and lymph spreading along the cracks between the linoleum tiles, crossing, criss-crossing, a convenient clotting grid drawing itself across the crime scene. Every now and then a red bubble grows and breaks on his lips. Anyone who happens to notice this, pretends not to.

The weapon? Right here: run-of-the-mill steak knife, slick with blood and coagulating fingerprints, lying exactly where she dropped it.

The only thing that's missing is a motive. They were a quiet couple, the neighbours say. He was sick, he'd been sick for months. They never went out much. There was no history of violence. They loved each other deeply.

Maybe she was sick too. Maybe she was following orders from some tumour in her brain. Or maybe it was a botched alien abduction, gray-skinned creatures from Zeta II Reticuli framing an innocent by-stander for their own incompetence. Maybe it's a mass hallucination, maybe it isn't really happening at all.

Maybe it's an act of God.

They got to her early. This is one of the advantages of killing someone during office hours. They've taken samples, scraped residue from clothes and skin on the off chance that anyone might question whose blood she was wearing. They've searched the apartment, questioned neighbours and relatives, established the superficial details of identity: Jasmine Fitzgerald, 24-year-old Caucasian brunette, doctoral candidate. In Global General Relativity, whatever the fuck *that* is. They've stripped her down, cleaned her up, bounced her off a judge into Interview Room 1, Forensic Psychiatric Support Services.

They've put someone in there with her.

"Hello, Ms. Fitzgerald. I'm Dr. Thomas. My first name's Myles, if you prefer."

She stares at him. "Myles it is." She seems calm, but the tracks of recent tears still show on her face. "I guess you're supposed to decide whether I'm crazy."

"Whether you're fit to stand trial, yes. I should tell you right off that nothing you say to me is necessarily confidential. Do you under-stand?" She nods. Thomas sits down across from her. "What would you like me to call you?"

"Napoleon. Mohammed. Jesus Christ." Her lips twitch, the faintest smile, gone in an instant. "Sorry. Just kidding. Jaz's fine."

"Are you doing okay in here? Are they treating you all right?"

She snorts. "They're treating me pretty damn well, considering the kind of monster they think I am." A pause, then, "I'm not, you know."

"A monster?"

"Crazy. I've—I've just recently undergone a paradigm shift, you know? The whole world looks different, and my head's there but sometimes my gut—I mean, it's so hard to *feel* differently about things..."

"Tell me about this paradigm shift," Thomas suggests. He makes it a point not to take notes. He doesn't even have a notepad. Not that it matters. The microcassette recorder in his blazer has very sensitive ears.

"Things make sense now," she says. "They never did before. I think, for the first time in my life, I'm actually happy." She smiles again, for longer this time. Long enough for Thomas to marvel at how genuine it seems.

"You weren't very happy when you first came here," he says gently. "They say you were very upset."

"Yeah." She nods, seriously. "It's tough enough to do that shit to yourself, you know, but to risk someone else, someone you really care about—" She wipes at one eye. "He was dying for over a year, did you know that? Each day he'd hurt a little more. You could almost see it spreading through him, like some sort of—leaf, going brown. Or maybe that was the chemo. Never could decide which was worse." She shakes her head. "Heh. At least *that's* over now."

"Is that why you did it? To end his suffering?" Thomas doubts it. Mercy killers don't generally disembowel their beneficiaries. Still, he asks.

She answers. "Of course I fucked up, I only ended up making things worse." She clasps her hands in front of her. "I miss him already. Isn't that crazy? It only happened a few hours ago, and I know it's no big deal, but I still miss him. That head-heart thing again."

"You say you fucked up," Thomas says.

She takes a deep breath, nods. "Big time."

"Tell me about that."

"I don't know shit about debugging. I thought I did, but when you're dealing with organics—all I really did was go in and mess randomly with the code. You make a mess of everything, unless you know exactly what you're doing. That's what I'm working on now."

"Debugging?"

"That's what I call it. There's no real word for it yet."

Oh yes there is. Aloud: "Go on."

Jasmine Fitzgerald sighs, her eyes closed. "I don't expect you to believe this under the circumstances, but I really loved him. No: I *love* him." Her breath comes out in a soft snort, a whispered laugh. "There I go again. That bloody past tense."

"Tell me about debugging."

"I don't think you're up for it, Myles. I don't even think you're all that interested." Her eyes open, point directly at him. "But for the record, Stu was dying. I tried to save him. I failed. Next time I'll do better, and better still the time after that, and eventually I'll get it right."

"And what happens then?" Thomas says.

"Through your eyes or mine?"

"Yours."

"I repair the glitches in the string. Or if it's easier, I replicate an undamaged version of the subroutine and insert it back into the main loop. Same difference."

"Uh huh. And what would *I* see?"

She shrugs. "Stu rising from the dead."

What's wrong with this picture?

Spread out across the table, the mind of Jasmine Fitzgerald winks back from pages of standardised questions. Somewhere in here, presumably, is a monster.

These are the tools used to dissect human psyches. The WAIS. The MMPI. The PDI. Hammers, all of them. Blunt chisels posing as microtomes. A copy of the DSM-IV sits off to one side, a fat paperback volume of symptoms and pathologies. A matrix of pigeonholes. Perhaps Fitzgerald fits into one of them. Intermittent Explosive, maybe? Battered Woman? Garden-variety Sociopath?

The test results are inconclusive. It's as though she's laughing up from the page at him. *True or false: I sometimes hear voices that no one else hears.* False, she's checked. *I have been feeling unusually depressed lately.* False. *Sometimes I get so angry I feel like hitting something.* True, and a hand-written note in the margin: Hey, doesn't everyone?

There are snares sprinkled throughout these tests, linked questions designed to catch liars in subtle traps of self-contradiction. Jasmine Fitzgerald has avoided them all. Is she unusually honest? Is she too smart for the tests? There doesn't seem to be anything here that—

Wait a second.

Who was Louis Pasteur? asks the WAIS, trying to get a handle on educational background.

A virus, Fitzgerald said.

Back up the list. Here's another one, on the previous page: *Who was Winston Churchill?* And again: a virus.

And fifteen questions before *that*: *Who was Florence Nightingale?*

A famous nurse, Fitzgerald responded to that one. And her responses to all previous questions on historical personalities are unremarkably correct. But everyone after Nightingale is a virus.

Killing a virus is no sin. You can do it with an utterly clear conscience. Maybe she's redefining the nature of her act. Maybe that's how she manages to live with herself these days.

Just as well. That raising-the-dead shtick didn't cut any ice at all.

She's slumped across the table when he enters, her head resting on folded arms. Thomas clears his throat. "Jasmine."

No response. He reaches out, touches her lightly on the shoulder. Her head comes up, a fluid motion containing no hint of grogginess. She settles back into her chair and smiles. "Welcome back. So, am I crazy or what?"

Thomas smiles back and sits down across from her. "We try to avoid prejudicial terms."

"Hey, I can take it. I'm not prone to tantrums."

A picture flashes across the front of his mind: beloved husband, entrails spread-eagled like butterfly wings against a linoleum grid. *Of course not. No tantrums for you. We need a whole new word to describe what it is you do.*

"Debugging," wasn't it?

"I was going over your test results," he begins.

"Did I pass?"

"It's not that kind of test. But I was intrigued by some of your answers."

She purses her lips. "Good."

"Tell me about viruses."

That sunny smile again. "Sure. Mutable information strings that can't replicate without hijacking external source code."

"Go on."

"Ever hear of Core Wars?"

"No."

"Back in the early eighties some guys got together and wrote a bunch of self-replicating computer programs. The idea was to put them into the same block of memory and have them compete for space. They all had their own little tricks for self-defence and reproduction and, of course, eating the competition."

"Oh, you mean *computer* viruses," Thomas says.

"Actually, before all that." Fitzgerald pauses a moment, cocks her head to one side. "You ever wonder what it might be like to *be* one of those little programs? Running around laying eggs and dropping logic bombs and interacting with other viruses?"

Thomas shrugs. "I never even knew about them until now. Why? Do you?"

"No," she says. "Not any more."

"Go on."

Her expression changes. "You know, talking to *you* is a bit like talking to a program. All you ever say is *go on* and *tell me more* and—I mean, Jesus, Myles, they wrote therapy programs back in the *sixties* that had more range than you do! In BASIC even! Register an *opinion*, for Chrissake!"

"It's just a technique, Jaz. I'm not here to get into a debate with you, as interesting as that might be. I'm trying to assess your fitness to stand trial. *My* opinions aren't really at issue."

She sighs, and sags. "I know. I'm sorry, I know you're not here to keep me entertained, but I'm *used* to being able to—

"I mean, *Stuart* would always be so—

"Oh, God. I miss him so *much*," she admits, her eyes shining and unhappy.

She's a killer, he tells himself. *Don't let her suck you in. Just assess her, that's all you have to do.*

Don't start liking her, for Christ's sake.

"That's—understandable," Thomas says.

She snorts. "Bullshit. You don't understand at all. You know what he did, the first time he went in for chemo? I was studying for my comps, and he stole my textbooks."

"Why would he do that?"

"Because he knew I wasn't studying at home. I was a complete wreck. And when I came to see him at the hospital he pulls these bloody books out from under his bed and starts quizzing me on Dirac and the Bekenstein bound. He was *dying*, and all he wanted to do was help me prepare for some stupid test. I'd do anything for him."

Well, Thomas doesn't say, *you certainly did more than most.*

"I can't wait to see him again," she adds, almost as an afterthought.

"When will that be, Jaz?"

"When do you think?" She looks at him, and the sorrow and despair he thought he saw in those eyes is suddenly nowhere to be seen.

"Most people, if they said that, would be talking about the afterlife."

She favours him with a sad little smile. "This *is* the afterlife, Myles. This is Heaven, and Hell, and Nirvana. Whatever we choose to make it. Right here."

"Yes," Thomas says after a moment. "Of course."

Her disappointment in him hangs there like an accusation.

"You don't believe in God, do you?" she asks at last.

"Do you?" he ricochets.

"Didn't used to. Turns out there's clues, though. Proof, even."

"Such as?"

"The mass of the top quark. The width of the Higgs boson. You can't read them any other way when you know what you're looking for. Know anything about quantum physics, Myles?"

He shakes his head. "Not really."

"Nothing really exists, not down at the subatomic level. It's all just probability waves. Until someone looks at it, that is. Then the wave collapses and you get what we call *reality*. But it can't happen without an observer to get things started."

Thomas squints, trying to squeeze some sort of insight into his brain. "So if we weren't here looking at this table, it wouldn't exist?"

Fitzgerald nods. "More or less." That smile peeks around the corner of her mouth for a second.

He tries to lure it back. "So God's the observer, is that what you're saying? God watches all the atoms so the universe can exist?"

"Huh. I never thought about it that way before." The smile morphs into a frown of concentration. "More metaphoric than mathematical, but it's a cool idea."

"Was God watching you yesterday?"

She looks up, distracted. "Huh?"

"Does He—does It communicate with you?"

Her face goes completely expressionless. "Does God tell me to do things, you mean. Did God tell me to carve Stu up like—like—" Her breath hisses out between her teeth. "No, Myles. I don't hear voices. Charlie Manson doesn't come to me in my dreams and whisper sweet nothings. I answered all those questions on your test already, so give me a fucking break, okay?"

He holds up his hands, placating. "That's not what I meant, Jasmine." *Liar.* "I'm sorry if that's how it sounded, it's just—you know, God, quantum mechanics—it's a lot to swallow at once, you know? It's—mind-blowing."

She watches him through guarded eyes. "Yeah. I guess it can be. I forget, sometimes." She relaxes a fraction. "But it's all true. The math is inevitable. You can change the nature of reality, just by *looking* at it. You're right. It's mind-blowing."

"But only at the subatomic level, right? You're not *really* saying we could make this table disappear just by ignoring it, are you?"

Her eye flickers to a spot just to the right and behind him, about where the door should be.

"Well, no," she says at last. "Not without a lot of practise."

What's wrong with this picture?

Besides the obvious, of course. Besides the vertical incision running from sternum to approximately two centimetres below the navel, penetrating the abdominal musculature and extending through into the visceral coelom. Beyond the serrations along its edge which suggest the use of some sort of blade. Not, evidently, a very sharp one.

No. We're getting ahead of ourselves here. The coroner's art is nothing if not systematic. Very well, then: Caucasian male, mid-twenties. External morphometrics previously noted. Hair loss and bruising consistent with chemotherapeutic toxicity. Right index and ring fingernails missing, same notation. The deceased was one sick puppy at time of demise. Sickened by the disease, poisoned by the cure. And just when you thought things couldn't get any worse...

Down and in. The wound swallows the coroner's rubberised hands like some huge torn vagina, its labia clotted and crystallised. The usual viscera glisten inside, repackaged by medics at the site who had to reel in all loose ends for transport. Perhaps evidence was lost in the process. Perhaps the killer had arranged the entrails in some significant pattern, perhaps the arrangement of the GI tract spelled out some clue or unholy name. No matter. They took pictures of everything.

Mesentery stretches like thin latex, binding loops of intestine one to the other. A bit too tightly, in fact. There appear to be—fistulas of some sort, scattered along the lower ileum. Loops seem fused together at several spots. What could have caused that?

Nothing comes to mind.

Note it, record it, take a sample for detailed histological analysis. Move on. The scalpel passes through the tract as easily as through overcooked pasta. Stringy bile and pre-fecal lumps slump tiredly into a collecting dish. Something bulges behind them from the dorsal wall. Something shines white as bone where no bone should be. Slice, resect. There. A mass of some kind covering the right kidney, approximately fifteen centimetres by ten, extending down to the bladder. Quite heterogeneous, it's got some sort of *lumps* in it. A tumour? Is this what Stuart MacLennan's doctors were duelling with when they pumped him full of poison? It doesn't look like any tumour the coroner's seen.

For one thing—and this is really kind of strange—it's looking *back* at him.

———

His desk is absolutely spartan. Not a shred of paper out of place. Not a shred of paper even in evidence, actually. The surface is as featureless as a Kubrick monolith, except for the Sun workstation positioned dead centre and a rack of CDs angled off to the left.

"I *thought* she looked familiar," he says. "When I saw the papers. Didn't know quite where to place her, though."

Jasmine Fitzgerald's graduate supervisor.

"I guess you've got a lot of students," Thomas suggests.

"Yes." He leans forward, begins tapping at the workstation keyboard. "I've yet to meet all of them, actually. One or two in Europe I correspond with exclusively over the net. I hope to meet them this summer in Berne—ah, yes. Here she is; doesn't look anything like the media picture."

"She doesn't live in Europe, Dr. Russell."

"No, right here. Did her field work at CERN, though. Damn hard getting anything done here since the supercollider fell through. Ah."

"What?"

"She's on leave. I remember her now. She put her thesis on hold about a year and a half ago. Illness in the family, as I recall." Russell stares at the monitor; something he sees there seems to sink in, all at once. "She killed her husband? She *killed* him?"

Thomas nods.

"My God." Russell shakes his head. "She didn't seem the type. She always seemed so—well, so cheery."

"She still does, sometimes."

"My God," he repeats. "And how can I help you?"

"She's suffering from some very elaborate delusions. She couches them in a lot of technical terminology I don't understand. I mean, for all I know she could actually be making *sense*—no, no. Scratch that. She *can't* be, but I don't have the background to really understand her, well, *claims*."

"What sort of *claims*?"

"For one thing, she keeps talking about bringing her husband back from the dead."

"I see."

"You don't seem surprised."

"Should I be? You said she was delusional."

Thomas takes a deep breath. "Dr. Russell, I've been doing some reading the past couple of days. Popular cosmology, quantum mechanics for beginners, that sort of thing."

Russell smiles indulgently. "I suppose it's never too late to start."

"I get the impression that a lot of the stuff that happens down at the subatomic level almost has quasi-religious overtones. Spontaneous appearance of matter, simultaneous existence in different states. Almost spiritual."

"Yes, I suppose that's true. After a fashion."

"Are cosmologists a religious lot, by and large?"

"Not really." Russell drums fingers on his monolith. "The field's so strange that we don't really *need* religious experience on top of it. Some of the eastern religions make claims that sound vaguely quantum-mechanical, but the similarities are pretty superficial."

"Nothing more, well, Christian? Nothing that would lead someone to believe in a single omniscient God who raises the dead?"

"God no. Oh, except for that Tipler fellow." Russell leans forward. "Why? Jasmine Fitzgerald hasn't become a Christian, has she?" Murder is one thing, his tone suggests, but *this*...

"I don't think so," Thomas reassures him. "Not unless Christianity's broadened its tenets to embrace human sacrifice."

"Yes. Quite." Russell leans back again, apparently satisfied.

"Who's Tipler?" Thomas asks.

"Mmmm?" Russell blinks, momentarily distracted. "Oh, yes. Frank Tipler. Cosmologist from Tulane, claimed to have a testable mathematical proof of the existence of God. And the afterlife too, if I recall. Raised a bit of a stir a few years back."

"I take it you weren't impressed."

"Actually, I didn't follow it very closely. Theology's not that interesting to me. I mean, if physics proves that there is or there isn't a god that's fine, but that's not really the point of the exercise, is it?"

"I couldn't say. Seems to me it'd be a hell of a spin-off, though."

Russell smiles.

"I don't suppose you've got the reference?" Thomas suggests.

"Of course. Just a moment." Russell feeds a CD to the workstation and massages the keyboard. The Sun purrs. "Yes, here it is: *The Physics of Immortality: Modern Cosmology, God and the Resurrection of the Dead.* 1994, Frank J. Tipler. I can print you out the complete citation if you want."

"Please. So what was his proof?"

The professor displays something akin to a very small smile.

"In thirty words or less," Thomas adds. "For idiots."

"Well," Russell says, "basically, he argued that some billions of years hence, life will incorporate itself into a massive quantum-effect computing device to avoid extinction when the universe collapses."

"I thought the universe wasn't *going* to collapse," Thomas interjects. "I thought they proved it was just going to keep expanding..."

"That was last year," Russell says shortly. "May I continue?"

"Yes, of course."

"Thank you. As I was saying, Tipler claimed that billions of years hence, life will incorporate itself into a massive quantum-effect computing device to avoid extinction when the universe collapses. An integral part of this process involves the exact reproduction of everything that ever happened in the universe up to that point, right down to the quantum level, as well as all possible variations of those events."

Beside the desk, Russell's printer extrudes a paper tongue. He pulls it free and hands it over.

"So God's a supercomputer at the end of time? And we'll all be resurrected in the mother of all simulation models?"

"Well—" Russell wavers. The caricature seems to cause him physical pain. "I suppose so," he finishes, reluctantly. "In thirty words or less, as you say."

"Wow." Suddenly Fitzgerald's ravings sound downright pedestrian. "But if he's right—"

"The consensus is he's not," Russell interjects hastily.

"But *if*. If the model's an exact reproduction, how could you tell the difference between real life and afterlife? I mean, what would be the *point*?"

"Well, the point is avoiding ultimate extinction, supposedly. As to how you'd tell the difference..." Russell shakes his head. "Actually, I never finished the book. As I said, theology doesn't interest me all that much."

Thomas shakes his head. "I can't believe it."

"Not many could," Russell says. Then, almost apologetically, he adds: "Tipler's theoretical proofs were quite extensive, though, as I recall."

"I bet. Whatever happened to him?"

Russell shrugs. "What happens to anyone who's stupid enough to come up with a new way of looking at the world? They tore into him like sharks at a feeding frenzy. I don't know where he ended up."

What's wrong with this picture?

Nothing. Everything. Suddenly awake, Myles Thomas stares around a darkened studio and tries to convince himself that nothing has changed.

Nothing *has* changed. The faint sounds of late-night traffic sound the same as ever. Gray parallelograms stretch across wall and ceiling, a faint luminous shadow of his bedroom window cast by some distant streetlight. Natalie's still gone from the left side of his bed, her departure so far removed by now that he doesn't even have to remind himself of it.

He checks the LEDs on his bedside alarm: 2:35a.

Something's different.

Nothing's changed.

Well, maybe one thing. Tipler's heresy sits on the night stand, its plastic dustcover reflecting slashes of red light from the alarm clock. *The Physics of Immortality: Modern Cosmology, God and the Resurrection of the Dead.* It's too dark to read the lettering but you don't forget a title like that. Myles Thomas signed it out of the library this afternoon, opened it at random:

...Lemma 1, and the fact that, $f_{ij} = \sum_{k=1}^{\infty} f_{ij}^{(k)} \leq 1$ we have

$$\sum_{n=1}^{\infty} p_{ij}^{(n)} = \sum_{n=1}^{\infty} \sum_{k=1}^{n} f_{ij}^{(k)} p_{jj}^{(n-k)} = \sum_{k=1}^{\infty} f_{ij}^{(k)} \sum_{n=0}^{\infty} p_{jj}^{(n)}$$

$$= f_{ij} \sum_{n=0}^{\infty} p_{jj}^{(n)} \leq \sum_{n=0}^{\infty} p_{jj}^{(n)} < \infty$$

which is just (*E*.3), and (*E*.3) can hold only if...

—and threw it into his briefcase, confused and disgusted. He doesn't even know why he went to the effort of getting the fucking thing. Jasmine Fitzgerald is delusional. It's that simple. For reasons that it is not Myles Thomas's job to understand, she vivisected her husband on the kitchen floor. Now she's inventing all sorts of ways to excuse herself, to undo the undoable, and the fact that she cloaks her delusions in cosmological gobbledegook does not make them any more credible. What does he expect to do, turn into a quantum mechanic overnight? Is he going to learn even a fraction of what he'd need to find the holes in her carefully constructed fantasy? Why did he even bother?

But he did. And now *Modern Cosmology, God and the Resurrection of the Dead* looms dimly in front of him at two thirty in the fucking morning, and something's changed, he's almost *sure* of it, but try as he might he can't get a handle on what it is. He just feels different, somehow. He just feels...

Awake. That's what you feel. You couldn't get back to sleep now if your life depended on it.

Myles Thomas sighs and turns on the reading lamp. Squinting as his pupils shrink against the light, he reaches out and grabs the offending book.

Parts of it, astonishingly, almost make sense.

"She's not here," the orderly tells him. "Last night we had to move her next door."

Next door: the hospital. "Why? What's wrong?"

"Not a clue. Convulsions, cyanosis—we thought she was toast, actually. But by the time the doctor got to her she couldn't find anything wrong."

"That doesn't make any sense."

"Tell me about it. Nothing about that crazy b—nothing about her makes sense." The orderly wanders off down the hall, frowning.

Jasmine Fitzgerald lies between sheets tucked tight as a straitjacket, stares unblinking at the ceiling. A nurse sits to one side, boredom and curiosity mixing in equal measures on his face.

"How is she?" Thomas asks.

"Don't really know," the nurse says. "She seems okay now."

"She doesn't look okay to me. She looks almost catatonic."

"She isn't. Are you, Jaz?"

"We're sorry," Fitzgerald says cheerfully. "The person you are trying to reach is temporarily unavailable. Please leave a message and we'll get back to you." Then: "Hi, Myles. Good to see you." Her eyes never waver from the acoustic tiles overhead.

"You better blink one of these days," Thomas remarks. "Your eyeballs are going to dry up."

"Nothing a little judicious editing won't fix," she tells him.

Thomas glances at the nurse. "Would you excuse us for a few minutes?"

"Sure. I'll be in the caf if you need me."

Thomas waits until the door swings shut. "So, Jaz. What's the mass of the Higgs boson?"

She blinks.

She smiles.

She turns to look at him.

"Two hundred twenty-eight GeV," she says. "All *right*. Someone actually *read* my thesis proposal."

"Not just your proposal. That's one of Tipler's testable predictions, isn't it?"

Her smile widens. "The critical one, actually. The others are pretty self-evident."

"And you tested it."

"Yup. Over at CERN. So how'd you find his book?"

"I only read parts of it," Thomas admits. "It was pretty tough slogging."

"Sorry. My fault," Fitzgerald says.

"How so?"

"I thought you could use some help, so I souped you up a bit. Increased your processing speed. Not enough, I guess."

Something shivers down his back. He ignores it.

"I'm not—". Thomas rubs his chin; he forgot to shave this morning "—exactly sure what you mean by that."

"Sure you do. You just don't believe it." Fitzgerald squirms up from between the sheets, props her back against a pillow. "It's just a semantic difference, Myles. You'd call it a *delusion*. Us physics geeks would call it a *hypothesis*."

Thomas nods, uncertainly.

"Oh, just say it, Myles. I know you're dying to."

"Go on," he blurts, strangely unable to stop himself.

Fitzgerald laughs. "If you insist, Doctor. I figured out what I was doing wrong. I thought I had to do everything myself, and I just can't. Too many variables, you see, even if you access them individually there's no way you can keep track of 'em all at once. When I tried, I got mixed up and everything—"

A sudden darkness in her face now. A memory, perhaps, pushing up through all those careful layers of contrivance.

"Everything went wrong," she finishes softly.

Thomas nods, keeps his voice low and gentle. "What are you remembering right now, Jaz?"

"You know damn well what I'm remembering," she whispers. "I—I cut him open—"

"Yes."

"He was dying. He was *dying*. I tried to fix him, I tried to fix the code but something went wrong, and..."

He waits. The silence stretches.

"...and I didn't know what. I couldn't fix it if I couldn't see what I'd done wrong. So I—I cut him open..." Her brow furrows suddenly. Thomas can't tell with what: remembrance, remorse?

"I really overstepped myself," she says at last.

No. Concentration. She's rebuilding her defences, she's pushing the tip of that bloody iceberg back below the surface. It can't be easy. Thomas can see it, ponderous and massively buoyant, pushing up from the depths while Jasmine Fitzgerald leans down and desperately pretends not to strain.

"I know it must be difficult to think about," Thomas says.

She shrugs. "Sometimes." *Going...* "When my head slips back into the old school. Old habits die hard." *Going...* "But I get over it."

The frown disappears.

Gone.

"You know when I told you about Core Wars?" she asks brightly.

After a moment, Thomas nods.

"All viruses replicate, but some of the better ones can write macros—*micros*, actually, would be a better name for them—to other addresses, little subroutines that autonomously perform simple tasks. And some of *those* can replicate too. Get my drift?"

"Not really," Thomas says quietly.

"I really should have souped you up a bit more. Anyway, those little routines, they can handle all the book-keeping. Each one tracks a few variables, and each time they replicate that's a few more, and pretty soon there's no limit to the size of the problem you can handle. Hell, you could rewrite the whole damn operating system from the inside out and not have to worry about any of the details, all your little daemons are doing that for you."

"Are we all just viruses to you, Jaz?"

She laughs at that, not unkindly. "Ah, Myles. It's a technical term, not a moral judgement. Life's information, shaped by natural selection. That's all I mean."

"And you've learned to—rewrite the code," Thomas says.

She shakes her head. "Still learning. But I'm getting better at it all the time."

"I see." Thomas pretends to check his watch. He still doesn't know the jargon. He never will. But at least, at last, he knows where she's coming from.

Nothing left but the final platitudes.

"That's all I need right now, Jasmine. I want to thank you for being so co-operative. I know how tough this must be on you."

She cocks her head at him, smiling. "This is goodbye then, Myles? You haven't come *close* to curing me."

He smiles back. He can almost feel each muscle fibre contracting, the increased tension on facial tendons, soft tissue stretching over bone. The utter insincerity of a purely mechanical process. "That's not what I'm here for, Jaz."

"Right. You're assessing my fitness."

Thomas nods.

"Well?" she asks after a moment. "Am I fit?"

He takes a breath. "I think you have some problems you haven't faced. But you can understand counsel, and there's no doubt you could follow any proceedings the court is likely to throw at you. Legally, that means you can stand trial."

"Ah. So I'm not sane, but I'm not crazy enough to get off, eh?"

"I hope things work out for you." That much, at least, is sincere.

"Oh, they will," she says easily. "Never fear. How much longer do I stay here?"

"Maybe another three weeks. Thirty days is the usual period."

"But you've finished with me. Why so long?"

He shrugs. "Nowhere else to put you, for now."

"Oh." She considers. "Just as well, I guess. It'll give me more time to practice."

"Goodbye, Jasmine."

"Too bad you missed Stuart," she says behind him. "You'd have liked him. Maybe I'll bring him around to your place sometime."

The doorknob sticks. He tries again.

"Something wrong?" she asks.

"No," Thomas says, a bit too quickly. "It's just—"

"Oh, right. Hang on a sec." She rustles in her sheets.

He turns his head. Jasmine Fitzgerald lies flat on her back, unblinking, staring straight up. Her breath is fast and shallow.

The doorknob seems subtly warmer in his hand.

He releases it. "Are you okay?"

"Sure," she says to the ceiling. "Just tired. Takes a bit out of you, you know?"

Call the nurse, he thinks.

"Really, I just need some rest." She looks at him one last time, and giggles. "But Myles to go before I sleep..."

"Dr. Desjardins, please."

"Speaking."

"You performed the autopsy on Stuart MacLennan?"

A brief silence. Then: "Who is this?"

"My name's Myles Thomas. I'm a psychologist at FPSS. Jasmine Fitzgerald is—was a client of mine."

The phone sits there in his hand, silent.

"I was looking at the case report, writing up my assessment, and I just noticed something about your findings—"

"They're preliminary," Desjardins interrupts. "I'll have the full report, um, shortly."

"Yes, I understand that, Dr. Desjardins. But my understanding is that MacLennan was, well, mortally wounded."

"He was gutted like a fish," Desjardins says.

"Right. But your r—your *preliminary* report lists cause of death as 'undetermined.'"

"That's because I haven't determined the cause of death."

"Right. I guess I'm a bit confused about what else it could have been. You didn't find any toxins in the body, at least none that weren't involved in MacLennan's chemo, and no other injuries except for these fistulas and teratomas—"

The phone barks in Thomas's hand, a short ugly laugh. "Do you know what a teratoma *is*?" Desjardins asks.

"I assumed it was something to do with his cancer."

"Ever hear the term *primordial cyst*?"

"No."

"Hope you haven't eaten recently," Desjardins says. "Every now and then you get a clump of proliferating cells floating around in the coelomic cavity. Something happens to activate the dormant genes—could be a lot of things, but the upshot is you sometimes get these growing blobs of tissue sprouting teeth and hair and bone. Sometimes they get as big as grapefruits."

"My God. MacLennan had one of those in him?"

"I thought, maybe. At first. Turned out to be a chunk of his kidney. Only there was an eye growing out of it. And most of his abdominal lymph nodes, too, the ducts were clotted with hair and something like fingernail. It was keratinised, anyway."

"That's horrible," Thomas whispers.

"No shit. Not to mention the perforated diaphragm, or the fact that half the loops of his small intestine were fused together."

"But I thought he had leukaemia."

"He did. That wasn't what killed him."

"So you're saying these teratomas might have had some role in MacLennan's death?"

"I don't see how," Desjardins says.

"But—"

"Look, maybe I'm not making myself clear. I have my doubts that Stuart MacLennan died from his wife's carving skills because any *one* of the abnormalities I found should have killed him more or less instantly."

"But that's pretty much impossible, isn't it? I mean, what did the investigating officers say?"

"Quite frankly, I don't think they read my report," Desjardins grumbles. "Neither did you, apparently, or you would have called me before now."

"Well, it wasn't really central to my assessment, Dr. Desjardins. And besides, it seemed so obvious—"

"For sure. You see someone laid open from crotch to sternum, you don't need any report to know what killed him. Who cares about any of this congenital abnormality bullshit?"

Congen—"You're saying he was *born* that way?"

"Except he couldn't have been. He'd never have even made it to his first breath."

"So you're saying—"

"I'm saying Stuart MacLennan's wife couldn't have killed him, because physiologically there's no way in hell that he could have been alive to start with."

Thomas stares at the phone. It offers no retraction.

"But—he was twenty-eight years old! How could that be?"

"God only knows," Desjardins tells him. "You ask me, it's a fucking miracle."

What's wrong with this picture?

He isn't quite certain, because he doesn't quite know what he was expecting. No opened grave, no stone rolled dramatically away from the sepulchre. Of course not. Jasmine Fitzgerald would probably say that her powers are too subtle for such obvious theatre. Why leave a pile of shovelled earth, an opened coffin, when you can just rewrite the code?

She sits cross-legged on her husband's undisturbed grave. Whatever powers she lays claim to, they don't shield her from the light rain falling on her head. She doesn't even have an umbrella.

"Myles," she says, not looking up. "I thought it might be you." Her sunny smile, that radiant expression of happy denial, is nowhere to be seen. Her face is as expressionless as her husband's must be, two meters down.

"Hello, Jaz," Thomas says.

"How did you find me?" she asks him.

"FPSS went ballistic when you disappeared. They're calling everyone who had any contact with you, trying to figure out how you got out. Where you might be."

Her fingers play in the fresh earth. "Did you tell them?"

"I didn't think of this place until after," he lies. Then, to atone: "And I don't *know* how you got out."

"Yes you do, Myles. You do it yourself all the time."

"Go on," he says, deliberately.

She smiles, but it doesn't last. "We got here the same way, Myles. We copied ourselves from one address to another. The only difference is, you still have to go from A to B to C. I just cut straight to Z."

"I can't accept that," Thomas says.

"Ever the doubter, aren't you? How can you enjoy heaven when you can't even recognise it?" Finally, she looks up at him. "*You should be told the difference between empiricism and stubbornness, Doctor.* Know what that's from?"

He shakes his head.

"Oh well. It's not important." She looks back at the ground. Wet tendrils of hair hang across her face. "They wouldn't let me come to the funeral."

"You don't seem to need their permission."

"Not now. That was a few days ago. I still hadn't worked all the bugs out then." She plunges one hand into wet dirt. "You know what I did to him."

Before the knife, she means.

"I'm not—I don't really—"

"You know," she says again.

Finally he nods, although she isn't looking.

The rain falls harder. Thomas shivers under his windbreaker. Fitzgerald doesn't seem to notice.

"So what now?" he asks at last.

"I'm not sure. It seemed so straightforward at first, you know? I loved Stuart, completely, without reservation. I was going to bring him back as soon as I learned how. I was going to do it right this time. And I still love him, I really do, but damn it all I don't love *everything* about him, you know? He was a slob, sometimes. And I hated his taste in music. So now that I'm here, I figure, why stop at just bringing him back? Why not, well, fine-tune him a bit?"

"Is that what you're going to do?"

"I don't know. I'm going through all the things I'd change, and when it comes right down to it maybe it'd be better to just start again from scratch. Less—intensive. Computationally."

"I hope you *are* delusional." Not a wise thing to say, but suddenly he doesn't care. "Because if you're not, God's a really callous bastard."

"Is it," she says, without much interest.

"Everything's just information. We're all just subroutines interacting in a model somewhere. Well nothing's really all that important then, is it? You'll get around to debugging Stuart one of these days. No hurry. He can wait. It's just microcode, nothing's irrevocable. So nothing really *matters*, does it? How could God give a shit about anything in a universe like that?"

Jasmine Fitzgerald rises from the grave and wipes the dirt off her hands. "Watch it, Myles." There's a faint smile on her face. "You don't want to piss me off."

He meets her eyes. "I'm glad I still can."

"*Touché.*" There's still a twinkle there, behind her soaked lashes and the runnels of rainwater coursing down her face.

"So what are you going to do?" he asks again.

She looks around the soaking graveyard. "Everything. I'm going to clean the place up. I'm going to fill in the holes. I'm going to rewrite Planck's constant so it makes *sense*." She smiles at him. "Right now, though, I think I'm just going to go somewhere and think about things for a while."

She steps off the mound. "Thanks for not telling on me. It wouldn't have made any difference, but I appreciate the thought. I won't forget it." She begins to walk away in the rain.

"Jaz," Thomas calls after her.

She shakes her head, without looking back. "Forget it, Myles. Nobody handed *me* any miracles." She stops, then, turns briefly. "Besides, you're not ready. You'd probably just think I hypnotised you or something."

I should stop her, Thomas tells himself. *She's dangerous. She's deluded. They could charge me with aiding and abetting. I should stop her.*

If I can.

She leaves him in the rain with the memory of that bright, guiltless smile. He's almost sure he doesn't feel anything pass through him then. But maybe he does. Maybe it feels like a ripple growing across some stagnant surface. A subtle reweaving of electrons. A small change in the way things are.

I'm going to clean the place up. I'm going to fill in the holes.

Myles Thomas doesn't know exactly what she meant by that. But he's afraid that soon—far too soon—there won't be anything wrong with this picture.

A WORD FOR HEATHENS

I am the hand of God.

His Spirit fills me even in this desecrated place. It saturates my very bones, it imbues my sword-arm with the strength of ten. The cleansing flame pours from my fingertips and scours the backs of the fleeing infidels. They boil from their hole like grubs exposed by the dislodging of a rotten log. They writhe through the light, seeking only darkness. As if there could be any darkness in the sight of God—did they actually think He would be blind to the despoiling of a place of *worship*, did they think He would not notice this wretched burrow dug out beneath His very *altar*?

Now their blood erupts steaming from the blackened crusts of their own flesh. The sweet stink of burning meat wafts faintly through my filter. Skin peels away like bits of blackened parchment, swirling in the updrafts. One of the heathens lurches over the lip of the hole and collapses at my feet. *Look past the faces*, they told us on the training fields, but today that advice means nothing; this abomination *has* no face, just a steaming clot of seared meat puckered by a bubbling fissure near one end. The fissure splits, revealing absurdly white teeth behind. Something between a whine and a scream, barely audible over the roar of the flames: *Please,* maybe. Or *Mommy*.

I swing my truncheon in a glorious backhand. Teeth scatter across the room like tiny dice. Other bodies crawl about the floor of the chapel, leaving charred bloody streaks on the floor like the slime trails of giant slugs. I don't think I've *ever* been so overpowered by God's presence in my life. I am Saul, massacring the people of Amolek. I am Joshua butchering the Amorites. I am Asa exterminating the Ethiopians. I hold down the stud and sweep the room with great gouts of fire. I am so filled with divine love I feel ready to burst into flame myself.

"Praetor!"

Isaiah claps my shoulder from behind. His wide eyes stare back at me, distorted by the curve of his faceplate. "Sir, they're dead! We need to put out the fire!"

For the first time in what seems like ages I notice the rest of my guard. The prefects stand around the corners of the room as I arranged them, covering the exits, the silver foil of their uniforms writhing with fragments of reflected flame. They grip not flamethrowers, but dousers. Part of me wonders how they could have held back; how could *anyone* feel the Spirit in this way, and not bring down the fire? But the Spirit recedes in me even now, and descending from that peak I can see that God's work is all but finished here. The heathens are dead, guttering stick-figures on the floor. Their refuge has been cleansed, the altar that once concealed it lies toppled on the floor where I kicked it just—

Was it only a few minutes ago? It seems like forever.

"Sir?"

I nod. Isaiah gives the sign; the prefects step forward and spray the chapel with fire-suppressants. The flames vanish; the light goes gray. Crumbling semicremated corpses erupt in clouds of wet hissing steam as the chemicals hit.

Isaiah watches me through the smoky air. It billows around us like a steam bath. "Are you all right, sir?" The sudden moisture lends a hiss to his voice; his respirator needs a new filter.

I nod. "The Spirit was so—so..." I'm lost for words. "I've never felt it so strong before."

There's a hint of a frown behind his mask. "Are you—I mean, are you *sure?*"

I laugh, delighted. "Am I *sure?* I felt like Trajan himself!"

Isaiah looks uncomfortable, perhaps at my invocation of Trajan's name. His funeral was only yesterday, after all. Yet I meant no disrespect—if anything, I acted today in his memory. I can see him standing at God's side, looking down into this steaming abattoir and nodding with approval. Perhaps the very heathen that murdered him lies here at my feet. I can see Trajan turning to the Lord and pointing out the worm that killed him.

I can hear the Lord saying, *Vengeance is mine.*

An outcast huddles at the far end of the Josephus platform, leaning across the barrier in a sad attempt to bathe in the tram's maglev field. The action is both pointless and pitiful; the generators are shielded, and even if they weren't the Spirit moves in so many different ways. It never ceases to amaze me how people can fail at such simple distinctions: shown that electromagnetic fields, precisely modulated, can connect us with the divine, they somehow conclude that *any* coil of wire and energy opens the door to redemption.

But the fields that move chariots are not those that grace us with the Rapture. Even if this misguided creature were to get his wish, even if by some perverse miracle the shielding were to vanish around the tram's coils, the best he could hope for would be nausea and disorientation. The worst—and it happens more than some would admit, these days—could be outright possession.

I've seen the possessed. I've dealt with the demons who inhabit them. The outcast is luckier than he knows.

I step onto the tram. The Spirit pushes the vehicle silently forward, tied miraculously to a ribbon of track it never touches. The platform slides past; the pariah and I lock eyes for a moment before distance disconnects us.

Not shame on his face: dull, inarticulate *rage.*

My armor, I suppose. It was someone like me who arrested him, who denied him a merciful death and left his body lingering in the world, severed from its very soul.

A pair of citizens at my side point at the dwindling figure and giggle. I glare at them: they notice my insignia, my holstered shockprod, and fall silent. I see nothing ridiculous in the outcast's desperation. Pitiful, yes. Ineffective. Irrational. And yet, what would any of us do, cut off from grace? Would any straw be too thin to grasp, for a chance at redemption?

Everything is so utterly clear in the presence of God. The whole universe makes sense, like a child's riddle suddenly solved; you see forever, you wonder how all these glorious pieces of creation could ever have confused you. At the moment, of course, those details are lost to me. All that remains is the indescribable memory of how it felt to have *understood*, absolutely and perfectly...and that memory, hours old, feels more real to me than *now*.

The tram glides smoothly into the next station. The newsfeed across the piazza replays looped imagery of Trajan's funeral. I still can't believe he's dead. Trajan was so strong in the Spirit we'd begun to think him invulnerable. That he could be bested by some *thing* built in the Backlands—it seems almost blasphemous.

Yet there he rests. Blessèd in the eyes of God and Man, a hero to both rabble and elite, a commoner who rose from Prefecthood to Generalship in under a decade: killed by an obscene contraption of levers and pellets and explosions of stinking gas. His peaceful face fills the feed. The physicians have hidden all signs of the thing that killed him, leaving only the marks of honorable injury for us to remember. The famous puckered line running down forehead to cheekbone, the legacy of a dagger than almost blinded him at twenty-five. The angry mass of scars crawling up his shoulder from beneath the tunic: a lucky shockprod strike during the Essene Mutiny. A crescent line on his right temple—a reminder of some other conflict whose name escapes me now, if indeed I ever knew it.

The view pulls back. Trajan's face recedes into an endless crowd of mourners as the tram starts up again. I barely knew the man. I met him a few times at Senate functions, where I'm sure I made no impression at all. But he made an impression on me. He made an impression on everyone. His conviction filled the room. The moment I met him, I thought: *Here is a man untroubled by doubt.*

There was a time when I had doubts.

Never about God's might or goodness, of course. Only, sometimes, whether we were truly doing His will. I would confront the enemy, and see not blasphemers but people. Not traitors-in-waiting, but children. I would recite the words of our savior: Did not the Christ Himself say *I come not bringing peace, but a sword?* Did not Holy Constantine baptize his troops with their sword-arms raised? I knew the scriptures, I'd known them from the crèche—and yet sometimes, God help me, they seemed only words, and the enemy had *faces*.

None so blind as those who will not see.

Those days are past. The Spirit has burned brighter in me over the past month than ever before. And this morning—this morning it burned brighter still. In Trajan's memory.

I get off the tram at my usual stop. The platform is empty but for a pair of constables. They do not board. They approach me, their feet clicking across the tiles with the telltale disciplined rhythm of those in authority. They wear the insignia of the priesthood.

I study their faces as they block my way. The memory of the Spirit fades just enough to leave room for a trickle of apprehension.

"Forgive the intrusion, Praetor," one of them says, "but we must ask you to come with us."

Yes, they are sure they have the right man. No, there is no mistake. No, it cannot wait. They are sorry, but they are simply following orders from the bishop. No, they do not know what this concerns.

In that, at least, they are lying. It isn't difficult to tell; *colleagues* and *prisoners* are accorded very different treatment in this regime, and they are not treating me as a colleague. I am not shackled, at least. I am not under arrest, my presence is merely required at the temple. They have accused me of nothing.

That, perhaps, is the most frustrating thing of all: accused, I could at least deny the charges.

Their cart winds through Constantinople, coasting from rail to rail with a click and a hum. I stand at the prow, forward of the control column. My escorts stand behind. Another unspoken accusation, this arrangement; I have not been ordered to keep my eyes front, but if I faced them—if I asserted the right to look *back*—how long would it be before a firm hand came down on my shoulder and turned me forward again?

"This is not the way to the temple," I say over my shoulder.

"Origen's blocked to Augustine. Cleaning up after the funeral."

Another lie. My own company guarded the procession down Augustine not two days ago. We left no obstructions. The constables probably know this. They are not trying to mislead me; they are showing me that they don't care enough to bother with a convincing lie.

I turn to confront them, and am preempted before I can speak: "Praetor, I must ask you to remove your helmet."

"You're joking."

"No sir. The bishop was quite explicit."

Stupefied and disbelieving, I undo the chin strap and lift the instrument from my skull. I begin to tuck it under my arm, but the constable reaches out and takes it from me.

"This is insane," I tell him. Without the helmet I'm as blind and deaf as any heathen. "I've done nothing wrong. What possible reason—"

The constable at the wheel turns us left onto a new track. The other puts his hand on my shoulder, and firmly turns me around.

Golgotha Plaza. Of course.

This is where the Godless come to die. The loss of my helmet is moot here; no one feels the presence of the Lord in this place. Our cart slides silently past the ranks of the heretics and the demon-possessed on their crosses, their eyes rolled back in their heads, bloody rivulets trickling from the spikes hammered through their wrists. Some have probably been here since before Trajan died; crucifixion could take days even in the days before anesthetics, and now we are a more civilized nation. We do not permit needless suffering even among our condemned.

It's an old trick, and a transparent one; many prisoners, paraded past these ranks, have chosen to cooperate before interrogation even begins. Do these two think I don't see through them? Do they think I haven't done this *myself*, more times than I can count?

Some of the dying cry out as we pass—not with pain, but with the voices of the demons in their heads. Even now, they preach. Even now, they seek to convert others to their Godless ways. No wonder the Church damps this place—for what might a simple man think, feeling the Divine Presence while hearing sacrilege?

And yet, I almost *can* feel God's presence. It should be impossible, even if the constables hadn't confiscated my helmet. But there it is: a trickle of the Divine, like a thin, bright shaft of sunlight breaking through the roof of a storm. It doesn't overpower; God's presence does not flood through me as it did earlier. But there is comfort, nonetheless. He is everywhere. He is even here. We do not banish Him with damper fields, any more than we turn off the sun by closing a window.

God is telling me, *Have strength. I am with you.*

My fear recedes like an ebbing tide. I turn back to my escorts and smile; God is with them too, if they'd only realize it.

But I don't believe they do. Something changes in their faces when they look at me. The last time I turned to face them, they were merely grim and uncooperative.

Now, for some reason, they almost look afraid.

They take me to the temple, but not to the bishop. They send me through the tunnel of light instead. They tell me it is entirely routine, although I went through the tunnel only four months ago and am not due again for another eight.

My armor is not returned to me afterwards. Instead, they escort me into the bishop's sanctum, through an ornate doorway embellished with the likeness of a fiery cross and God's commandment to Constantine: *In hoc signo vinces.* In this sign, conquer.

They leave me alone, but I know the procedure. There are guards outside.

The sanctum is dark and comforting, all cushions and velvet drapes and mahogany bones. There are no windows. A screen on one wall glows with a succession of volumetric images. Each lingers for a few moments before dissolving hypnotically into the next: the Sinai foothills; Prolinius leading the charge against the Hindus; the Holy Grotto itself, where God showed Moses the Burning Bush, where He showed all of us the way of the Spirit.

"Imagine that we had never found it."

I turn to find the bishop standing behind me as if freshly materialized. He holds a large envelope the color of ivory. He watches me with the faintest trace of a smile on his lips.

"Teacher?" I say.

"Imagine that Constantine never had his vision, that Eusebius never sent his expedition into Sinai. Imagine that the Grotto had never been rediscovered after Moses. No thousand-year legacy, no technological renaissance. Just another unprovable legend about a prophet hallucinating in the mountains, and ten commandments handed down with no tools to enforce them. We'd be no better than the heathens."

He gestures me towards a settee, a decadent thing, overstuffed and wine-colored. I do not wish to sit, but neither do I wish to give offense. I perch carefully on one edge.

The bishop remains standing. "I've been there, you know," he continues. "In the very heart of the Grotto. Kneeling in the very place Moses Himself must have knelt."

He's waiting for a response. I clear my throat. "It must have been... indescribable."

"Not really." He shrugs. "You probably feel closer to God during your morning devotionals. It's...unrefined, after all. Raw ore. Astounding enough that a natural formation could induce *any* kind of religious response, much less one consistent enough to base a culture on. Still, the effect is...weaker than you might expect. Overrated."

I swallow and hold my tongue.

"Of course, you could say the same thing about the religious experience in principal," he continues, blandly sacrilegious. "Just an electrical hiccough in the temporal lobe, no more *divine* than the force that turns compass needles and draws iron filings to a magnet."

I remember the first time I heard such words: with the rest of my crèche, just before our first Communion. *It's like a magic trick,* they said. *Like static interfering with a radio. It confuses the part of your brain that keeps track of your edges, of where you* stop *and everything else begins—and when that part gets confused, it thinks you go on forever, that you and creation are one. It tricks you into believing you're in the very presence of God.* They showed us a picture of the brain sitting like a great wrinkled prune within the shadowy outline of a human head, arrows and labels drawing our attention to the relevant parts.

They opened up wands and prayer caps to reveal the tiny magnets and solenoids inside, all the subtle instrumentality that had subverted an entire race.

Not all of us got it at first. When you're a child, *electromagnet* is just another word for *miracle*. But they were patient, repeating the essentials in words simple enough for young minds, until we'd all grasped the essential point: we were but soft machines, and God was a malfunction.

And then they put the prayer caps on our heads and opened us to the Spirit and we knew, beyond any doubting, that God was real. The experience transcended debate, transcended logic. There was no room for argument. We *knew*. Everything else was just words.

Remember, they said afterwards. *When the heathens would tell you our God is a lie, remember this moment.*

I cannot believe that the bishop is playing the same games with me now. If he is joking, it is in very bad taste. If he is testing my conviction he falls laughably short. Neither alternative explains my presence here.

But he won't take silence for an answer: "Don't you agree?" he presses.

I tread carefully. "I was taught that the Spirit lives within iron filings and compass needles as much as in our minds and our hearts. That makes it no less Divine." I take a breath. "I mean no disrespect, Teacher, but why am I here?"

He glances at the envelope in his hand. "I wished to discuss your recent...exemplary performance."

I wait, not taken in. My guards did not treat me as an *exemplary* performer.

"You," he continues, "are why we prevail against the heathens. It's not just the technology that the Spirit provides, it's the *certainty*. We *know* our God. He is empirical, He can be tested and proven and experienced. We have no doubt. *You* have no doubt. That is why we have been unstoppable for a thousand years, that is why neither Backland spies nor heathen flying machines nor the very breadth of an ocean will keep us from victory."

They are not words that need corroboration.

"Imagine what it must be like to have to *believe*." The bishop shakes his head, almost sadly. "Imagine the doubt, the uncertainty, the discord and petty strife over which dreams are divine and which are blasphemous. Sometimes I almost pity the heathens. What a terrible thing it must be, to need *faith*. And yet they cling to it. They creep into our towns and they wear our clothes and they move among us, and they *shield* themselves from the very presence of God." He sighs. "I confess I do not entirely understand them."

"They ingest some sort of herb or fungus," I tell him. "They claim it connects them with their own *god*."

The bishop *mmmm*s. Doubtless he knew this already. "I would like to see their *fungus* move a monorail. Or even turn a compass needle. And yet, surrounded by evidence of the Lord's hand, they continue to cut themselves off from it. This is not widely known, but we've received reports that they can successfully scramble entire rooms. Whole villas, even."

He runs one long fingernail along the envelope, slitting it lengthwise.

"Like the chapel you purged this morning, Praetor. It was scrambled. The Spirit could not manifest."

I shake my head. "You are mistaken, Teacher. I've never felt the Spirit more strongly than—"

The grim-faced escorts. The detour through Golgotha. The shaft of inexplicable sunlight. Everything falls into place.

A yawning chasm opens in the pit of my stomach.

The bishop extracts a sheet of film from the envelope: a snapshot of my passage through the Tunnel of Light. "You are possessed," he says.

No. There is some mistake.

He holds up the snapshot, a ghostly, translucent image of my head rendered in grays and greens. I can see the demon clearly. It festers within my skull, a malign little lump of darkness just above my right ear. A perfect spot from which to whisper lies and treachery.

I am unarmed. I am imprisoned: I will not leave this place a free man. There are guards beyond the door, and unseen priestholes hidden in the dark corners of the room. If I so much as raise a hand to the bishop I am dead.

I am dead anyway. I am possessed.

"No," I whisper.

"I am the way, the truth, and the light," the bishop intones. *"None can come to the Father except through me."* He stabs at the lump on the plate with one accusing finger. "Is *this* of the Christ? Is it of His Church? How then can it be real?"

I shake my head, dumbly. I cannot believe this is happening. I cannot believe what I see. I felt the Spirit today. I *felt* it. I am as certain of that as I have been of anything.

Is it me thinking these thoughts? Is it the demon, whispering to me?

"It seems there are more of them every day," the bishop remarks sadly. "And they are not content to corrupt the soul. They kill the body as well."

They force the *Church* to kill the body, he means. The Church is going to kill me.

But the bishop shakes his head, as though reading my mind. "I speak literally, Praetor. The demon will take your life. Not immediately—it may seduce you with this false rapture for some time. But then you will feel pain, and your mind will go. You will change; not even your loved ones will recognize you by your acts. Perhaps, near the end, you will become a drooling infant, squalling and soiling yourself. Or perhaps the pain will simply grow unbearable. Either way, you will die."

"How—how long?"

"A few days, a few weeks...I know of one poor soul who was ridden for nearly a year before she was saved."

Saved. Like the heretics at Golgotha.

And yet, whispers a tiny inner voice, *even a few days spent in that Presence would be easily worth a lifetime...*

I bring my hand to my temple. The demon lurks in there, festering in wet darkness only a skull's thickness away. I stare at the floor. "It can't be."

"It is. But it does not *have* to be."

It takes me a moment to realize what he's just said. I look up and meet his eyes.

He's smiling. "There is another way," he says. "Yes, usually the body must die that the soul can be saved—crucifixion is infinitely kinder than the fate that usually awaits the possessed. But there's an alternative, for those with—potential. I will not mislead you, Praetor. There are risks. But there have been successes as well."

"An...an alternative...?"

"We may be able to exorcise the demon. We may be able to *remove* it, physically, from your head. If it works we can both save your life and return you to the Lord's presence."

"If it works..."

"You are a soldier. You know that death is always a possibility. It is a risk here, as in all things." He takes a deep, considered breath. "On the cross, death would be a certainty."

The demon in my head does not argue. It whispers no blasphemies, makes no desperate plea against the prospect of its extraction. It merely opens the door to Heaven a crack, and bathes my soul in a sliver of the Divine.

It shows me the Truth.

I *know*, as I knew in the crèche, as I knew this morning. I am in the presence of God, and if the bishop cannot see it then the bishop is a babbling charlatan, or worse.

I would gladly go to the cross for just such a moment as this.

I smile and shake my head. "Do you think me *blind*, Bishop? You would wrap your wretched plottings up in Scripture, that I would not see them for what they are?" And I *do* see them now, laid bare in the Spirit's radiance. Of course these vile Pharisees would trap the Lord in trinkets and talismans if they could. They would ration God through a spigot to which only they have access—and those to whom He would speak without their consent, they would brand *possessed*.

And I *am* possessed, but not by any demon. I am possessed by Almighty God. And neither He nor His Sons are hermit crabs, driven to take up residence in the shells of idols and machinery.

"Tell me, Bishop," I cry. "Was Saul wearing one of your *prayer caps* on the road to Damascus? Did Elisha summon his bears with one of your wands? Or were *they* possessed of demons as well?"

He shakes his head, feigning sadness. "It is not the Praetor that speaks."

He's right. God speaks through me, as he spoke through the Prophets of old. I am God's voice, and it doesn't matter that I am unarmed and unarmored, it doesn't matter that I am deep in the devil's sanctum. I need only raise my hand and God will strike this blasphemer down.

I raise my fist. I am fifty cubits high. The bishop stands before me, an insect unaware of its own insignificance. He has one of his ridiculous machines in one hand.

"Down, devil!" we both cry, and there is blackness.

I awaken into bondage. Broad straps hold me against the bed. The left side of my face is on fire. Smiling physicians lean into view and tell me all is well. Someone holds up a mirror. My head has been shaved on the right side; a bleeding crescent, inexplicably familiar, cuts across my temple. Crosses of black thread sew my flesh together as though I were some torn garment, clumsily repaired.

The exorcism was successful, they say. I will be back with my company within the month. The restraints are merely a precaution. I will be free of them soon, as I am free of the demon.

"Bring me to God," I croak. My throat burns like a desert.

They hold a prayer wand to my head. I feel nothing.

I feel *nothing*.

The wand is in working order. The batteries are fully charged. It's probably nothing, they say. A temporary aftereffect of the exorcism. Give it time. Probably best to leave the restraints for the moment, but there's nothing to worry about.

Of course they are right. I have dwelt in the Spirit, I know the mind of the Almighty—after all, were not all of us chosen made in His image? God would never abandon even the least of his flock. I do not have to believe this, it is something I *know*. Father, you will not forsake me.

It will come back. It will come back.

They urge me to be patient. After three days they admit that they've seen this before. Not often, mind you; it was a rare procedure, and this is an even rarer consequence. But it's possible that the demon may have injured the part of the mind that lets us truly know God. The physicians recite medical terms which mean nothing to me. I ask them about the others that preceded me down this path: How long before *they* were restored to God's sight? But it seems there are no hard and fast rules, no overall patterns.

Trajan burns on the wall beside my bed. Trajan burns daily there and is never consumed, a little like the Burning Bush itself. My keepers have been replaying his cremation daily, a thin gruel of recorded images thrown against the wall; I suspect they are meant to be inspirational. It is always just past sundown in these replays. Trajan's fiery passing returns a kind of daylight to the piazza, an orange glow reflecting in ten thousand upturned faces.

He is with God now, forever in His presence. Some say that was true even before he passed, that Trajan lived his whole life in the Spirit. I don't know whether that's true; maybe people just couldn't explain his zeal and devotion any other way.

A whole lifetime in the presence of God. I'd give a lifetime now for even a minute.

We are in unexplored territory, they say. That is where they are, perhaps.

I am in Hell.

Finally they admit it: none of the others have recovered. They have been lying to me all along. I have been cast into darkness, I am cut off from God. And they called this butchery a *success*.

"It will be a test of your faith," they tell me. My *faith*. I gape like a fish at the word. It is a word for heathens, for people with made-up gods. The cross would have been infinitely preferable. I would kill these smug meat-cutters with my bare hands, if my bare hands were free.

"Kill me," I beg. They refuse. The bishop himself has commanded that I be kept alive and in good health. "Then summon the bishop," I tell them. "Let me talk to him. Please."

They smile sadly and shake their heads. One does not *summon* the bishop.

More lies, perhaps. Maybe the bishop has forgotten that I even exist, maybe these people just enjoy watching the innocent suffer. Who else, after all, would dedicate their lives to potions and bloodletting?

The cut in my head keeps me awake at night, itches maddeningly as scar tissue builds and puckers along its curved edges. I still can't remember where I've seen its like before.

I curse the bishop. He told me there would be risks, but he only mentioned death. Death is not a risk to me here. It is an aspiration.

I refuse food for four days. They force-feed me liquids through a tube in my nose.

It's a strange paradox. There is no hope here; I will never again know God, I am denied even surcease. And yet these butchers, by the very act of refusing me a merciful death, have somehow awakened a tiny spark that wants to live. It is *their* sin I am suffering for, after all. This darkness is of *their* making. I did not turn away from God; they hacked God out of me like a gobbet of gangrenous flesh. It can't be that they want me to live, for there is no living apart from God. It can only be that they want me to *suffer*.

And with this realization comes a sudden desire to deny them that satisfaction.

They will not let me die. Perhaps, soon, they will wish they had.

God damn them.

God damn them. Of course.

I've been a fool. I've forgotten what really matters. I've been so obsessed by these petty torments that I've lost sight of one simple truth: God does not turn on his children. God does not abandon His own.

But *test* them—yes. God tests us all the time. Did He not strip Job of all his worldly goods and leave him picking his boils in the dust? Did He not tell Abraham to kill his own son? Did He not restore them to His sight, once they had proven worthy of it?

I believe that God rewards the righteous. I believe that the Christ said *Bless*é*d are those who believe even though they have* not *seen*. And now, at last, I believe that perhaps *faith* is not the obscenity I once thought, for it can give strength when one is cut off from the truth.

I am not abandoned. I am *tested*.

I send for the bishop. Somehow, this time I know he'll come.

He does.

"They say I've lost the Spirit," I tell him. "They're wrong."

He sees something in my face. Something changes in his.

"Moses was denied the Promised Land," I continue. "Constantine saw the flaming cross but twice in his lifetime. God spoke to Saul of Tarsus only once. Did *they* lose faith?"

"They moved the world," the bishop says.

I bare my teeth. My conviction fills the room. "So will I."

He smiles gently. "I believe you."

I stare at him, astonished by my own blindness. "You knew this would happen."

He shakes his head. "I could only hope. But yes, there is a—strange truth we are only learning now. I'm still not sure I believe it myself. Sometimes it isn't the *experience* of redemption that makes the greatest champions, but the *longing* for it."

On the panel beside me, Trajan burns and is not consumed. I wonder briefly if my fall from grace was entirely accidental. But in the end it does not matter. I remember, at last, where I once saw a scar like mine.

Before today, the acts I committed in God's name were pale, bloodless things. No longer. I will return to the Kingdom of Heaven. I will raise my sword-arm high and I will not lay it down until the last of the unbelievers has been slaughtered. I will build mountains of flesh in His name. Rivers will flow from the throats that I cut. I will not stop until I have earned my way back into His sight.

The bishop leans forward and loosens my straps. "I don't think we need these any more."

They couldn't hold me anyway. I could tear them like paper.

I am the fist of God.

HOME

It has forgotten what it was.

Not that that matters, down here. What good is a name when there's nothing around to use it? This one doesn't remember where it came from. It doesn't remember the murky twilight of the North Pacific Drift, or the noise and gasoline aftertaste that drove it back below the thermocline. It doesn't remember the gelatinous veneer of language and culture that once sat atop its spinal cord. It doesn't even remember the long, slow dissolution of that overlord into dozens of autonomous, squabbling subroutines. Now, even those have fallen silent.

Not much comes down from the cortex any more. Low-level impulses flicker in from the parietal and occipital lobes. The motor strip hums in the background. Occasionally, Broca's area mutters to itself. The rest is mostly dead and dark, worn smooth by a sluggish black ocean cold as antifreeze. All that's left is pure reptile.

It pushes on, blind and unthinking, oblivious to the weight of four hundred liquid atmospheres. It eats whatever it can find. Desalinators and recyclers keep it hydrated. Sometimes, old mammalian skin grows sticky with secreted residues; newer skin, laid on top, opens pores to the ocean and washes everything clean with aliquots of distilled seawater.

The reptile never wonders about the signal in its head that keeps it pointing the right way. It doesn't know where it's headed, or why. It only knows, with pure brute instinct, how to get there.

It's dying, of course, but slowly. It wouldn't care much about that even if it knew.

Now something is tapping on its insides. Infinitesimal, precisely spaced shock waves are marching in from somewhere ahead and drumming against the machinery in its chest.

The reptile doesn't recognize the sound. It's not the intermittent grumble of conshelf and seabed pushing against each other. It's not the low-frequency ATOC pulses that echo dimly past en route to the Bering. It's a pinging noise—*metallic*, Broca's area murmurs, although it doesn't know what that means.

Abruptly, the sound intensifies.

The reptile is blinded by sudden starbursts. It tries to blink, a vestigial act from a time it doesn't remember. The caps on its eyes darken automatically. The pupils beneath, hamstrung by the speed of reflex, squeeze to pinpoints a few seconds later.

A copper beacon glares out from the darkness ahead—too coarse, too steady, far brighter than the bioluminescent embers that sometimes light the way. Those, at least, are dim enough to see by; the reptile's augmented eyes can boost even the faint twinkle of deepwater fish and turn it into something resembling twilight. But this new light turns the rest of the world stark black. Light is never this bright, not since—

From the cortex, a shiver of recognition.

It floats motionless, hesitating. It's almost aware of faint urgent voices from somewhere nearby. But it's been following the same course for as long it can remember, and that course points only one way.

It sinks to the bottom, stirring a muddy cloud as it touches down. It crawls forward along the ocean floor.

The beacon shines down from several meters above the seabed. At closer range it resolves into a string of smaller lights stretched in an arc, like photophores on the flank of some enormous fish.

Broca sends down more noise: *Sodium floods.* The reptile burrows on through the water, panning its face from side to side.

And freezes, suddenly fearful. Something huge looms behind the lights, bloating gray against black. It hangs above the seabed like a great smooth boulder, impossibly buoyant, encircled by lights at its equator. Striated filaments connect it to the bottom.

Something else, changes.

It takes a moment for the reptile to realize what's happened: the drumming against its chest has stopped. It glances nervously from shadow to light, light to shadow.

"You are approaching Linke Station, Aleutian Geothermal Array. We're glad you've come back."

The reptile shoots back into the darkness, mud billowing behind it. It retreats a good twenty meters before a dim realization sinks in.

Broca's area knows those sounds. It doesn't understand them— Broca's never much good at anything but mimicry—but it has heard something like them before. The reptile feels an unaccustomed twitch. It's been a long time since curiosity was any use.

It turns and faces back from where it fled. Distance has smeared the lights into a diffuse, dull glow. A faint staccato rhythm vibrates in its chest.

The reptile edges back towards the beacon. One light divides again into many; that dim, ominous outline still lurks behind them.

Once more the rhythm falls silent at the reptile's approach. The strange object looms overhead in its girdle of light. It's smooth in some places, pockmarked in others. Precise rows of circular bumps, sharp-angled protuberances appear at closer range.

"You are approaching Linke Station, Aleutian Geothermal Array. We're glad you've come back."

The reptile flinches, but stays on course this time.

"We can't get a definite ID from your sonar profile." The sound fills the ocean. "You might be Deborah Linden. Deborah Linden. Please respond if you are Deborah Linden."

Deborah Linden. That brings memory: something with four familiar limbs, but standing upright, moving against gravity and bright light and making strange harsh sounds—

—laughter—

"Please respond—"

It shakes its head, not knowing why.

"—if you are Deborah Linden."

Judy Caraco, says something else, very close.

"Deborah Linden. If you can't speak, please wave your arms."

The lights overhead cast a bright scalloped circle on the ocean floor. There on the mud rests a box, large enough to crawl into. Two green pinpoints sparkle from a panel on one of its sides.

"Please enter the emergency shelter beneath the station. It contains food and medical facilities."

One end of the box gapes open; delicate jointed things can be seen folded up inside, hiding in shadow.

"Everything is automatic. Enter the shelter and you'll be all right. A rescue team is on the way."

Automatic. That noise, too, sticks out from the others. *Automatic* almost means something. It has personal relevance.

The reptile looks back up at the thing that's hanging overhead like, like,

—like a fist—

like a fist. The underside of the sphere is a cool shadowy refuge; the equatorial lights can't reach all the way around its convex surface. In the overlapping shadows on the south pole, something shimmers enticingly.

The reptile pushes up off the bottom, raising another cloud.

"Deborah Linden. The station is locked for your own protection."

It glides into the cone of shadow beneath the object and sees a bright shiny disk a meter across, facing down, held inside a circular rim. The reptile looks up into it.

Something looks back.

Startled, the reptile twists down and away. The disk writhes in the sudden turbulence.

A bubble. That's all it is. A pocket of gas, trapped underneath the

—airlock.

The reptile stops. It knows that word. It even understands it, some-how. Broca's not alone any more, something else is reaching out from the temporal lobe and tapping in. Something up there actually knows what Broca is talking about.

"Please enter the emergency shelter beneath the station—"

Still nervous, the reptile returns to the airlock. The air pocket shines silver in the reflected light. A black wraith moves into view within it, almost featureless except for two empty white spaces where eyes should be. It reaches out to meet the reptile's outstretched hand. Two sets of fingertips touch, fuse, disappear. One arm is grafted onto its own reflection at the wrist. Fingers, on the other side of the looking glass, touch metal.

"—locked for your own protection. Deborah Linden."

It pulls back its hand, fascinated. Inside, forgotten parts are stirring. Other parts, more familiar, try to send them away. The wraith floats overhead, empty and untroubled.

It draws its hand to its face, runs an index finger from one ear to the tip of the jaw. A very long molecule, folded against itself, unzips.

The wraith's smooth black face splits open a few centimeters; what's underneath shows pale gray in the filtered light. The reptile feels the familiar dimpling of its cheek in sudden cold.

It continues the motion, slashing its face from ear to ear. A great smiling gash opens below the eyespots. Unzipped, a flap of black membrane floats under its chin, anchored at the throat.

There's a pucker in the center of the skinned area. The reptile moves its jaw; the pucker opens.

By now most of its teeth are gone. It swallowed some, spat others out if they came loose when its face was unsealed. No matter. Most of the things it eats these days are even softer than it is. When the occasional mollusc or echinoderm proves too tough or too large to swallow whole, there are always hands. Thumbs still oppose.

But this is the first time it's actually seen that gaping, toothless ruin where a mouth used to be. It knows this isn't right, somehow.

"—Everything is automatic—"

A sudden muffled buzz cuts into the noise, then fades. Welcome silence returns for a moment. Then different sounds, quieter than before, almost hushed:

"Christ, Judy, is that you?"

It knows that sound.

"Judy Caraco? It's Jeannette Ballard. Remember? We went through prelim together. Judy? Can you speak?"

That sound comes from a long time ago.

"Can you hear me, Judy? Wave if you can hear me."

Back when this one was part of something larger, not an *it* at all, then, but—

"The machine didn't recognize you, you know? It was only programmed for locals."

—she.

Clusters of neurons, long dormant, sparkle in the darkness. Old, forgotten subsystems stutter and reboot.

I—

"You've come—my God, Judy, do you know where you are? You went missing off Juan de Fuca! You've come over three thousand kilometers!"

It knows my name. She can barely think over the sudden murmuring in her head.

"Judy, it's me. Jeannette. God, Judy, how did you last this long?"

She can't answer. She's just barely starting to understand the question. There are parts of her still asleep, parts that won't talk, still other parts completely washed away. She doesn't remember why she never gets thirsty. She's forgotten the tidal rush of human breath. Once, for a little while, she knew words like *photoamplification* and *myoelectric*; they were nonsense to her even then.

She shakes her head, trying to clear it. The new parts—no, the old parts, the very old parts that went away and now they've come back *and won't shut the fuck up*—are all clamoring for attention. She reaches into the bubble again, past her own reflection; once again, the ventral airlock pushes back.

"Judy, you can't get into the station. No one's there. Everything's automated now."

She brings her hand back to her face, tugs at the line between black and gray. More shadow peels back from the wraith, leaving a large pale oval with two smaller ovals, white and utterly featureless, inside. The flesh around her mouth is going prickly and numb.

My face! something screams. *What happened to my eyes?*

"You don't want to go inside anyway, you couldn't even stand up. We've seen it in some of the other runaways, you lose your calcium after a while. Your bones go all punky, you know?"

My eyes—

"We're airlifting a 'scaphe out to you. We'll have a team down there in fifteen hours, tops. Just go down into the shelter and wait for them. It's state of the art, Judy, it'll take care of everything."

She looks down into the open box. Words appear in her head: *Leg. Hold. Trap.* She knows what they mean.

"They—they made some mistakes, Judy. But things are different now. We don't have to change people any more. You just wait there, Judy. We'll put you back to rights. We'll bring you home."

The voices inside grow quiet, suddenly attentive. They don't like the sound of that word. *Home.* She wonders what it means. She wonders why it makes her feel so cold.

More words scroll through her mind: *The lights are on. Nobody's home.*

The lights come on, flickering.

She can catch glimpses of sick, rotten things squirming in her head. Old memories grind screeching against years of corrosion. Something lurches into sudden focus: worms, clusters of twitching, eyeless, pulpy snouts reaching out for her across the space of two decades. She stares, horrified, and remembers what the worms were called. They were called "fingers."

Something gives way with a snap. There's a big room and a hand puppet clenched in one small fist. Something smells like mints and worms are surging up between her legs and they *hurt* and they're whispering *shhh it's not really that bad is it,* and it is but she doesn't want to let him down *after all I've done for you* so she shakes her head and squeezes her eyes shut and just waits. It's years and years before she opens her eyes again and when she does he's back, so much smaller now, he doesn't remember he doesn't even fucking *remember* it's all *my dear how you've grown how long has it been?* So she tells him as the taser wires hit and he goes over, she tells him as his muscles lock tight in a twelve-thousand-volt orgasm; she shows him the blade, shows him up real close and his left eye deflates with a wet tired sigh but she leaves the other one, jiggling hilariously in frantic little arcs, so he can watch but shit for once there really is a cop around when you need one and here come the worms again, a hard clenched knot of them driving into her kidney like a piston, worms grabbing her hair, and they take her not to the nearest precinct but to some strange clinic where voices in the next room murmur about *optimal post-traumatic environments* and *endogenous dopamine addiction.* And then someone says *There's an alternative Ms. Caraco, a place you could go that's a little bit dangerous but then you'd be right at home there, wouldn't you? And you could make a real contribution, we need people who can live under a certain kind of stress without going, you know...*

And she says *okay, okay, just fucking do it.*

And the worms burrow into her chest, devour her soft parts and replace them with hard-edged geometries of plastic and metal that cut her insides.

And then dark cold, life without breath, four thousand meters of black water pressing down like a massive sheltering womb...

"Judy, will you just for God's sake *talk* to me? Is your vocoder broken? Can't you answer?"

Her whole body is shaking. She can't do anything except watch her hand rise, an autonomous savior, to take the black skin floating around her face. The reptile presses edges together, here, and here. Hydrophobic side chains embrace; a slippery black caul stitches itself back together over rotten flesh. Muffled voices rage faintly inside.

"Judy, please just *wave* or something! Judy, what are you—where are you going?"

It doesn't know. All it's ever done is travel to this place. It's forgotten why.

"Judy, you can't wander too far away... Don't you remember, our instruments can't see very well this close to an active rift—"

All it wants is to get away from the noise and the light. All it wants is to be alone again.

"Judy, wait—we just want to help—"

The harsh artificial glare fades behind it. Ahead there is only the sparse twinkle of living flashlights.

A faint realization teeters on the edge of awareness and washes away forever:

She knew this was home years before she ever saw an ocean.

THE EYES OF GOD

I am not a criminal. I have done nothing wrong.

They've just caught a woman at the front of the line, mocha-skinned, mid-thirties, eyes wide and innocent beneath the brim of her La Senza beret. She dosed herself with oxytocin from the sound of it, tried to subvert the meat in the system—a smile, a wink, that extra chemical nudge that bypasses logic and whispers right to the brainstem: *This one's a friend, no need to put* her *through the machines...*

But I guess she forgot: we're all machines here, tweaked and tuned and retrofitted down to the molecules. The guards have been immunised against argument and aerosols. They lead her away, indifferent to her protests. I try to follow their example, harden myself against whatever awaits her on the other side of the white door. What was she thinking, to try a stunt like that? Whatever hides in her head must be more than mere inclination. They don't yank paying passengers for evil fantasies, not yet anyway, not yet. She must have done something. She must have *acted*.

Half an hour before the plane boards. There are at least fifty law-abiding citizens ahead of me and they haven't started processing us yet. The buzz box looms dormant at the front of the line like a great armoured crab, newly installed, mouth agape. One of the guards in its shadow starts working her way up the line, spot-checking some passengers, bypassing others, feeling lucky after the first catch of the day. In a just universe I would have nothing to fear from her. I'm not a criminal, I have done nothing wrong. The words cycle in my head like a defensive affirmation.

I am not a criminal. I have done nothing wrong.

But I know that fucking machine is going to tag me anyway.

At the head of the queue, the Chamber of Secrets lights up. A canned female voice announces the dawning of preboard security, echoing through the harsh acoustics of the terminal. The guards slouch to attention. We gave up everything to join this line: smart tags, jewellery, my pocket office, all confiscated until the far side of redemption. The buzz box needs a clear view into our heads; even an earring can throw it off. People with medical implants and antique mercury fillings aren't welcome here. There's a side queue for those types, a special room where old-fashioned interrogations and cavity searches are still the order of the day.

The omnipresent voice orders all Westjet passengers with epilepsy, cochlear dysfunction, or Grey syndrome to identify themselves to Security prior to entering the scanner. Other passengers who do not wish to be scanned may opt to forfeit their passage. Westjet regrets that it cannot offer refunds in such cases. Westjet is not responsible for neurological side effects, temporary or otherwise, that may result from use of the scanner. Use of the scanner constitutes acceptance of these conditions.

There *have* been side effects. A few garden-variety epileptics had minor fits in the early days. A famous Oxford atheist—you remember, the guy who wrote all the books—caught a devout and abiding faith in the Christian God from a checkpoint at Heathrow, although some responsibility was ultimately laid at the feet of the pre-existing tumour that killed him two months later. One widowed grandmother from St. Paul's was all over the news last year when she emerged from a courthouse buzz box with an insatiable sexual fetish for running shoes. That could have cost Sony a lot, if she hadn't been a forgiving soul who chose not to litigate. Rumours that she'd used SWank just prior to making that decision were never confirmed.

THE EYES OF GOD | 109

"Destination?"

The guard has arrived while I wasn't looking. Her laser licks my face with biometric taste buds. I blink away the afterimages.

"Destination," she says again.

"Uh, Yellowknife."

She scans her handpad. "Business or pleasure?" There's no point to these questions, they're not even according to script. SWank has taken us beyond the need for petty interrogation. She just doesn't like the look of me, I bet. Maybe she just *knows* somehow, even if she can't put her finger on it.

"Neither," I say. She looks up sharply. Whatever her initial suspicions, my obvious evasiveness has cemented them. "I'm attending a funeral," I explain.

She moves along without a word.

I know you're not here, Father. I left my faith back in childhood. Let others hold to their feeble-minded superstitions, let them run bleating to the supernatural for comfort and excuses. Let the cowardly and the weak-minded deny the darkness with the promise of some imagined afterlife. I have no need for invisible friends. I know I'm only talking to myself. If only I could stop.

I wonder if that machine will be able to eavesdrop on our conversation.

I stood with you at your trial, as you stood with me years before when I had no other friend in the world. I swore on your sacred book of fairy tales that you'd never touched me, not once in all those years. Were the others lying, I wonder? I don't know. Judge not, I guess.

But you were judged, and found wanting. It wasn't even newsworthy—child-fondling priests are more cliché than criminal these days, have been for years, and no one cares what happens in some dickass town up in the Territories anyway. If they'd quietly transferred you just one more time, if you'd managed to lay low just a little longer, it might not have even come to this. They could have fixed you.

Or not, now that I think of it. The Vatican came down on SWank like it came down on cloning and the Copernican solar system before it. Mustn't fuck with the way God built you. Mustn't compromise free choice, no matter how freely you'd choose to do so.

I notice that doesn't extend to tickling the temporal lobe, though. St. Michael's just spent seven million equipping their nave for Rapture on demand.

Maybe suicide was the only option left to you, maybe all you could do was follow one sin with another. It's not as though you had anything to lose; your own scriptures damn us as much for desire as for doing. I remember asking you years ago, although I'd long since thrown away my crutches: What about the sin not made manifest? What if you've coveted thy neighbour's wife or warmed yourself with thoughts of murder, but kept it all inside? You looked at me kindly, and perhaps with far greater understanding than I ever gave you credit for, before condemning me with the words of an imaginary superhero. If you've done any of these things in your heart, you said, then you've done them in the eyes of God.

I feel a sudden brief chime between my ears. I could really use a drink about now; the woody aroma of a fine old scotch curling through my sinuses would really hit the spot. I glance around, spot the billboard that zapped me. Crown Royal. Fucking head spam. I give silent thanks for legal standards outlawing the implantation of brand names; they can stick cravings in my head, but hooking me on trademarks would cross some arbitrary threshold of *free will*. It's a meaningless gesture, a sop to the civil-rights fanatics. Like the chime that preceded it: it tells me, the courts say, that I am still autonomous. As long as I *know* I'm being hacked, I've got a sporting chance to make my own decisions.

Two spots ahead of me, an old man sobs quietly. He seemed fine just a moment ago. Sometimes it happens. The ads trigger the wrong connections. SWank can't lay down hi-def sensory panoramas without a helmet, these long-range hits don't *instil* so much as *evoke*. Smell's key, they say—primitive, lobes big enough for remote targeting, simpler to hack than the vast gigapixel arrays of the visual cortex. And so *primal*, so much closer to raw reptile. They spent millions finding the universal triggers. Honeysuckle reminds you of childhood; the scent of pine recalls Christmas. They can mood us up for Norman Rockwell or the Marquis de Sade, depending on the product. Nudge the right receptor neurons and the brain builds its *own* spam.

For some people, though, honeysuckle is what you smelled when your mother got the shit beaten out of her. For some, Christmas was when you found your sister with her wrists slashed open.

It doesn't happen often. The ads provoke mild unease in one of a thousand of us, true distress in a tenth as many. Some thought even that price was too high. Others quailed at the spectre of machines instilling not just sights and sounds but *desires*, opinions, religious beliefs. But commercials featuring cute babies or sexy women also plant desire, use sight and sound to bypass the head and go for the gut. Every debate, every argument is an attempt to literally *change someone's mind*, every poem and pamphlet a viral tool for the hacking of opinions. *I'm doing it right now*, some Mindscape™ flak argued last month on MacroNet. *I'm trying to change your neural wiring using the sounds you're hearing. You want to ban SWank just because it uses sounds you* can't?

The slope is just too slippery. Ban SWank and you might as well ban art as well as advocacy. You might as well ban free speech itself.

We both know the truth of it, Father. Even words can bring one to tears.

The line moves forward. We shuffle along with smooth, ominous efficiency, one after another disappearing briefly into the buzz box, reappearing on the far side, emerging reborn from a technological baptism that elevates us all to temporary sainthood.

Compressed ultrasound, Father. That's how they cleanse us. You probably saw the hype a few years back, even up there. You must have seen the papal bull condemning it, at least. Sony filed the original patent as a game interface, just after the turn of the century; soon, they told us, the eyephones and electrodes of yore would give way to affordable little boxes that tracked you around your living room, bypassed eyes and ears entirely and planted five-dimensional sensory experience directly into your brain. (We're still waiting for those, actually; the tweaks may be ultrasonic but the system keeps your brain in focus by tracking EM emissions, and not many consumers Faraday their homes.) In the meantime, hospitals and airports and theme parks keep the dream alive until the price comes down. And the spin-offs—Father, the spin-offs are everywhere. The deaf can hear. The blind can see. The post-traumatised have all their acid memories washed away, just as long as they keep paying the connection fee.

That's the rub, of course. It doesn't last: the high frequencies excite some synapses and put others to sleep, but they don't actually change any of the pre-existing circuitry. The brain eventually bounces back to normal once the signal stops. Which is not only profitable for those doling out the waves, but a lot less messy in the courts. There's that whole integrity-of-the-self thing to worry about. Having your brain rewired every time you hopped a commuter flight might raise some pretty iffy legal issues.

Still. I've got to admit it speeds things up. No more time-consuming background checks, no more invasive "random" searches, no litany of questions designed to weed out the troublemakers in our midst. A dash of transcranial magnetism; a squirt of ultrasound; *next*. A year ago I'd have been standing in line for hours. Today I've been here scarcely fifteen minutes and I'm already in the top ten. And it's more than mere convenience: it's security, it's safety, it's a sigh of relief after a generation of Russian roulette. No more Edmonton Infernos, no more Rio Insurrections, no more buildings slagged to glass or cities sickening in the aftermath of some dirty nuke. There are still saboteurs and terrorists loose in the world, of course. Always will be. But when they strike at all, they strike in places unprotected by SWanky McBuzz. Anyone who flies *these* friendly skies is as harmless as—as I am.

Who can argue with results like that?

In the old days I could have wished I was a psychopath. They had it easy back then. The machines only looked for emotional responses: eye saccades, skin galvanism. Anyone without a conscience could stare them down with a wide smile and an empty heart. But SWank inspired a whole new generation. The tech looks under the surface now. Prefrontal cortex stuff, glucose metabolism. Now, fiends and perverts and would-be saboteurs all get caught in the same net.

Doesn't mean they don't let us go again, of course. It's not as if sociopathy is against the law. Hell, if they screened out everyone with a broken conscience, Executive Class would be empty.

There are children scattered throughout the line. Most are accompanied by adults. Three are not, two boys and a girl. They are nervous and beautiful, like wild animals, easily startled. They are not used to being on their own. The oldest can't be more than nine, and he has a freckle on the side of his neck.

I can't stop watching him.

Suddenly children roam free again. For months now I've been seeing them in parks and plazas, unguarded, innocent and so *vulnerable*, as though SWank has given parents everywhere an excuse to breathe. No matter that it'll be years before it trickles out of airports and government buildings and into the places children play. Mommy and Daddy are tired of waiting, take what comfort they can in the cameras mounted on every street corner, panning and scanning for all the world as if real people stood behind them. Mommy and Daddy can't be bothered to spend five minutes on the web, compiling their own predator's handbook on the use of laser pointers and blind spots to punch holes in the surveillance society. Mommy and Daddy would rather just take all those bromides about "civil safety" on faith.

For so many years we've lived in fear. By now people are so desperate for any pretence of safety that they'll cling to the promise of a future that hasn't even arrived yet. Not that that's anything new; whether you're talking about a house in the suburbs or the browning of Antarctica, Mommy and Daddy have *always* lived on credit.

If something *did* happen to their kids it would serve them right.

The line moves forward. Suddenly I'm at the front of it.

A man with Authority waves me in. I step forward as if to an execution. I do this for you, Father. I do this to pay my respects. I do this to dance on your grave. If I could have avoided this moment—if this cup could have passed from me, if I could have *walked* to the Northwest Territories rather than let this obscene technology into my head—

Someone has spray-painted two words in stencilled black over the mouth of the machine: *The Shadow*. Delaying, I glance a question at the guard.

"It knows what evil lurks in the hearts of men," he says. "Bwahaha. Let's move it along."

I have no idea what he's talking about.

The walls of the booth glimmer with a tight weave of copper wire. The helmet descends from above with a soft hydraulic hiss; it sits too lightly on my head for such a massive device. The visor slides over my eyes like a blindfold. I am in a pocket universe, alone with my thoughts and an all-seeing God. Electricity hums deep in my head.

I'm innocent of any wrongdoing. I've never broken the law. Maybe God will see that if I think it hard enough. Why does it have to see anything, why does it have to *read* the palimpsest if it's just going to scribble over it again? But brains don't work like that. Each individual *is* individual, wired up in a unique and glorious tangle that must be read before it can be edited. And motivations, intents—these are endless, multiheaded things, twining and proliferating from frontal cortex to cingulate gyrus, from hypothalamus to claustrum. There's no LED that lights up when your plans are nefarious, no Aniston Neuron for mad bombers. For the safety of everyone, they must read it all. For the safety of everyone.

I have been under this helmet for what seems like forever. Nobody else took this long.

The line is not moving forward.

"Well," Security says softly. "Will you look at that."

"I'm not," I tell him. "I've never—"

"And you're not about to. Not for the next nine hours, anyway."

"I never *acted* on it." I sound petulant, childish. "Not once."

"I can see that," he says, but I know we're talking about different things.

The humming changes subtly in pitch. I can feel magnets and mosquitoes snapping in my head. I am changed by something not yet cheap enough for the home market: an ache evaporates, a dull longing so chronic I feel it now only in absentia.

"There. Now we could put you in charge of two Day Cares and a chorus of altar boys, and you wouldn't even be tempted."

The visor rises; the helmet floats away. Authority stares back at me from a gaggle of contemptuous faces.

"This is wrong," I say quietly.

"Is it now."

"I haven't done anything."

"We haven't either. We haven't locked down your pervert brain, we haven't changed who you are. We've protected your precious constitutional rights and your God-given identity. You're as free to diddle kiddies in the park as you ever were. You just won't *want* to for a while."

"But I haven't *done* anything." I can't stop saying it.

"Nobody does, until they do." He jerks his head towards Departure. "Get out of here. You're cleared."

I am not a criminal. I have done nothing wrong. But my name is on a list now, just the same. Word of my depravity races ahead of me, checkpoint after checkpoint, like a fission of dominoes. They'll be watching, though they have to let me pass.

That could change before long. Even now, Community Standards barely recognise the difference between what we do and what we are; nudge them just a hair further and every border on the planet might close at my approach. But this is only the dawning of the new enlightenment, and the latest rules are not yet in place. For now, I am free to stand at your unconsecrated graveside, and mourn on my own recognizance.

You always were big on the power of forgiveness, Father. Seventy times seven, the most egregious sins washed away in the sight of the Lord. All it took, you insisted, was true penitence. All you had to do was accept His love.

Of course, it sounded a lot less self-serving back then.

But even the unbelievers get a clean slate now. My redeemer is a machine, and my salvation has an expiry date—but then again, I guess yours did too.

I wonder about the machine that programmed *you*, Father, that great glacial contraption of dogma and moving parts, clacking and iterating its way through two thousand years of bloody history. I can't help but wonder at the way it rewired *your* synapses. Did it turn you into a predator, weigh you down with lunatic strictures that no sexual being could withstand, deny your very nature until you snapped? Or were you already malfunctioning when you embraced the Church, hoping for some measure of strength you couldn't find in yourself?

I knew you for years, Father. Even now, I tell myself I know you— and while you may have been many things, you were never a coward. I refuse to believe that you opted for death because it was the easy way out. I choose to believe that in those last days, you found the strength to rewrite your own programming, to turn your back on obsolete algorithms two millennia out of date, and decide for yourself the difference between a mortal sin and an act of atonement.

You loathed yourself, you loathed the things you had done. And so, finally, you made absolutely certain you could never do them again. You *acted*.

You acted as I never could, though I'd pay so much smaller a price.

There is more than this temporary absolution, you see. We have machines now that can burn the evil right out of a man, deep-focus microwave emitters that vaporise the very pathways of depravity. No one can force them on you; not yet, anyway. Members' bills wind through Parliament, legislative proposals that would see us pre-emptively reprogrammed for good instead of evil, but for now the procedure is strictly voluntary. It *changes* you, you see. It violates some inalienable essence of selfhood. Some call it a kind of suicide in its own right.

I kept telling the man at Security: I never *acted* on it. But he could see that for himself.

I never had it fixed. I must *like* what I am.

I wonder if that makes a difference.

I wonder which of us is more guilty.

FLESH MADE WORD

Wescott was glad when it finally stopped breathing.

It had taken hours, this time. He had waited while it wheezed out thick putrid smells, chest heaving and gurgling and filling the room with stubborn reminders that it was only dying, not yet dead, not yet. He had been patient. After ten years, he had learned to be patient; and now, finally, the thing on the table was giving up.

Something moved behind him. He turned, irritated; the dying hear better than the living, a single spoken word could ruin hours of observation. But it was only Lynne, slipping quietly into the room. Wescott relaxed. Lynne knew the rules.

For a moment he even wondered why she was there.

Wescott turned back to the body. Its chest had stopped moving. *Sixty seconds*, he guessed. *Plus or minus ten.*

It was already dead by any practical definition. But there were still a few embers inside, a few sluggish nerves twitching in a brain choked with dead circuitry. Wescott's machines showed him the landscape of that dying mind: a topography of luminous filaments, eroding as he watched.

The cardiac thread shuddered and lay still.

Thirty seconds. Give or take five. The qualifiers came automatically. There is no truth. There are no facts. There is only the envelope of the confidence interval.

He could feel Lynne waiting invisibly behind him.

Wescott glanced at the table for a moment, looked away again; the lid over one sunken eye had crept open a crack. He could almost imagine he had seen nothing looking out.

Something changed on the monitors. *Here it comes...*

He didn't know why it scared him. They were only nerve impulses, after all; a fleeting ripple of electricity, barely detectable, passing from midbrain to cortex to oblivion. Just another bunch of doomed neurons, gasping.

And now there was only flesh, still warm. A dozen lines lay flat on the monitors. Wescott leaned over and checked the leads connecting meat to machine.

"Dead at nineteen forty-three," he said into his recorder. The machines, intelligent in their own way, began to shut themselves down. Wescott studied the dead face, peeled back the unclenched eyelid with a pair of forceps. The static pupil beneath stared past him, fixed at infinity.

You took the news well, Wescott thought.

He remembered Lynne. She was standing to one side, her face averted.

"I'm sorry," she said. "I know this is never a good time, but it's—"

He waited.

"It's Zombie," she went on. "There was an accident, Russ, he wandered out on the road and—and I took him into the vet's and she says he's too badly hurt but she won't put him to sleep without your consent, you never listed me as an owner—"

She stopped, like a flash flood ending.

He looked down at the floor. "Put him to sleep?"

"She said it's almost certain anything they tried wouldn't work, it would cost thousands and he'd probably die anyway—"

"You mean kill him. She won't kill him without my consent." Wescott began stripping the leads from the cadaver, lining them up on their brackets. They hung there like leeches, their suckers slimy with conductant.

"—and all I could think was, after eighteen years he shouldn't die alone, someone should be there with him, but I can't, you know, I just—"

Somewhere at the base of his skull, a tiny voice cried out, *My Christ don't I go through enough of this shit without having to watch it happen to my own cat?* But it was very far away, and he could barely hear it.

He looked at the table. The corpse stared its cyclopean stare.

"Sure," Wescott said after a moment. "I'll take care of it." He allowed himself a half-smile. "All in a day's work."

The workstation sat in one corner of the living room, an ebony cube of tinted perspex, and for the past ten years it had spoken to him in Carol's voice. That had hurt at first, so much that he had nearly changed the program; but he had fought the urge, and beaten it, and endured the synthetic familiarity of her voice like a man doing penance for some great sin. Somewhere in the past decade the pain had faded below the level of conscious recognition. Now he heard it list the day's mail, and felt nothing.

"Jason Mosby called again from Southam," it said, catching Carol's intonation perfectly. "He s-still wants to interview you. He left a conversational program in my stack. You can run it any time you want."

"What else?"

"Zombie's collar stopped transmitting at nine-sixteen, and Zombie didn't s-show up for his afternoon feed. Y-You might want to call around."

"Zombie's gone," he said.

"That's what I said."

"No, I mean—" *Christ, Carol. You never were much for euphemisms, were you?* "Zombie got hit by a car. He's dead."

Even when we tried using them on you.

"Oh. Shit." The computer paused a moment, some internal clock counting off a precise number of nanosecs. "I'm sorry, Russ."

It was a lie, of course, but a fairly convincing one all the same.

Outside, Wescott smiled faintly. "It happens. Just a matter of time for all of us."

There was a sound from behind. He turned away from the cube; Lynne stood in the doorway. He could see sympathy in her eyes, and something else.

"Russ," she said. "I'm so sorry."

He felt a twitch at the corner of his mouth. "So's the computer."

"How are you feeling?"

He shrugged. "Okay, I guess."

"I doubt it. You had him all those years."

"Yeah. I—miss him." There was a hard knot of vacuum in his throat. He examined the feeling, distantly amazed, and almost felt a kind of gratitude.

She padded across the room to him, took his hands. "I'm sorry I wasn't there at the end, Russ. It was all I could do to take him in. I just couldn't, you know—"

"It's okay," Wescott said.

"—and you had to be there anyway, you—"

"It's okay," he said again.

Lynne straightened and rubbed one hand across her cheek. "Would you rather not talk about it?" Which meant, of course, *I want to talk about it.*

He wondered what he could say that wouldn't be utterly predictable: and realised that he could afford to tell the truth.

"I was thinking," he said, "he had it coming to him."

Lynne blinked.

"I mean, he'd spread enough carnage on his own. Remember how every couple of days he'd bring in a wounded vole or a bird, and I never let him actually kill any of them—"

"You didn't want to see anything suffer," Lynne said.

"—so I'd kill them myself." One blow with a hammer, brains scrambled instantly, nothing left that *could* suffer after that. "I always spoiled his fun. It's such a drag having to play with dead things, he'd bitch at me for hours..."

She smiled sadly. "He was suffering, Russ. He wanted to die. I know you loved the little ingrate, we both did."

Something flared where the vacuum had been. "It's okay, Lynne. I watch *people* die all the time, remember? I'm in no great need of therapy over a fucking cat. And if I was, you could—"

—have at least been there this morning.

He caught himself. *I'm angry,* he realised. *Isn't that strange. I haven't used this feeling for years.*

It seemed odd that anything so old could have such sharp edges.

"Sorry," he said evenly. "I didn't mean to snap. It's just—I heard enough platitudes at the vet, you know? I'm sick of people saying *He wants to die* when they mean *It would cost too much*. And I'm especially sick of people saying *love* when they mean *economics*."

Lynne put her arms around him. "There was nothing they could have done."

He stood there, swaying slightly, almost oblivious to her embrace.

Carol, how much did I pay to keep you breathing? And when did I decide you weren't worth the running tab?

"It's always economics," he said. And brought his arms up to hold her.

"You want to read minds."

Not Carol's voice, this time. This time it belonged to that guy from Southam...Mosby, that was it. Mosby's program sat in memory, directing a chorus of electrons that came out sounding like he did, a cheap auditory clone. Wescott preferred it to the original.

"Read minds?" He considered. "Actually, right now I'm just trying to build a working model of one."

"Like me?"

"No. You're just a fancy menu. You ask questions; depending on how I answer them you branch to certain others. You're linear. Minds are more...distributed."

"Thoughts are not signals, but the intersections of signals."

"You've read Penthorne."

"I'm reading him now. I've got Biomedical Abstracts online."

"Mmmm."

"I'm also reading Gödel," the program said. "If he's right, you'll never get an accurate model of the human brain, because no box is big enough to hold itself."

"So simplify it. Throw away the details, but preserve the essence. You don't want to make your model too big anyway; if it's as complicated as the real thing, it's just as hard to understand."

"So you just cut away at the brain until you end up with something simple enough to deal with?"

Wescott winced. "If you've got to keep it to vidbits, I guess that's as good as any."

"And what's left is still complex enough to teach you anything about human behaviour?"

"Look at you."

"Just a fancy menu."

"Exactly. But you know more than the real Jason Mosby. You're a better conversationalist, too; I met him once. I bet you'd even score higher on a Turing test. Am I right?"

A barely perceptible pause. "I don't know. Possibly."

"As far as I can tell you're better than the original, and with only a few percent of the processing power."

"Getting back to—"

"And if the original screams and fights when somebody tries to turn him off," Wescott went on, "it's just because he's been programmed to think he can suffer. He puts a bit more effort into keeping his subroutines running. Maybe not much of a difference after all, hmmm?"

The program fell silent. Wescott started counting: *One one thousand, two one thousand, three—*

"That actually brings up another subject I wanted to ask you about," the menu said.

Almost four seconds to respond, and even then it had had to change the subject. It had limits. Good program, though.

"You haven't published anything on your work at VanGen," Mosby's proxy remarked. "I'm unable to access your NSERC proposal, of course, but judging from the public abstract, you've been working on dead people."

"Not dead. Dying."

"Near-death experiences? Levitation, tunnel of light, that sort of thing?"

"Symptoms of anoxia," Wescott said. "Mostly meaningless. We go further."

"Why?"

"A few basic patterns are easier to record after other brain functions have shut down."

"What patterns? What do they tell you?"

They tell me there's only one way to die, Mosby. It doesn't matter what kills you, age or violence or disease, we all sing out the same damn song before we cash in. You don't even have to be human; as long as you've got a neocortex you're part of the club.

And you know what else, Mosby? We can almost read the lyric sheet. Come by in person, say a month from now, and I could preview your own last thoughts for you. I could give you the scoop of the decade.

"Dr. Wescott?"

He blinked. "Sorry?"

"What patterns? What do they tell you?"

"What do you think?" Wescott said, and started counting again.

"I think you watch people die," the program answered, "and you take pictures. I don't know why. But I think our subscribers would like to."

Wescott was silent for a few moments.

"What's your release number?" he asked at last.

"Six point five."

"You're just out, aren't you?"

"April fifteenth," the program told him.

"You're better than six four."

"We're improving all the time."

From behind, the sound of an opening door. "Stop," Wescott said.

"Do you want to c-cancel the program or just suspend it?" Carol's voice asked from the cube.

"Suspend." Wescott stared at the computer, vaguely jarred by the change in voice. *Do they ever feel crowded in there?*

"Can you hear it?" Lynne said from behind him.

He turned in his chair. She was taking off her shoes by the front door.

"Hear what?" Wescott asked.

She came across the room. "The way her voice sort of—catches, sometimes?"

He frowned.

"Like she was in pain when she made the recording," she went on. "Maybe it was before she was even diagnosed. But when she programmed that machine, it picked up on it. You've never heard it? In all these years?"

Wescott said nothing.

Lynne put her hands on his shoulders. "You sure it isn't time to change the personality in that thing?" she asked gently.

"It's not a personality, Lynne."

"I know. Just a pattern-matching algorithm. You keep saying that."

"Look, I don't know what you're so worried about. It's no threat to you."

"I didn't mean—"

"Eleven years ago she talked to it for a while. It uses her speech patterns. It isn't her. I know that. It's just an old operating system that's been obsolete for the better part of a decade."

"Russ—"

"That lousy program Mosby sent me is ten times more sophisticated. And you can go out and buy a psyche simulator that will put *that* to shame. But this is all I have left, okay? The least you can do is grant me the freedom to remember her the way I choose."

She pulled back. "Russ, I'm not trying to fight with you."

"I'm glad." He turned back to the workstation. "Resume."

"Suspend," Lynne said. The computer waited silently.

Wescott took a slow breath and turned back to face her.

"I'm not one of your patients, Lynne." His words were measured, inflectionless. "If you can't leave your work downtown, at least find someone else to practise on."

"Russ..." Her voice trailed off.

He looked back at her, utterly neutral.

"Okay, Russ. See you later." She turned and walked back to the door. Wescott noted the controlled tetanus in her movements, imagined the ratchet contraction of actomyosin as she reached for her shoes.

She's running, he thought, fascinated. *My words did that to her. I make waves in the air and a million nerves light up her brain like sheet lightning. How many ops/sec happening in there? How many switches opening, closing, rerouting, until some of that electricity runs down her arm and makes her hand turn the doorknob?*

He watched her intricate machinery close the door behind itself.

She's gone, he thought. *I've won again.*

Wescott watched Hamilton strap the chimp onto the table and attach the leads to its scalp. The chimp was used to the procedure; it had been subject to such indignities on previous occasions, and had always survived in good health and good spirits. There was no reason for it to expect anything different this time.

As Hamilton snugged the straps, the smaller primate stiffened and hissed.

Wescott studied a nearby monitor. "Damn, it's nervous." Cortical tracings, normally languorous, scrambled across the screen in epileptic spasms. "We can't start until it calms down. *Unless* it calms down. Shit. This could scotch the whole recording."

Hamilton pulled one of the restraints a notch tighter. The chimp, its back pulled flat against the table, flexed once and went suddenly limp.

Wescott looked back at the screen. "Okay, it's relaxing. Showtime, Pete; you're on in about thirty seconds."

Hamilton held up the hypo. "Ready."

"Okay, getting baseline—now. Fire when ready."

Needle slid into flesh. Wescott reflected on the obvious unhumanity of the thing on the table; too small and hairy, all bow legs and elongate simian arms. *A machine. That's all it is. Potassium ions jumping around in a very compact telephone switchboard.*

But the eyes, when he slipped and looked at them, looked back.

"Midbrain signature in fifty seconds," Wescott read off. "Give or take ten."

"Okay," Hamilton said. "It's going through the tunnel."

Just a machine, running out of fuel. A few nerves sputter and the system thinks it sees lights, feels motion—

"There. Thalamus," Hamilton reported. "Right on time. Now it's in the ret." A pause. "Neocortex, now. Same damn thing every time."

Wescott didn't look. He knew the pattern. He had seen its hand-writing in the brains of half a dozen species, watched that same familiar cipher scurry through dying minds in hospital beds and operating theatres and the twisted wreckage of convenient automobiles. By now he didn't even need the machines to see it. He only had to look at the eyes.

Once, in a moment of reckless undiscipline, he'd wondered if he were witnessing the flight of the soul, come crawling to the surface of the mind like an earthworm flushed by heavy rains. Another time he'd thought he might have captured the EEG of the Grim Reaper.

He no longer allowed himself such unbridled licence. Now he only stared at the widening pupils within those eyes, and heard the final panicked bleating of the cardiac monitor.

Something behind the eyes went out.

What were you? he wondered.

"Dunno yet," Hamilton said beside him. "But another week, two at the outside, and we've got it nailed."

Wescott blinked.

Hamilton started unstrapping the carcass. After a moment he looked up. "Russ?"

"It knew." Wescott stared at the monitor, all flat lines and static now.

"Yeah." Hamilton shrugged. "I wish I knew what tips them off sometimes. Save a lot of time." He dumped the chimp's body into a plastic bag. Its dilated pupils stared out at Wescott in a grotesque parody of human astonishment.

"—Russ? You okay?"

He blinked; the dead eyes lost control. Wescott looked up and saw Hamilton watching him with a strange expression.

"Sure," he said easily. "Never better."

There was this cage. Something moved inside that he almost recognised, a small furred body that looked familiar. But up close he could see his mistake. It was only a wax dummy, or maybe an embalmed specimen the undergrads hadn't got to yet. There were tubes running into it at odd places, carrying sluggish aliquots of yellow fluid. The specimen jaundiced, bloated as he watched. He reached through the bars of the cage...he could do that somehow, even though the gaps were only a few centimeters wide... and touched the thing inside. Its eyes opened and stared past him, blank

and blind with pain; and their pupils were not vertical as he had expected,
but round and utterly human...

He felt her awaken in the night beside him, and not move.

He didn't have to look. He heard the change in her breathing, could almost feel her systems firing up, her eyes locking onto him in the near darkness. He lay on his back, looking up at a ceiling full of shadow, and did not acknowledge her.

He turned his face to stare at the faint gray light leaking through the window. Straining, he could just hear distant city sounds.

He wondered, for a moment, if she hurt as much as he did; then realised that there was no contest. The strongest pain he could summon was mere aftertaste.

"I called the vet today," he said. "She said they didn't need my consent. They didn't need me there at all. They would have shut Zombie down the moment you brought him in, only you told them not to."

Still she did not move.

"So you lied. You fixed it so I'd have to be there, watching one more piece of my life getting—" he took a breath, "—chipped away—"

At last she spoke: "Russ—"

"But you don't hate me. So why would you put me through that? You must have thought it would be good for me, somehow."

"Russ, I'm sorry. I didn't mean to hurt you."

"I don't think that's entirely true," he remarked.

"No. I guess not." Then, almost hopefully, "It did hurt, didn't it?"

He blinked against a brief stinging in his eyes. "What do you think?"

"I think, nine years ago I moved in with the most caring, humane person I'd ever known. And two days ago I didn't know if he'd give a damn about the death of a pet he'd had for eighteen years. I really didn't know, Russ, and I'm sorry but I had to find out. Does that make sense?"

He tried to remember. "I think you were wrong from the start. I think you gave me too much credit nine years ago."

He felt her head shake. "Russ, after Carol died I was afraid *you* were going to. I remember hoping I'd never be able to hurt that much over another human being. I fell in love with you because you could."

"Oh, I loved her all right. Hundreds of thousands of dollars worth at least. Never did get around to figuring out her final worth."

"That's not why you did it! You remember how she was suffering!"

"Actually, no. She had all those—painkillers, cruising through her system. That's what they told me. By the time they started cutting pieces out of her she was—numb..."

"Russ, I was there too. They said there was no hope, she was in constant pain, they said she'd want to die—"

"Oh yes. Later, that's what they said. When it was time to decide. Because they knew..."

He stopped.

"They knew," he said again, "what I wanted to hear."

Beside him, Lynne grew very still.

He laughed once, softly. "I shouldn't have been so easy to convince, though. I knew better. We're not hardwired for Death with Dignity; life's been kicking and clawing and doing anything it can to take a few more breaths, for over three billion years. You can't just decide to turn yourself off."

She slid an arm across his chest. "People turn themselves off all the time, Russ. Too often. You know that."

He didn't answer. A distant siren poisoned the emptiness.

"Not Carol," he said after a while. "I made that decision for her."

Lynne put her head on his shoulder. "And you've spent ten years trying to find out if you guessed right. But they're not *her*, Russ, all the people you've recorded, all the animals you've...put down, they're not *her*—"

"No. They're not." He closed his eyes. "They don't linger on month after month. They don't...shrivel up...you *know* they're going to die, and it's always quick, you don't have to come in day after day, watching them change into something that, that *rattles* every time it breathes, that doesn't even know who you are and you wish it would just—"

Wescott opened his eyes.

"I keep forgetting what you do for a living," he said.

"Russ—"

He looked over at her, calmly. "Why are you doing this to me? You think I haven't already been over it enough?"

"Russ, I'm only—"

"Because it won't work, you know. It's too late. It took long enough, but I know how the mind works now, and you know what? It's nothing special after all. It's not spiritual, it's not even quantum. It's just a bunch of switches wired together. So it doesn't matter if people can't speak their minds. Pretty soon I'll be able to *read* them."

His voice was level and reasoned. He kept his eyes on the ceiling; the darkened light fixture there seemed to waver before his eyes. He blinked, and the room swam suddenly out of focus.

She reached up to touch the wetness on his face. "It scares you," she whispered. "You've been chasing it for ten years and you've almost got it and it scares the shit out of you."

He smiled and wouldn't look at her. "No. That isn't it at all."

"What, then?"

He took a breath. "I just realised. I don't care one way or the other any more."

He came home, clutching the printout, and knew from the sudden emptiness of the apartment that he had been defeated here as well.

The workstation slept in its corner. Several fitful readouts twinkled on one of its faces, a sparse autonomic mosaic. He walked towards it; and halfway there one face of the cube flashed to life.

Lynne, from the shoulders up, looked out at him from the screen.

Wescott glanced around the room. He almost called out.

On the cube, Lynne's lips moved. "Hello, Russ," they said.

He managed a short laugh. "Never thought I'd see you in there."

"I finally tried one of these things. You were right, they've come a long way in ten years."

"You're a real simulation? Not just a fancy conversational routine?"

"Uh huh. It's pretty amazing. It ate all sorts of video footage, and all my medical and academic records, and then I had to talk with it until it got a feel for who I was."

And who is that? he wondered absently.

"It changed right there while I was talking to it, Russ. It was really spooky. It started out in this dead monotone, and as we talked it started mimicking my voice, and my mannerisms, and in a little while it sounded just like me, and here it is. It went from machine to human in about four hours."

He smiled, not easily, because he knew what was coming next.

"It—actually, it was a bit like watching a time-lapse video of you over the past few years," the model said. "Played backwards."

He kept his voice exactly level. "You're not coming home."

"Sure I am, Russ. Only home isn't here any more. I wish it were, you don't know how badly I wish it were, but you just can't let it go and I can't live with that any more."

"You still don't understand. It's just a program that happens to sound like Carol did. It's nothing. I'll—wipe it if it's that important to you—"

"That's not all I'm talking about, Russ."

He thought of asking for details, and didn't.

"Lynne—" he began.

Her mouth widened. It wasn't a smile. "Don't ask, Russ. I can't come back until you do."

"But I'm right here!"

She shook her head. "The last time I saw Russ Wescott, he cried. Just a little. And I think—I think he's been hunting something for ten years, and he finally caught a glimpse of it and it was too big, so he went away and left some sort of autopilot in charge. And I don't blame him, and you're a very good likeness, really you are but there's nothing in you that knows how to feel."

Wescott thought of acetylcholinesterase and endogenous opioids. "You're wrong, Carol. I know more about feelings than almost anyone in the world."

On the screen, Lynne's proxy sighed through a faint smile.

The simulation was wearing new earrings; they looked like antique printed circuits. Wescott wanted to comment on them, to compliment or criticise or do anything to force the conversation into less dangerous territory. But he was afraid that she had worn them for years and he just hadn't noticed, so he said nothing.

"Why couldn't you tell me yourself?" he said at last. "Don't I deserve that much? Why couldn't you at least leave me in person?"

"This *is* in person, Russ. It's as in person as you ever let anyone get with you any more."

"That's bullshit! Did I *ask* you to go out and get yourself simmed? You think I see you as some sort of cartoon? My Christ, Lynne—"

"I don't take it personally, Russ. We're all cartoons as far as you're concerned."

"What in Christ's name are you talking about?"

"I don't blame you, really. Why learn 3D chess when you can reduce it down to tic-tac-toe? You understand it perfectly, and you always win. Except it isn't that much fun to play, of course..."

"Lynne—"

"Your models only simplify reality, Russ. They don't re-create it."

Wescott remembered the printout in his hand. "Sure they do. Enough of it, anyway."

"So." The image looked down for a moment. *Uncanny, the way it fakes and breaks eye contact like that—*"You have your answer."

"*We* have the answer. Me, and a few terabytes of software, and a bunch of colleagues, Lynne. People. Who work with me, face to face."

She looked up again, and Wescott was amazed that the program had even mimicked the sudden sad brightness her eyes would have had in that moment. "So what's the answer? What's at the end of the tunnel?"

He shrugged. "Not much, after all. An anticlimax."

"I hope it was more than that, Russ. It killed us."

"Or it could've just been an artefact of the procedure. The old observer effect, maybe. Common sense could have told us as much, I could've saved myself the—"

"Russ."

He didn't look at the screen.

"There's nothing down there at all," he said, finally. "Nothing that thinks. I never liked it down there, it's all just...raw instinct, at the center. Left over from way back when the limbic system *was* the brain. Only now it's just unskilled labour, right? Just one small part of the whole, to do all that petty autonomic shit the upstart neocortex can't be bothered with. I never even considered that it might still be somehow...alive..."

His voice trailed off. Lynne's ghost waited silently, perhaps unequipped to respond. Perhaps programmed not to.

"You die from the outside in, did you know that?" he said, when the silence hurt more than the words. "And then, just for a moment, the center is all you are again. And down there, nobody wants to...you know, even the suicides, they were just fooling themselves. Intellectual games. We're so fucking proud of thinking ourselves to death that we've forgotten all about the old reptilian part sleeping inside, the part that doesn't calculate ethics or quality of life or burdens on the next of kin, it just wants to *live*, that's all it's programmed for, you know? And at the very end, when we aren't around to keep it in line any more, it comes up and looks around and at that last moment it knows it's been betrayed, and it...screams..."

He thought he heard someone speak his name, but he didn't look up to find out.

"That's what we always found," he said. "Something waking up after a hundred million years, scared to death..."

His words hung there in front of him.

"You don't know that." Her voice was distant, barely familiar, with a sudden urgency to it. "You said yourself it could be an artefact. She might not have felt that way at all, Russ. You don't have the data."

"Doesn't matter," he murmured. "Wetware always dies the same way—"

He looked up at the screen.

And the image was for Chrissakes *crying*, phosphorescent tears on artificial cheeks in some obscene parody of what Lynne would do if she had been there. Wescott felt sudden hatred for the software that wept for him, for the intimacy of its machine intuition, for the precision of its forgery. For the simple fact that it *knew* her.

"No big deal," he said. "Like I said, an anticlimax. Anyhow, I suppose you have to go back and report to your—body—"

"I can stay if you want. I know how hard this must be for you, Russ—"

"No you don't." Wescott smiled. "Lynne might have. You're just accessing a psych database somewhere. Good try, though."

"I don't have to go, Russ—"

"Hey, that's not who I am any more. Remember?"

"—we can keep talking if you want."

"Right. A dialogue between a caricature and an autopilot."

"I don't have to leave right away."

"Your algorithm's showing," he said, still smiling. And then, tersely: "Stop."

The cube darkened.

"Do y-ou want to cancel the program or just suspend it?" Carol asked.

He stood there for a while without answering, staring into that black featureless cube of perspex. He could see nothing inside but his own reflection.

"Cancel," he said at last. "And delete."

NIMBUS

She's been out there for hours now, listening to the clouds. I can see the RadioShack receiver balanced on her knees, I can see the headphone wires snaking up and cutting her off from the world. Or connecting her, I suppose. Jess is hooked into the sky now, in a way I'll never be. She can hear it talking. The clouds advance, threatening gray anvils and mountains boiling in ominous slow motion, and the 'phones fill her head with alien grumbles and moans.

God she looks like her mother. I catch her profile and for a moment it *is* Anne there, gently chiding, *Of course not, Jess, there aren't any spirits. They're just clouds.* But now I see her face and eight years have passed in a flash, and I know this can't be Anne. Anne knew how to smile.

I should go out and join her. It's still safe enough, we've got a good half hour before the storm hits. Not that it's really going to hit *us*; it's just passing through, they say, on its way to some other target. Still, I wonder if it knows we're in the way. I wonder if it cares.

I *will* join her. For once, I will not be a coward. My daughter sits five meters away in our own back yard, and I am damn well going to be there for her. It's the least I can do before I go.

I wonder if that will mean anything to her.

An aftermath, before the enlightenment.

It was as though somebody had turned the city upside down and shaken it. We waded through a shallow sea of detritus: broken walls, slabs of torn roofing, toilets and sofas and shattered glass. I walked behind Anne, Jess bouncing on my shoulders making happy gurgling noises; just over a year old, not quite talking yet but plenty old enough for continual astonishment. You could see it in her eyes. Every blown newspaper, every bird, every step was a new experience in wonder.

Also every loaded shotgun. Every trigger-happy National Guardsman. This was a time when people still thought they owned things. They saw their homes strewn across two city blocks and the enemy they feared was not the weather, but each other. Hurricanes were accidents, freaks of nature. The experts were still blaming volcanoes and the greenhouse effect for everything. Looters, on the other hand, were real. They were tangible. They were a problem with an obvious solution.

The volunteers' shelter squatted in the distance like a circus tent at Armageddon. A tired-looking woman inside had given us shovels and pitchforks, and directed us to the nearest pile of unmanned debris. We began to pitch pieces of someone's life into an enormous blue dumpster. Anne and I worked side by side, stopping occasionally to pass Jessica back and forth.

I wondered what new treasures I was about to unearth. Some priceless family heirloom, miraculously spared? A complete collection of Jethro Tull CDs? Just a game, of course; the whole area had been combed, the owners had come and despaired of salvage, there was only wreckage beneath the wreckage. Still, every now and then I thought I saw something shining in the dirt, a bottle cap or a gum wrapper or a Rolex—

My pitchfork punched through a chunk of plaster and slid into something soft. It dropped suddenly under my weight, as if lubricated. It stopped.

I heard the muted hiss of escaping gas. Something smelled, very faintly, of rotten meat.

This isn't what I think it is. The crews have already been here. They used trained dogs and infrared scopes and they've already found all the bodies, they couldn't have missed anything, there's nothing here but wood and plaster and cement—

I tightened my grip on the pitchfork, pulled up on the shaft. The tines rose up from the plaster, slick, dark, wet.

Anne was laughing. I couldn't believe it. I looked up, but she wasn't looking at me or the pitchfork or the coagulating stain. She was looking across the wreckage to a Ford pickup, loaded with locals and their rifles, inching its way down a pathway cleared in the road.

"Get a load of the bumper," she said, oblivious to my discovery.

There was a bumper sticker on the driver's side. I saw the caricature of a storm cloud, inside the classic red circle with diagonal slash. And a slogan.

A warning, to whom it may concern: *Clouds, we're gonna kick your ass.*

Jess takes off the headphones as I join her. She touches a button on the receiver. Cryptic wails, oddly familiar, rise from a speaker on the front of the device. We sit for a moment without speaking, letting the sounds wash over us.

Everything about her is so pale. I can barely see her eyebrows.

"Do they know where it's headed?" Jess asks at last.

I shake my head. "There's Hanford, but they've never gone after a reactor before. They say it might be trying to get up enough steam to go over the mountains. Maybe it's going after Vancouver or SeaTac again." I tap the box on her knees. "Hey, it might be laying plans even as we speak. You've been listening to that thing long enough, you should know what it's saying by now."

A distant flicker of sheet lightning strobes on the horizon. From Jessica's receiver, a dozen voices wail a discordant crescendo.

"Or you could even talk to it," I continue. "I saw the other day, they've got two-ways now. Like yours, only you can send as well as receive."

Jess fingers the volume control. "It's just a gimmick, Dad. These things couldn't put out enough power to get heard over all the other stuff in the air. TV, and radio, and..." She cocks her head at the sounds coming from the speaker. "Besides, nobody understands what they're saying anyway."

"Ah, but *they* could understand *us*," I say, trying for a touch of mock drama.

"Think so?" Her voice is expressionless, indifferent.

I push on anyway. Talking at least helps paper over my fear a bit. "Sure. The big ones could understand, anyway. A storm this size must have an IQ in the six digits, easy."

"I suppose," Jess says.

Inside, something tears a little. "Doesn't it *matter* to you?"

She just looks at me.

"Don't you want to know?" I say. "We're sitting here underneath this huge thing that nobody understands, we don't know what it's doing or why, and you sit there listening while it shouts at itself and you don't seem to care that it changed everything overnight—"

But of course, she doesn't remember that. Her memory doesn't go back to when we thought that clouds were just...clouds. She never knew what it was like to rule the world, and she never expects to.

My daughter is indifferent to defeat.

Suddenly, unbearably, I just want to hold her. *God Jess, I'm sorry we messed up so badly.* With effort, I control myself. "I just wish you could remember the way it was."

"Why?" she asks. "What was so different?"

I look at her, astonished. "Everything!"

"It doesn't sound like it. They say we *never* understood the weather. There were hurricanes and tornadoes even before, and sometimes they'd smash whole cities, and nobody could stop them then either. So what if it happens because the sky's alive, or just because it's, you know, random?"

Because your mother is dead, Jess, and after all these years I still don't know what killed her. Was it just blind chance? Was it the reflex of some slow, stupid animal that was only scratching an itch?

Can the sky commit murder?

"It matters," is all I tell her. Even if it doesn't make a difference.

The front is almost directly overhead now, like the mouth of a great black cave crawling across the heavens. West, all is clear. Above, the squall line tears the sky into jagged halves.

East, the world is a dark, murky green.

I feel so vulnerable out here. I glance back over my shoulder. The armoured house crouches at our backs, only the biggest trees left to keep it company. It's been eight years and the storms still haven't managed to dig us out. They got Mexico City, and Berlin, and the whole damn golden horseshoe, but our little house hangs in there like a festering cyst embedded in the landscape.

Then again, they probably just haven't noticed us yet.

Reprieved. The thing in the sky had gone to sleep, at least in our corner of the world. The source of its awareness—sources, rather, for they were legion—had convected into the stratosphere and frozen, a billion crystalline motes of suspended intellect. By the time they came back down they'd be on the other side of the world, and it would take days for the rest of the collective conscious to fill the gap.

We used the time to ready our defences. I was inspecting the exoskeleton the contractors had just grafted onto the house. Anne was around front, checking the storm shutters. Our home had become monstrous, an angular fortress studded with steel beams and lightning rods. A few years earlier we would have sued anyone who did this to us. Today, we had gone into hock to pay for the retrofit.

I looked up at a faint roar from overhead. The sun reflected off a cluster of tiny cruciform shapes drawing contrails across the sky.

Cloud seeders. A common enough sight. In those days we still thought we could fight back.

"They won't work," Jess said seriously at my elbow.

I look down, startled. "Hey, Jess. Didn't see you sneaking up on me."

"They're just getting the clouds mad," she said, with all the certainty a four-year-old can muster. She squinted up into the blue expanse. "They're just trying to kill the, um, the messenger."

I squatted down, regarded her eye to eye. "And who told you that?" Not her mother, anyway.

"That woman. Talking to Mom."

Not just a woman, I saw as I rounded the corner into the front yard. A couple: early twenties, mildly scruffy, both bearing slogans on their t-shirts. *Love Your Mother* the woman's chest told me, over a decal of the earth from lunar orbit. The man's shirt was more verbose: *Unlimited growth, the creed of carcinoma.* No room for a picture on that one.

Gaianists. Retreating across the lawn, facing Anne, as if afraid to turn their backs. Anne was smiling and waving, the very picture of inoffence, but I really felt for the poor bastards. They probably never knew what hit them.

Sometimes, when Seventh-day Adventists came calling, Anne would actually invite them in for a little target practise. It was usually the Adventists who asked to leave.

"Did they have anything worthwhile to say?" I asked her now.

"Not really." Anne stopped waving and turned to face me. Her smile morphed into a triumphant smirk. "We're angering the sky gods, you know that? Thou shalt not inhabit a single-family dwelling. Thou shalt honour thy environmental impact, to keep it low."

"They could be right," I remarked. At least, there weren't many people around to argue the point. Most of our former neighbours had already retreated into hives. Not that *their* environmental impact had had much to do with it.

"Well, I'll grant it's not as flakey as some of the things they come up with," Anne admitted. "But if they're going to blame me for the revenge of the cloud demons, they damn well better have a rational argument or two waiting in the wings."

"I take it they didn't."

She snorted. "The same hokey metaphors. Gaia's leaping into action to fight the human disease. I guess hurricanes are supposed to be some sort of penicillin."

"No crazier than some of the things the experts say."

"Yeah, well, I don't necessarily believe them either."

"Maybe you should," I said. "I mean, *we* sure as hell don't know what's going on."

"And you think *they* do? Just a couple of years ago they were denying everything, remember? Life can't exist without stable organized structure, they said."

"I sort of thought they'd learned a few things since then."

"No kidding." Anne's eyes grew round with enlightenment. "And all this time I thought they were just making up trendy buzzwords."

Jess wandered between us. Anne scooped her up; Jess scrambled onto her mother's shoulders and surveyed the world from dizzying adult height.

I glanced back at the retreating evangelists. "So how did you handle those two?"

"I agreed with them," Anne said.

"Agreed?"

"Sure. We're a disease. Fine. Only some of us have mutated." She jerked a thumb at our castle. "Now, we're resistant to antibiotics."

We are resistant to antibiotics. We've encysted ourselves like hermit crabs. We've been pruned, cut back, decimated but not destroyed. We are only in remission.

But now, outside the battlements, we're naked. Even at this range the storm could reach out and swat us both in an instant. How can Jess just sit there?

"I can't even enjoy sunny days any more," I admit to her.

She looks at me, and I know her perplexity is not because I can't enjoy clear skies, but because I would even think it worthy of comment. I keep talking, refusing the chronic realization that we're aliens to each other. "The sky can be pure blue and sunshine, but if there's even one fluffy little cumulus bumping along I can't help feeling...watched. It doesn't matter if it's too small to think on its own, or that it'll dissipate before it gets a chance to upload. I keep thinking it's some sort of spy, it's going to report back somewhere."

"I don't think they can see," Jess says absently. "They just sense big things like cities and smokestacks, hot spots or things that...itch. That's all."

The wind breathes, deceptively gentle, in her hair. Above us a finger of gray vapour crawls between two towering masses of cumulonimbus. What's happening up there? A random conjunction of water droplets? A 25,000-baud data dump between processing nodes? Even after all this time it sounds absurd.

So many eloquent theories, so many explanations for our downfall. Everyone's talking about order from chaos: fluid geometry, bioelectric microbes that live in the clouds, complex behaviours emerging from some insane alliance of mist and electrochemistry. It looks scientific enough on paper, but spoken aloud it always sounds like an incantation...

And none of it helps. The near distance is lit with intermittent flashes of light. The storm walks toward us on jagged fractal legs. I feel like an insect under the heel of a descending boot. Maybe that's a positive sign. Would I be afraid if I had really given up?

Maybe. Maybe the situation is irrelevant. Maybe cowards are *always* afraid.

Jess's receiver is crying incessantly. "Whale songs," I hear myself say, and the tremor in my voice is barely discernible. "Humpback whales. That's what they sound like."

Jess fixes her eyes back on the sky. "They don't *sound* like anything, Dad. It's just electricity. Only the receiver sort of...makes it sound like something we know."

Another gimmick. We've fallen from God's chosen to endangered species in only a decade, and the hustlers still won't look up from their market profiles. I can sympathize. Looming above us, right now, are the ones who threw us into the street. The forward overhang is almost upon us. Ten kilometers overhead, winds are screaming past each other at sixty meters a second.

So far the storm isn't even breathing hard.

There was a banshee raging through the foothills. It writhed with tornados; Anne and I had watched the whirling black tentacles tearing at the horizon before we'd fled underground. Tornados were impossible during the winter, we'd been assured just a year before. Yet here we were, huddling together as the world shook, and all our reinforcements might as well have been made of paper if one of those figments came calling.

Sex is instinctive at times like those. Jeopardy reduces us to automata; there is no room for love when the genes reassert themselves.

Even pleasure is irrelevant. We were just another pair of mammals, trying to maximize our fitness before the other shoe dropped.

Afterwards, at least, we were still allowed to feel. We clung together, blind and invisible in the darkness, almost crushing each other with the weight of our own desperation. We couldn't stop crying. I gave silent thanks that Jess had been trapped at daycare when the front came through. I wouldn't have stood the strain of a brave facade that night.

After a while, Anne stopped shaking. She lay in my arms, sniffling quietly. Dim floaters of virtual light swarmed maddeningly at the edge of my vision.

"The gods have come back," she said at last.

"Gods?" Anne was usually so bloody empirical.

"The old ones," she said. "The Old Testament gods. The Greek pantheon. Thunderbolts and fire and brimstone. We thought we'd outgrown them, you know? We thought..."

I felt a deep, trembling breath.

"*I* thought," she continued. "I thought we didn't need them any more. But we did. We fucked up so horribly on our own. There was nobody to keep us in line, and we trampled everything..."

I stroked her back. "Old news, Annie. You know we've cleaned things up. Hardly any cities allow gasoline any more, extinctions have levelled off. I even heard the other day that rainforest biomass increased last year."

"That's not *us*." A sigh whispered across my cheek. "We're no better than we ever were. We're just afraid of a spanking. Like spoiled kids caught drawing naughty pictures on the walls."

"Anne, we still don't know for sure if the clouds are really alive. Even if they are, that doesn't make them intelligent. Some people still say this is all just a weird side-effect of chemicals in the atmosphere."

"We're begging for mercy, Jon. That's all we're doing."

We breathed against dark, distant roaring for a few moments.

"At least we're doing something," I said at last. "Maybe we're not doing it for all the enlightened reasons we should be, but at least we're cleaning up. That's something."

"Not enough," she said. "We threw shit at something for centuries.

How can a few prayers and sacrifices make it just go away and leave us alone? If it even exists. And if it *does* have any more brains than a flatworm. I guess you get the gods you deserve."

I tried to think of something to say, some twig of false reassurance. But, as usual, I wasn't fast enough. Anne picked herself up first:

"At least we've learned a little humility. And who knows? Maybe the gods will answer our prayers before Jess grows up..."

They didn't. The experts tell us now that our supplications are on indefinite hold. We're praying to something that shrouds the whole planet, after all. It takes time for such a huge system to assimilate new information, more time to react. The clouds don't live by human clocks. We swarm like bacteria to them, doubling our numbers in an instant. How fast the response, from our microbial perspective? How long before the knee jerks? The experts mumble jargon among themselves and guess: decades. Maybe fifty years. This monster advancing on us now is answering a summons from the last century.

The sky screams down to fight with ghosts. It doesn't see me. If it sees anything at all, it is only the afterimage of some insulting sore, decades old, that needs to be disinfected. I lean against the wind. Murky chaos sweeps across something I used to call property. The house recedes behind me. I don't dare look but I know it must be kilometers away, and somehow I'm paralysed. This blind seething medusa claws its way towards me and its face covers the whole sky; how can I *not* look?

"Jessica..."

I can see her from the corner of my eye. With enormous effort, I move my head a little and she comes into focus. She is looking at the heavens, but her expression is not terrified or awed or even curious.

Slowly, smooth as an oiled machine, she lowers her eyes to earth and switches off the receiver. It hardly matters any more. The thunder is continuous, the wind is an incessant roar, the first hailstones are pelting down on us. If we stay out here we'll be dead in two hours. Doesn't she know it? Is this some sort of test, am I supposed to prove my love for her by facing down God like this?

Maybe it doesn't matter. Maybe now's the time. Maybe—

Jessica puts her hand on my knee. "Come on," she says, like a parent. "Let's go inside."

I am remembering the last time I saw Anne. I have no choice; the moment traps me when I'm not looking, embeds me in a cross-section of time stopped dead when the lightning hit ten meters behind her:

The world is a flat mosaic in blinding black-and-white, strobe-lit, motionless. Sheets of gray water are suspended in the act of slamming the earth. Anne is just out of reach, head down, her determination as clear as a Kodalith snapshot in perfect focus: she is damn well going to make it to safety and she doesn't care what gets in her way. And then the lightning implodes into darkness, the world jerks back into motion with a sound like Hiroshima and the stench of burning electricity, but my eyes are shut tight, still fixed on that receding instant. There is sudden pain, small fingernails gouging the flesh of my palm, and I know that Jessica has not closed her eyes, that she knows more of this moment than I can bear to. I pray, for the only time in my life I pray to the sky *please let me be mistaken take someone else take me take the whole fucking city only please give her back I'm sorry I didn't believe...*

Forty or fifty years from now, according to some, it might hear that. Too late for Anne. Too late even for me.

It's still out there. Just passing through, it drums its fingers on the ground and all our reinforced talismans can barely keep it out. Even here, in this underground sanctum, the walls are shaking.

It doesn't scare me any more.

There was another time, long ago, when I wasn't afraid. Back then the shapes in the sky were friendly; snow-covered mountains, magical kingdoms, once I even saw Anne up there. But now I only see something malign and hideous, ancient, something slow to anger and impossible to appease. In the thousands of years we spent watching the clouds, after all the visions and portents we read there, never once did we see the thing that was really looking back.

We see it now.

I wonder which epitaphs they'll be reading tomorrow. What city is about to be shattered by impossible tornados, how many will die in this fresh onslaught of hailstones and broken glass? I don't know. I don't even care. That surprises me. Just a few days ago, I think it would have mattered. Now, even the realization that we are spared barely moves me to indifference.

Jess, how can you sleep through this? The wind tries to uproot us, bits of God's brain bash themselves against our shelter, and somehow you can just curl up in the corner and block it out. You're so much older than I am, Jess; you learned not to care years ago. Barely any of you shines out any more. Even the glimpses I catch only seem like old photographs, vague reminders of what you used to be. Do I really love you as much as I tell myself?

Maybe all I love is my own nostalgia.

I gave you a start, at least. I gave you a few soft years before things fell apart. But then the world split in two, and the part I can live in keeps shrinking. You slip so easily between both worlds; your whole generation is amphibious. Not mine. There's nothing left I can offer you, you don't need me at all. Before long I'd have dragged you down with me.

I won't let that happen. You're half Anne, after all.

The maelstrom covers the sound of my final ascent. I wonder what Anne would think of me now. She'd disapprove, I guess. She was too much of a fighter to *ever* give up. I don't think she had a suicidal thought in her whole life.

And suddenly, climbing the stairs, I realize that I can ask her right now if I want to. Anne is watching me from a far dark corner of the room, through weathered adolescent eyes opened to mere slits. Is she going to call me back? Is she going to berate me for giving in, say that she loves me? I hesitate. I open my mouth.

But she closes her eyes without a word.

MAYFLY

WITH DERRYL MURPHY

"I hate you."

A four-year-old girl. A room as barren as a fishbowl.

"I *hate* you."

Little fists, clenching: one of the cameras, set to motion-cap, zoomed on them automatically. Two others watched the adults, mother, father on opposite sides of the room. The machines watched the players: half a world away, Stavros watched the machines.

"*I hate you I hate you I HATE you!*"

The girl was screaming now, her face contorted in anger and anguish. There were tears at the edge of her eyes but they stayed there, never falling. Her parents shifted like nervous animals, scared of the anger, used to the outbursts but far from comfortable with them.

At least this time she was using words. Usually she just howled.

She leaned against the blanked window, fists pounding. The window took her assault like hard white rubber, denting slightly, then rebounding. One of the few things in the room that bounced back when she struck out; one less thing to break.

"Jeannie, hush..." Her mother reached out a hand. Her father, as usual, stood back, a mixture of anger and resentment and confusion on his face.

Stavros frowned. *A veritable pillar of paralysis, that man.*

And then: *They don't deserve her.*

The screaming child didn't turn, her back a defiant slap at Kim and Andrew Goravec. Stavros had a better view: Jeannie's face was just a few centimeters away from the southeast pickup. For all the pain it showed, for all the pain Jeannie had felt in the four short years of her physical life, those few tiny drops that never fell were the closest she ever came to crying.

"Make it *clear*," she demanded, segueing abruptly from anger to petulance.

Kim Goravec shook her head. "Honey, we'd love to show you outside. Remember before, how much you liked it? But you have to promise not to *scream* at it all the time. You didn't used to, honey, you—"

"*Now!*" Back to rage, the pure, white-hot anger of a small child.

The pads on the wall panel were greasy from Jeannie's repeated, sticky-fingered attempts to use them herself. Andrew flashed a begging look at his wife: *Please, let's just give her what she wants.*

His wife was stronger. "Jeannie, we know it's difficult—"

Jeannie turned to face the enemy. The north pickup got it all: the right hand rising to the mouth, the index finger going in. The defiant glare in those glistening, focused eyes.

Kim took a step forward. "Jean, honey, *no!*"

They were baby teeth, still, but sharp. They'd bitten to the bone before Mommy even got within touching distance. A red stain blossomed from Jeannie's mouth, flowed down her chin like some perverted re-enactment of mealtime messes as a baby, and covered the lower half of her face in an instant. Above the gore, bright angry eyes said *gotcha.*

Without a sound Jeannie Goravec collapsed, eyes rolling back in her head as she pitched forward. Kim caught her just before her head hit the floor. "Oh God Andy she's fainted she's in shock she—"

Andrew didn't move. One hand was buried in the pocket of his blazer, fiddling with something.

Stavros felt his mouth twitch. *Is that a remote control in your pocket or are you just glad to—*

Kim had the tube of liquid skin out, sprayed it onto Jeannie's hand while cradling the child's head in her lap. The bleeding slowed. After a moment Kim looked back at her husband, who was standing motionless and unhelpful against the wall. He had that look on his face, that giveaway look that Stavros was seeing so often these days.

"You turned her off," Kim said, her voice rising. "After everything we'd agreed on, you still turned her *off?*"

Andrew shrugged helplessly. "Kim..."

Kim refused to look at him. She rocked back and forth, tuneless breath whistling between her teeth, Jeannie's head still in her lap. Kim and Andrew Goravec with their bundle of joy. Between them, the cable connecting Jeannie's head to the server shivered on the floor like a disputed boundary.

Stavros had this metaphoric image of her: Jean Goravec, buried alive in the airless dark, smothered by tonnes of earth—finally set free. Jean Goravec coming up for air.

Another image, of himself this time: Stavros Mikalaides, liberator. The man who made it possible for her to experience, however briefly, a world where the virtual air was sweet and the bonds nonexistent. Certainly there'd been others in on the miracle—a dozen tech-heads, twice as many lawyers—but they'd all vanished over time, their interest fading with proof-of-principal or the signing of the last waiver. The damage was under control, the project was in a holding pattern; there was no need to waste more than a single Terracon employee on mere cruise control. So only Stavros remained—and to Stavros, Jeannie had never been a *project*. She was his as much as the Goravecs. Maybe more.

But even Stavros still didn't know what it was really like for her. He wondered if it was physically possible for *anyone* to know. When Jean Goravec slipped the leash of her fleshly existence, she awoke into a reality where the very laws of physics had expired.

It hadn't started that way, of course. The system had booted up with years of mundane, real-world environments on file, each lovingly rendered down to the dust motes. But they'd been flexible, responsive to the needs of any developing intellect. In hindsight, maybe too flexible. Jean Goravec had edited her personal reality so radically that even Stavros' mechanical intermediaries could barely parse it. This little girl could turn a forest glade into a bloody Roman coliseum with a thought. Unleashed, Jean lived in a world where all bets were off.

A thought-experiment in child abuse: place a newborn into an environment devoid of vertical lines. Keep her there until the brain settles, until the wiring has congealed. Whole assemblies of pattern-matching retinal cells, aborted for lack of demand, will be forever beyond recall. Telephone poles, the trunks of trees, the vertical aspects of skyscrapers—your victim will be neurologically blind to such things for life.

So what happens to a child raised in a world where vertical lines dissolve, at a whim, into circles or fractals or a favorite toy?

We're the impoverished ones, Stavros thought. *Next to Jean, we're blind.*

He could see what she started with, of course. His software read the patterns off her occipital cortex, translated them flawlessly into images projected onto his own tactical contacts. But images aren't *sight*, they're just...raw material. There are filters all along the path: receptor cells, firing thresholds, pattern-matching algorithms. Endless stores of past images, an experiential visual library to draw on. More than vision, sight is *interpretation*, a subjective stew of infinitesimal enhancements and corruptions. Nobody in the world could interpret Jean's visual environment better than Stavros Mikalaides, and he'd barely been able to make sense of those shapes for years.

She was simply, immeasurably, beyond him. It was one of the things he loved most about her.

Now, mere seconds after her father had cut the cord, Stavros watched Jean Goravec ascend into her true self. Heuristic algorithms upgraded before his eyes; neural nets ruthlessly pared and winnowed trillions of redundant connections; intellect emerged from primordial chaos. Namps-per-op dropped like the heavy end of a teeter-totter; at the other end of that lever, processing efficiency rose into the stratosphere.

This was Jean. *They have no idea*, Stavros thought, *what you're capable of.*

She woke up screaming.

"It's all right, Jean, I'm here." He kept his voice calm to help her come down.

Jean's temporal lobe flickered briefly at the input. "Oh, God," she said. "Another nightmare?"

"Oh, God." Breath too fast, pulse too high, adrenocortical analogs off the scale. It could have been the telemetry of a rape.

He thought of short-circuiting those responses. Half a dozen tweaks would make her happy. But half a dozen tweaks would also turn her into someone else. There is no personality beyond the chemical—and while Jean's mind was fashioned from electrons rather than proteins, analogous rules applied.

"I'm here, Jean," he repeated. A good parent knew when to step in, and when suffering was necessary for growth. "It's okay. It's okay."

Eventually, she settled down.

"Nightmare." There were sparks in the parietal subroutines, a tremor lingering in her voice. "It doesn't fit, Stav. Scary dreams, that's the definition. But that implies there's some *other* kind, and I can't—I mean, why is it *always* like this? Was it always like this?"

"I don't know." *No, it wasn't.*

She sighed. "These words I learn, none of them really seem to fit *anything* exactly, you know?"

"They're just symbols, Jean." He grinned. At times like this he could almost forget the source of those dreams, the stunted, impoverished existence of some half-self trapped in distant meat. Andrew Goravec's act of cowardice had freed her from that prison, for a while at least. She soared now, released to full potential. She *mattered*.

"Symbols. That's what *dreams* are supposed to be, but...I don't know. There're all these references to dreams in the library, and none of them seem that much different from just being awake. And when I *am* asleep, it's all just—screams, almost, only dopplered down. Really sludgy. And shapes. Red shapes." A pause. "I hate bedtime."

"Well, you're awake now. What are you up for today?"

"I'm not sure. I need to get away from this place."

He didn't know what place she meant. By default she woke up in the house, an adult residence designed for human sensibilities. There were also parks and forests and oceans, instantly accessible. By now, though, she'd changed them all past his ability to recognize.

But it was only a matter of time before her parents wanted her back. *Whatever she wants,* Stavros told himself. *As long as she's here. Whatever she wants.*

"I want out," Jean said.

Except that. "I know," he sighed.

"Maybe then I can leave these *nightmares* behind."

Stavros closed his eyes, wished there was some way to be with her. *Really* with her, with this glorious, transcendent creature who'd never known him as anything but a disembodied voice.

"Still having a hard time with that monster?" Jean asked.

"Monster?"

"You know. The *bureaucracy*."

He nodded, smiling—then, remembering, said, "Yeah. Always the same story, day in, day out."

Jean snorted. "I'm still not convinced that thing even exists, you know. I checked the library for a slightly less wonky definition, but now I think you and the library are *both* fucked in the head."

He winced at the epithet; it was certainly nothing he'd ever taught her. "How so?"

"Oh, right, Stav. Like natural selection would *ever* produce a hive-based entity whose sole function is to sit with its thumb up its collective butt being inefficient. Tell me another one."

A silence, stretching. He watched as microcurrent trickled through her prefrontal cortex.

"You there, Stav?" she said at last.

"Yeah, I'm here." He chuckled, quietly. Then: "You know I love you, right?"

"Sure," she said easily. "Whatever *that* is."

Jean's environment changed then; an easy unthinking transition for her, a gasp-inducing wrench between bizarre realities for Stavros. Phantoms sparkled at the edge of his vision, vanishing when he focused on them. Light bounced from a million indefinable facets, diffuse, punctuated by a myriad pinpoint staccatos. There was no ground or walls or ceiling. No restraints along any axis.

Jean reached for a shadow in the air and sat upon it, floating. "I think I'll read *Through the Looking Glass* again. At least *someone* else lives in the real world."

"The changes that happen here are your own doing, Jean," said Stavros. "Not the machinations of any, any God or Author."

"I know. But Alice makes me feel a little more—ordinary." Reality shifted abruptly once more; Jean was in the park now, or rather, what Stavros thought of as the park. Sometimes he was afraid to ask if her interpretation had stayed the same. Above, light and dark spots danced across a sky that sometimes seemed impressively vault-like, seconds later oppressively close, even its color endlessly unsettled. Animals large and small, squiggly yellow lines and shapes and color-shifting orange and burgundy pies. Other things that might have been representations of life, or mathematical theorems—or both—browsed in the distance.

Seeing through Jean's eyes was never easy. But all this unsettling abstraction was a small price to pay for the sheer pleasure of watching her read.

My little girl.

Symbols appeared around her, doubtless the text of *Looking Glass*. To Stavros it was gibberish. A few recognizable letters, random runes, formulae. They switched places sometimes, seamlessly shifting one into another, flowing around and through and beside—or even launching themselves into the air like so many dark-hued butterflies.

He blinked his eyes and sighed. If he stayed much longer the visuals would give him a headache that would take a day to shake. Watching a life lived at such speed, even for such a short time, took its toll.

"Jean, I'm gone for a little while."

"Company business?" she asked.

"You could say that. We'll talk soon, love. Enjoy your reading."

Barely ten minutes had passed in meatspace.

Jeannie's parents had put her on her own special cot. It was one of the few real pieces of solid geometry allowed in the room. The whole compartment was a stage, virtually empty. There was really no need for props; sensations were planted directly into Jean's occipital cortex, spliced into her auditory pathways, pushing back against her tactile nerves in precise forgeries of touchable things. In a world made of lies, real objects would be a hazard to navigation.

"God damn you, she's not a fucking *toaster*," Kim spat at her husband. Evidently the icy time-out had expired; the battle had resumed.

"Kim, what was I supposed to—"

"She's a *child*, Andy. She's *our* child."

"Is she." It was a statement, not a question.

"Of *course* she is!"

"Fine." Andrew took the remote from his pocket held it out to her. "*You* wake her up, then."

She stared at him without speaking for a few seconds. Over the pickups, Stavros heard Jeannie's body breathing into the silence.

"You prick," Kim whispered.

"Uh huh. Not quite up for it, are you? You'd rather let *me* do the dirty work." He dropped the remote: it bounced softly off the floor. "Then blame me for it."

Four years had brought them to this. Stavros shook his head, disgusted. They'd been given a chance no one else could have dreamed of, and look what they'd done with it. The first time they'd shut her off she hadn't even been two. Horrified at that unthinkable precedent, they'd promised never to do it again. They'd put her to sleep on schedule, they'd sworn, and no when else. She was, after all, their daughter. Not a fucking toaster.

That solemn pact had lasted three months. Things had gone downhill ever since; Stavros could barely remember a day when the Goravecs hadn't messed up one way or another. Now, when they put her down, the argument was pure ritual. Mere words—ostensibly wrestling with the evil of the act itself—didn't fool anybody. They weren't even arguments any more, despite the pretense. Negotiations, rather. Over whose turn it was to be at fault.

"I don't *blame* you, I just—I mean—oh, *God*, Andy, it wasn't supposed to *be* like this!" Kim smeared away a tear with a clenched fist. "She was supposed to be our *daughter*. They said the brain would mature normally, they said—"

"They said," Stavros cut in, "that you'd have the chance to be parents. They couldn't guarantee you'd be any *good* at it."

Kim jumped at the sound of his voice in the walls, but Andrew just gave a bitter smile and shook his head. "This is private, Stavros. Log off."

It was an empty command, of course; chronic surveillance was the price of the project. The company had put billions into the R&D alone. No way in hell were they going to let a couple of litigious grunts play with that investment unsupervised, settlement or no settlement.

"You had everything you needed." Stavros didn't bother to disguise the contempt in his voice. "Terracon's best hardware people handled the linkups. I modeled the virtual genes myself. Gestation was perfect. We did everything we could to give you a normal child."

"A *normal child*," Andrew remarked, "doesn't have a cable growing out of her head. A normal child isn't leashed to some cabinet full of—"

"Do you have any *idea* the baud rate it takes to run a human body by remote control? RF was out of the question. And she goes portable as soon as the state of the art and her own development allow it. As I've told you time and again." Which he had, although it was almost a lie. Oh, the state of the art would proceed as it always had, but Terracon was no longer investing any great R&D in the Goravec file. Cruise control, after all.

Besides, Stavros reflected, *we'd be crazy to trust you two to take Jeannie anywhere outside a controlled environment...*

"We—we know, Stav." Kim Goravec had stepped between her husband and the pickup. "We haven't forgotten—"

"We haven't forgotten it was Terracon who got us into this mess in the first place, either," Andrew growled. "We haven't forgotten whose negligence left me cooking next to a cracked baffle plate for forty-three minutes and sixteen seconds, or whose tests missed the mutations, or who tried to look the other way when our shot at the birth lottery turned into a fucking nightmare—"

"And have you forgotten what Terracon did to make things right? How much we spent? Have you forgotten the waivers you signed?"

"You think you're some kind of saints because you settled out of court? You want to talk about making things right? It took us *ten years* to win the lottery, and you know what your lawyers did when the tests came back? They offered to *fund the abortion*."

"Which doesn't mean—"

"Like another child was *ever* going to happen. Like anyone was going to give me another chance with my balls full of chunky codon soup. You—"

"The issue," Kim said, her voice raised, "is supposed to be *Jeannie*."

Both men fell silent.

"Stav," she continued, "I don't care what Terracon says. Jeannie isn't normal, and I'm not just talking about the obvious. We love her, we really love her, but she's become so *violent* all the time, we just can't take—"

"If someone turned me on and off like a microwave oven," Stavros said mildly, "I might be prone to the occasional tantrum myself."

Andrew slammed a fist into the wall. "Now *just a fucking minute*, Mikalaides. Easy enough for you to sit halfway around the world in your nice insulated office and lecture us. *We're* the ones who have to deal with Jeannie when she bashes her fists into her face, or rubs the skin off her hands until she's got hamburger hanging off the end of her arms, or stabs herself in the eye with a goddamn *fork*. She ate *glass* once, remember? A fucking three-year-old ate glass! And all you Terracon assholes could do was blame Kim and me for allowing 'potentially dangerous implements' into the playroom. As if *any* competent parent should expect their child to mutilate herself given half a chance."

"It's just insane, Stav," Kim insisted. "The doctors can't find anything wrong with the body, you insist there's nothing wrong with the mind, and Jeannie just keeps *doing* this. There's something seriously wrong with her, and you guys won't admit it. It's like she's daring us to turn her off, it's as though she *wants* us to shut her down."

Oh God, thought Stavros. The realization was almost blinding. *That's it. That's exactly it.*

It's my fault.

"Jean, listen. This is important. I've got—I want to tell you a story."

"Stav, I'm not in the mood right now—"

"*Please*, Jean. Just listen."

Silence from the earbuds. Even the abstract mosaics on his tacticals seemed to slow a little.

"There—there was this land, Jean, this green and beautiful country, only its people screwed everything up. They poisoned their rivers and they shat in their own nests and they basically made a mess of everything. So they had to hire people to try and clean things up, you know? These people had to wade though the chemicals and handle the fuel rods and sometimes that would change them, Jean. Just a little.

"Two of these people fell in love and wanted a child. They almost didn't make it, they were allowed only one chance, but they took it, and the child started growing inside, but something went wrong. I, I don't know exactly how to explain it, but—"

"An epigenetic synaptic defect," Jean said quietly. "Does that sound about right?"

Stavros froze, astonished and fearful.

"A single point mutation," Jean went on. "That'd do it. A regulatory gene controlling knob distribution along the dendrite. It would've been active for maybe twenty minutes, total, but by then the damage had been done. Gene therapy wouldn't work after that; would've been a classic case of barn-door-after-the-horse."

"Oh God, Jean," Stavros whispered.

"I was wondering when you'd get around to owning up to it," she said quietly.

"How could you possibly...did you—"

Jean cut him off: "I think I can guess the rest of the story. Right after the neural tube developed things would start to go—wrong. The baby would be born with a perfect body and a brain of mush. There would be—complications, not real ones, sort of made-up ones. *Litigation*, I think is the word, which is funny, because it doesn't even *remotely* relate to any moral implications. I don't really understand that part.

"But there was another way. Nobody knew how to build a brain from scratch, and even if they could, it wouldn't be the same, would it? It wouldn't be their *daughter*, it would be—something else."

Stavros said nothing.

"But there was this man, a scientist, and he figured out a work-around. *We* can't build a brain, he said, but the *genes* can. And genes are a lot simpler to fake than neural nets anyway. Only four letters to deal with, after all. So the scientist shut himself away in a lab where *numbers* could take the place of *things*, and he wrote a recipe in there, a recipe for a child. And miraculously he grew something, something that could wake up and look around and which was *legally*—I don't really understand that word either, actually—legally and genetically and developmentally the daughter of the parents. And this guy was very proud of what he'd accomplished, because even though he was just a glorified model-builder by trade, he hadn't *built* this thing at all. He'd grown it. And nobody had ever knocked up a computer before, much less coded the brain of a virtual embryo so it would actually *grow* in a server somewhere."

Stavros put his head in his hands. "How long have you known?"

"I still don't, Stav. Not all of it anyway, not for sure. There's this surprise ending, for one thing, isn't there? That's the part I only just figured out. You grew your own child in *here*, where everything's numbers. But she's supposed to be living somewhere *else*, somewhere where everything's—static, where everything happens a billion times slower than it does here. The place where all the words fit. So you had to hobble her to fit into that place, or she'd grow up overnight and spoil the illusion. You had to keep the clock speed way down."

"And you just weren't up for it, were you? You had to let me run free when my body was...*off*..."

There was something in her voice he'd never heard before. He'd seen anger in Jean before, but always the screaming inarticulate rage of a spirit trapped in flesh. This was calm, cold. *Adult*. This was *judgement*, and the prospect of that verdict chilled Stavros Mikalaides to the marrow.

"Jean, they don't love you." He sounded desperate even to himself. "Not for who you are. They don't *want* to see the real you, they want a *child*, they want some kind of ridiculous *pet* they can coddle and patronize and pretend with."

"Whereas you," Jean retorted, her voice all ice and razors, "just had to see what this baby could do with her throttle wide open on the straightaway."

"God, no! Do you think *that's* why I did it?"

"Why not, Stav? Are you saying you don't *mind* having your kickass HST commandeered to shuttle some brain-dead meat puppet around a room?"

"I did it because you're *more* than that! I did it because you should be allowed to develop at your own pace, not stunted to meet some idiotic parental expectation! They shouldn't force you to act like a *four-year-old!*"

"Except I'm not *acting* then, Stav. Am I? I really am four, which is just the age I'm supposed to be."

He said nothing.

"I'm *reverting*. Isn't that it? You can run me with training wheels or scramjets, but it's *me* both times. And that other me, I bet she's not very happy, is she? She's got a four-year-old brain, and four-year-old sensibilities, but she *dreams*, Stav. She dreams about some wonderful place where she can *fly*, and every time she wakes up she finds she's made out of clay. And she's too fucking stupid to know what any of it means—she probably can't even *remember* it. But she wants to get back there, she'd do anything to..." She paused, seemingly lost for a moment in thought.

"*I* remember it, Stav. Sort of. Hard to remember much of anything when someone strips away ninety-nine percent of who and what you are. You're reduced to this bleeding little lump, barely even an animal, and *that's* the thing that remembers. What remembers is on the wrong end of a cable somewhere. I don't belong in that body at all. I'm just— *sentenced* to it, on and off. On and off."

"Jean—"

"Took me long enough, Stav, I'm the first to admit it. But now I know where the nightmares come from."

In the background, the room telemetry bleated.

God no. Not now. Not now...

"What is it?" Jean said.

"They—they want you back." On a slave monitor, a pixellated echo of Andrew Goravec played the keypad in its hand.

"*No!*" Her voice rose, panic stirring the patterns that surrounded her. "*Stop* them!"

"I can't."

"Don't tell me that! You run *everything*! You *built* me, you bastard, you tell me you love me. They only *use* me! *Stop them!*"

Stavros blinked against stinging afterimages. "It's like a light-switch, it's physical; I can't stop them from here—"

There was a third image, to go with the other two. Jean Goravec, struggling as the leash, the noose, went around her throat. Jean Goravec, bubbles bursting from her mouth as something dark and so very, very *real* dragged her back to the bottom of the ocean and buried her there.

The transition was automatic, executed by a series of macros he'd slipped into the system after she'd been born. The body, awakening, pared the mind down to fit. The room monitors caught it all with dispassionate clarity: Jeannie Goravec, troubled child-monster, awakening into hell. Jeannie Goravec, opening eyes that seethed with anger and hatred and despair, eyes that glimmered with a bare fraction of the intelligence she'd had five seconds before.

Enough intelligence for what came next.

The room had been designed to minimize the chance of injury. There was the bed, though, one of its edges built into the east wall.

That was enough.

The speed with which she moved was breathtaking. Kim and Andrew never saw it coming. Their child darted beneath the foot of the bed like a cockroach escaping the light, scrambled along the floor, re-emerged with her cable wrapped around the bed's leg. Hardly any slack in that line at all, now. Her mother moved then, finally, arms outstretched, confused and still unsuspecting—

"Jeannie—"

—while Jean braced her feet against the edge of the bed and *pushed*.

Three times she did it. Three tries, head whipped back against the leash, scalp splitting, the cable ripping from her head in spastic, bloody, bone-cracking increments, blood gushing to the floor, hair and flesh and bone and machinery following close behind. Three times, despite obvious and increasing agony. Each time more determined than before.

And Stavros could only sit and watch, simultaneously stunned and unsurprised by that sheer ferocity. *Not bad for a bleeding little lump. Barely even an animal...*

It had taken almost twenty seconds overall. Odd that neither parent had tried to stop it. Maybe it was the absolute unexpected shock of it. Maybe Kim and Andrew Goravec, taken so utterly aback, hadn't had time to think.

Then again, maybe they'd had all the time they'd needed.

Now Andrew Goravec stood dumbly near the center of the room, blinking bloody runnels from his eyes. An obscene rainshadow persisted on the wall behind him, white and spotless; the rest of the surface was crimson. Kim Goravec screamed at the ceiling, a bloody marionette collapsed in her arms. Its strings—string, rather, for a single strand of fiberop carries much more than the required bandwidth—lay on the floor like a gory boomslang, gobbets of flesh and hair quivering at one end.

Jean was back off the leash, according to the panel. Literally now as well as metaphorically. She wasn't talking to Stavros, though. Maybe she was angry. Maybe she was catatonic. He didn't know which to hope for.

But either way, Jean didn't live over *there* any more. All she'd left behind were the echoes and aftermath of a bloody, imperfect death. Contamination, really; the scene of some domestic crime. Stavros cut the links to the room, neatly excising the Goravecs and their slaughterhouse from his life.

He'd send a memo. Some local Terracon lackey could handle the cleanup.

The word *peace* floated through his mind, but he had no place to put it. He focused on a portrait of Jean, taken when she'd been eight months old. She'd been smiling; a happy and toothless baby smile, still all innocence and wonder.

There's a way, that infant puppet seemed to say. *We can do anything, and nobody has to know—*

The Goravecs had just lost their child. Even if they'd wanted the body repaired, the mind reconnected, they wouldn't get their way. Terracon had made good on all legal obligations, and hell—even *normal* children commit suicide now and then.

Just as well, really. The Goravecs weren't fit to raise a hamster, let alone a beautiful girl with a four-digit IQ. But Jean—the *real* Jean, not that bloody broken pile of flesh and bone—she wasn't easy *or* cheap to keep alive, and there would be pressure to free up the processor space once the word got out.

Jean had never got the hang of that particular part of the real world. Contract law. Economics. It was all too arcane and absurd even for her flexible definition of reality. But that was what was going to kill her now, assuming that the mind had survived the trauma of the body. The monster wouldn't keep a program running if it didn't have to.

Of course, once Jean was off the leash she lived considerably faster than the real world. And bureaucracies...well, *glacial* applied sometimes, when they were in a hurry.

Jean's mind reflected precise simulations of real-world chromosomes, codes none-the-less real for having been built from electrons instead of carbon. She had her own kind of telomeres, which frayed. She had her own kind of synapses, which would wear out. Jean had been built to replace a human child, after all. And human children, eventually, age. They become adults, and then comes a day when they die.

Jean would do all these things, faster than any.

Stavros filed an incident report. He made quite sure to include a pair of facts that contradicted each other, and to leave three mandatory fields unfilled. The report would come back in a week or two, accompanied by demands for clarification. Then he would do it all again.

Freed from her body, and with a healthy increase in her clock-cycle priority, Jean could live a hundred-fifty subjective years in a month or two. And in that whole century and a half, she'd never have to experience another nightmare.

Stavros smiled. It was time to see just what this baby could do, with her throttle wide open on the straightaway.

He just hoped he'd be able to keep her tail-lights in view.

AMBASSADOR

First Contact was supposed to solve everything.

That was the rumour, anyway: gentle wizards from Epsilon Eridani were going to save us from the fire and welcome us into a vast Galactic Siblinghood spanning the Milky Way. Whatever diseases we'd failed to conquer, they would cure. Whatever political squabbles we hadn't outgrown, they would resolve. First Contact was going to fix it all.

It was not supposed to turn me into a hunted animal.

I didn't dwell much on the philosophical implications, at first; I was too busy running for my life. *Zombie* streaked headlong into the universe, slaved to a gibbering onboard infested with static. Navigation was a joke. Every blind jump I made reduced the chances of finding my way home by another order of magnitude. I did it anyway, and repeatedly; any jump I *didn't* make would kill me.

Once more out of the breach. Long-range put me somewhere in the cometary halo of a modest binary. In better times the computer would have shown me the system's planetary retinue in an instant; now it would take days to make the necessary measurements.

Not enough time. I could have fixed my position in a day or so using raw starlight even without the onboard, but whatever was after me had never given me the chance. Several times I'd made a start. The longest reprieve had lasted six hours; in that time I'd placed myself somewhere coreward of the Orion spur.

I'd stopped trying. Knowing my location at any moment would put me no further ahead at t+1. I'd be lost again as soon as I jumped.

And I always jumped. It always found me. I still don't know how; theoretically it's impossible to track anything through a singularity. But somehow space always opened its mouth and the monster dropped down on me, hungry and mysterious. It might have been easier to deal with if I'd known why.

What did I do, you ask. What did I do to get it so angry? Why, I tried to say hello.

What kind of intelligence could take offence at *that*?

Imagine a dead tree, three hundred fifty meters tall, with six gnarled branches worming their way from its trunk. Throw it into orbit around a guttering red dwarf that doesn't even rate a proper name. This is what I'd come upon; there were no ports, no running lights, no symbols on the hull. It hung there like some forgotten chunk of cosmic driftwood. Embers of reflected sunlight glinted occasionally from the surface; they only emphasised the shadows drowning the rest of the structure. I thought it was derelict at first.

Of course I went through the motions anyway. I reached out on all the best wavelengths, tried to make contact a hundred different ways. For hours it ignored me. Then it sent the merest blip along the hydrogen band. I fed it into the onboard.

What else do you do with an alien broadcast?

The onboard had managed one startled hiccough before it crashed. All the stats on my panel had blinked once, in impossible unison, and gone dark.

And then doppler had registered the first incoming missile.

So I'd jumped, blind. There really hadn't been a choice, then or the four times since. Sometime during that panicked flight, I had given my tormentor a name: *Kali*.

Unless *Kali* had gotten bored—hope springs eternal, even within puppets such as myself—I'd have to run again in a few hours. In the meantime I aimed *Zombie* at the binary and put her under thrust. Open space is impossible to hide in; a system, even a potential one, is marginally better.

Of course I'd have to jump long before I got there. It didn't matter. My reflexes were engineered to perform under all circumstances. *Zombie's* autopilot may have been disabled, but mine engaged smoothly.

It takes time to recharge between jumps. So far, it had taken longer for *Kali* to find me. At some point that was likely to change; the onboard had to be running again before it did.

I knew there wasn't a hope in hell.

A little forensic hindsight, here: How exactly did *Kali* pull it off?

I'm not exactly sure. But some of *Zombie's* diagnostic systems run at the scale of the merely electronic, with no reliance on quantum computation. The crash didn't affect them; they were able to paint a few broad strokes in the aftermath.

The Trojan signal contained at least one set of spatial co-ordinates. The onboard would have read that as a pointer of some kind: it would have opened the navigation files to see what resided at x-y-z. A conspicuous astronomical feature, perhaps? Some common ground to compare respective visions of time and space?

Zap. Nav files gone.

Once nav was down—or maybe before, I can't tell—the invading program told *Zombie* to update all her backups with copies of itself. Only then, with all avenues of recovery contaminated, had it crashed the onboard. Now the whole system was frozen, every probability wave collapsed, every qubit locked into P=1.00.

It was an astonishingly beautiful assault. In the time it had taken me to say hello, *Kali* had grown so intimate with my ship that she'd been able to seduce it into suicide. Such a feat was beyond my capabilities, far beyond those of the haphazard beasts that built me. I'd have given anything to meet the mind behind the act, if it hadn't been trying so hard to kill me.

Early in the hunt I'd tried jumping several times in rapid succession, without giving *Kali* the chance to catch up. I'd nearly bled out the reserves. All for nothing; the alien found me just as quickly, and I'd had barely enough power to escape.

I was still paying for that gamble. It would take two days at sublight for *Zombie* to recharge fully, and ninety minutes before I could even jump again. Now I didn't dare jump until the destroyer came for me; I lay in real space and hoarded whatever moments of peace the universe saw fit to grant.

This time the universe granted three and a half hours. Then short-range beeped at me; object ahead. I plugged into *Zombie*'s cameras and looked forward.

A patch of stars disappeared before my eyes.

The manual controls were still unfamiliar. It took precious seconds to call up the right numbers. Whatever eclipsed the stars was preceding *Zombie* on a sunwards course, decelerating fast. One figure refused to settle; the mass of the object was increasing as I watched. Which meant that it was coming through from somewhere else.

Kali was cutting her search time with each iteration.

Two thousand kilometres ahead, twisted branches turned to face me across the ether. One of them sprouted an incandescent bud.

Zombie's sensors reported the incoming missile to the onboard; the brainchips behind my dash asked for an impact projection. The onboard chittered mindlessly.

I stared at the approaching thunderbolt. *What do want with me? Why can't you just leave me alone?*

Of course I didn't wait for an answer. I jumped.

My creators left me a tool for this sort of situation: *fear*, they called it.

They didn't leave much else. None of the parasitic nucleotides that gather like dust whenever blind stupid evolution has its way, for example. None of the genes that build genitals; what would have been the point? They left me a sex drive, but they tweaked it; the things that get me off are more tightly linked to mission profiles than to anything so vulgar as procreation. I retain a smattering of chemical sexuality, mostly androgens so I won't easily take no for an answer.

There are genetic sequences, long and intricately folded, which code for loneliness. Thigmotactic hardwiring, tactile pleasure, pheromonal receptors that draw the individual into social groups. All gone from me.

They even tried to cut religion out of the mix but God, it turns out, is borne of fear. The loci are easy enough to pinpoint but the linkages are absolute: you can't exorcise faith without eliminating pure mammalian terror as well. And out here, they decided, fear was too vital a survival mechanism to leave behind.

So fear is what they left me with. Fear, and superstition. And try as I might to keep my midbrain under control, the circuitry down there kept urging me to grovel and abase itself before the omnipotence of the Great Killer God.

I almost envied *Zombie* as she dropped me into another impermanent refuge. *Zombie* moved on reflex alone, brain-dead, galvanic. She didn't know enough to be terrified.

For that matter, I didn't know much more.

What was *Kali*'s problem, anyway? Was its captain insane, or merely misunderstood? Was I being hunted by something innately evil, or just the product of an unhappy childhood?

Any intelligence capable of advanced spaceflight must also be able to understand peaceful motives; such was the wisdom of Human sociologists. Most had never left the solar system. None had actually encountered an alien. No matter. The logic seemed sound enough; any species incapable of controlling their aggression probably wouldn't survive long enough to escape their own system. The things that made me nearly didn't.

Indiscriminate hostility against anything that moves is not an evolutionary strategy that makes sense.

Maybe I'd violated some cultural taboo. Perhaps an alien captain had gone insane. Or perhaps I'd chanced upon a battleship engaged in some ongoing war, wary of doomsday weapons in sheep's clothing.

But what were the odds, really? In all the universe, what are the chances that our first encounter with another intelligence would happen to involve an alien lunatic? How many interstellar wars would have to be going on simultaneously before I ran significant odds of blundering into one at random?

It almost made more *sense* to believe in God.

I searched for another answer that fitted. I was still looking two hours later, when *Kali* bounced my signal from only a thousand kilometres off.

Somewhere else in space, the question and I appeared at the same time: *Is* everyone *out here like this?*

Assuming that I wasn't dealing with a statistical fluke—that I hadn't just happened to encounter one psychotic alien amongst a trillion sane ones, and that I hadn't blundered into the midst of some unlikely galactic war—there was one other alternative.

Kali was typical.

I put the thought aside long enough to check the Systems monitor; nearly two hours, this time, before I could jump again. *Zombie* was deeply interstellar, over six lightyears from the nearest system. Even I couldn't justify kicking in the thrusters at that range. Nothing to do but wait, and wonder—

Kali couldn't be typical. It made no sense. Maybe this was all just some fantastic cross-cultural miscommunication. Maybe *Kali* had mistaken my own transmission as some kind of attack, and responded in kind.

Right. An intelligence smart enough to rape my onboard in a matter of hours, yet too stupid to grasp signals expressly designed to be decipherable by *anyone*. *Kali* hadn't needed prime number sequences or pictograms to understand me or my overtures. It knew *Zombie*'s mind from the qubits up. It knew that I was friendly, too. It had to know.

It just didn't care.

And barely ten minutes past the jump threshold, it finally caught up with me.

I could feel space rippling almost before the short-range board lit up. My inner ears split into a dozen fragments, each insisting *up* was a different direction. At first I thought *Zombie* was jumping by herself; then I thought the onboard gravity was failing somehow.

Then *Kali* began materialising less than a hundred meters away. I was caught in her wake.

I moved without thinking. *Zombie* spun on her axis and leapt away under full thrust. Telltales sparkled in crimson protest. Behind me, the plasma cone of *Zombie*'s exhaust splashed harmlessly against the resolving monster.

Still wanting for solid substance, *Kali* turned to follow. Her malformed arms, solidifying, reached out for me.

It's going to grapple, I realised. Something subcortical screamed *Jump!*

Too close. I'd drag *Kali* through with me if I tried.

Jump!

Eight hundred meters between us. At that range my exhaust should have been melting it to ions.

Six hundred meters. *Kali* was whole again.

JUMP!

I jumped. *Zombie* leapt blindly out of space. For one sickening moment, geometry died. Then the vortex spat me out.

But not alone.

We came through together. Cat and mouse dropped into reality four hundred meters apart, coasting at about one-thousandth *c*. The momentum vectors didn't quite match; within ten seconds *Kali* was over a hundred kilometres away.

Then you destroyed her.

It took some time to figure that out. All I saw was the flash, so bright it nearly overwhelmed the filters; then the cooling shell of hydrogen that crested over me and dissipated into a beautiful, empty sky.

I couldn't believe that I was free.

I tried to imagine what might have caused *Kali*'s destruction. Engine malfunction? Sabotage or mutiny on board, for reasons I could never even guess at? Ritual suicide?

Until I played back the flight recorder, it never occurred to me that she might have been hit by a missile travelling at half the speed of light.

That frightened me more than *Kali* had. The short-range board gave me a clear view to five AUs, and there was nothing in any direction. Whatever had destroyed her must have come from a greater distance. It must have been en route before we'd even come through.

It had been expecting us.

I almost missed *Kali* in that moment. At least she hadn't been invisible. At least she hadn't been able to see the future.

There was no way of knowing whether the missile had been meant for my pursuer, or for me, or for anything else that wandered by. Was I alive because you didn't want me dead, or because you thought I was dead already? And if my presence went undetected now, what might give me away? Engine emissions, RF, perhaps some exotic property of advanced technology which my species has yet to discover? What did your weapons key on?

I couldn't afford to find out. I shut everything down to bare subsistence, and played dead, and watched.

I've been here for many days now. At last, things are becoming clear.

Mysterious contacts wander space at the limit of *Zombie*'s instruments, following cryptic trails. I have coasted through strands of invisible energy that defy analysis. There is also much background radiation here, of the sort *Kali* bled when she died. I have recorded the light of many fusion explosions: some lighthours distant, some less than a hundred thousand kilometres away.

Occasionally, such things happen at close range.

Strange artefacts appear in the paths of missiles sent from some source too distant to see. Almost always they are destroyed; but once, before your missiles reached it, a featureless sphere split into fragments which danced away like dust motes. Only a few of them fell victim to your appetite that time. And once, something that *shimmered*, as wide and formless as an ocean, took a direct hit without disappearing. It limped out of range at less than the speed of light, and you did not send anything to finish the job.

There are things in this universe that even you cannot destroy.

I know what this is. I am caught in a spiderweb. You snatch ships from their travels and deposit them here to face annihilation. I don't know how far you can reach. This is a very small volume of space, perhaps only two or three lightdays across. So many ships couldn't blunder across such a tiny reef by accident; you must be bringing them from a much greater distance. I don't know how. Any singularity big enough to manage such a feat would show up on my instruments a hundred lightyears away, and I can find nothing. It doesn't matter anyway, now that I know what you are.

You're *Kali*, but much greater. And only now do you make sense to me.

I've stopped trying to reconcile the wisdom of Earthbound experts with the reality I have encountered. The old paradigms are useless. I propose a new one: *technology implies belligerence.*

Tools exist for only one reason: to force the universe into unnatural shapes. They treat nature as an enemy, they are by definition a rebellion against the way things are. In benign environments technology is a stunted, laughable thing, it can't thrive in cultures gripped by belief in natural harmony. What need of fusion reactors if food is already abundant, the climate comfortable? Why force change upon a world which poses no danger?

Back where I come from, some peoples barely developed stone tools. Some achieved agriculture. Others were not content until they had ended nature itself, and still others until they'd built cities in space.

All rested, eventually. Their technology climbed to some complacent asymptote, and stopped—and so they do not stand before you now. Now even my creators grow fat and slow. Their environment mastered, their enemies broken, they can afford more pacifist luxuries. Their machines softened the universe for them, their own contentment robs them of incentive. They forget that hostility and technology climb the cultural ladder together, they forget that it's not enough to be smart.

You also have to be *mean.*

You did not rest. What hellish world did you come from, that drove you to such technological heights? Somewhere near the core, perhaps: stars and black holes jammed cheek to jowl, tidal maelstroms, endless planetary bombardment by comets and asteroids. Some place where no one can pretend that *life* and *war* aren't synonyms. How far you've come.

My creators would call you barbarians, of course. They know nothing. They don't even know me: I'm a recombinant puppet, they say. My solitary contentment is preordained, my choices all imaginary, automatic. Pitiable.

Uncomprehending, even of their own creations. How could they possibly understand you?

But I understand. And understanding, I can act.

I can't escape you. I'd die of old age before I drifted out of this abattoir on my current trajectory. Nor can I jump free, given your ability to snare ships exceeding lightspeed. There's only one course that may keep me alive.

I've traced back along the paths of the missiles you throw; they converge on a point a little less than three lightdays ahead. I know where you are.

We're centuries behind you now, but that may change. Even *your* progress won't be endless; and the more of a threat you pose to the rest of us, the more you spur our own advancement. Was that how you achieved your own exalted stature out here? Did you depose some earlier killer god whose attempts at eradication only made you stronger? Do you fear such a fate for yourselves?

Of course you do.

Even my masters may pose a threat, given time; they'll shake off their lethargy the moment they realise that you exist. You can rid yourself of that threat if you exterminate them while they are still weak. To do that, you need to know where they are.

Don't think you can kill me and learn what you need from my ship. I've destroyed any records that survived *Kali*'s assault; there weren't many. And I doubt that even you could deduce much from *Zombie*'s metallurgical makeup; my creators evolved under a very common type of star. You have no idea where I come from.

But I do.

My ship can tell you some of the technology. Only *I* can tell you where the nest is. And more than that; I can tell you of the myriad systems that Humanity has explored and colonised. I can tell you all about those pampered children of the womb who sent me into the maelstrom on their behalf. You'll learn little of them by examining me, for I was built to differ from the norm.

But you could always *listen* to me. You have nothing to lose.

I will betray them. Not because I bear them any ill will, but because the ethics of loyalty simply don't apply out here. I'm free of the ties that cloud the judgement of lesser creatures; when you're a sterile product of controlled genetics, *kin selection* is a meaningless phrase.

My survival imperative, on the other hand, is as strong as anyone's. Not automatic after all, you see. *Autonomous.*

I assume that you can understand this transmission. I'm sending it repeatedly in half-second bursts while thrusting. Wait for me; hold your fire.

I'm worth more to you *alive.*

Ready or not, here I come.

HILLCREST V. VELIKOVSKY

The facts of the case were straightforward. Lacey Hillcrest of Pensacola, fifty years old and a devout Pentecostal, had been diagnosed with inoperable lymphatic cancer and given six months to live. Five years later she was still alive, albeit frail. She attributed her survival to a decorative silver-plated cross received from her sister, Gracey Balfour. Witnesses attested that Mrs. Hillcrest's condition improved dramatically upon acquisition of the totem, a product of the Graceland Mint alleged to contain an embedded fragment of the original Crucifix of Golgotha.

On the morning of June 27, Mrs. Hillcrest and her sister patronised The Museum of Quackery and Pseudoscience, owned and managed by one Linus C. Velikovsky. The museum contained a variety of displays concerning discredited beliefs, theories, and outright hoaxes perpetrated throughout American history. Mrs. Balfour entered into a heated discussion with another museum patron at the Intelligent Design exhibit, temporarily losing track of her sister; they eventually reconnected at a display concerning psychosomatic phenomena, specifically placebo effects and faith healing. Mrs. Hillcrest had evidently spent some time perusing the display and was subsequently described as "subdued and uncommunicative." Within a month she was dead.

The charge against Mr. Velikovsky was negligent homicide.

The Prosecution called Dr. Andrew deTritus, a clinical psychologist with an impressive record of expert testimony on any (and sometimes conflicting) sides of a given issue. Dr. deTritus testified to the uncontested reality of the placebo effect, pointing out that "attitude" and "outlook"—like any other epiphenomenon—were ultimately electrochemical in nature. *Belief* literally rewired the brain, and the existence of placebo effects showed that such changes could have a real impact on human health.

Velikovsky took the stand in his own defence, which was straightforward: all claims presented by his displays were factually accurate and supported by scientific evidence. The prosecution objected to this point on the grounds of relevance but was, after some discussion, overruled.

Far from disputing Velikovsky's claims during cross-examination, however, the Prosecution used them to bolster its own case. The defendant had deliberately set up shop in "one of our great country's most devout regions, with no thought to the welfare of the Lacey Hillcrests of the world." By his own admission, Mr. Velikovsky had chosen Florida "because of all the creation museums," and had clearly been intent on rubbing people's noses in the alleged falsity of their beliefs. Furthermore, Mr. Velikovsky was obviously well-versed in placebo effects, having built an erudite display on the subject. What did he *think* would happen, the Prosecution thundered, when he forced his so-called *truth* down the throat of someone whose motto—knitted into her favourite throw-cushion—was *If ye have faith the size of a mustard seed, ye shall move mountains*? In telling "the truth" Velikovsky had knowingly and recklessly endangered the very *life* of another human being.

Velikovsky pointed out that he hadn't even known Lacey Hillcrest existed, adding that needlepointing something onto a pillowcase did not necessarily make it true. The Prosecution responded that the man who plants land mines in a playground doesn't know the names of his victims either, and asked if the defendant's needlepoint remark meant that he was now calling Jesus a liar.

The Defence objected repeatedly throughout.

The Defence had, in fact, fought an uphill battle ever since her client's swearing-in, during which Velikovsky had asked whether swearing to tell the truth on "a book of falsehoods" might undermine the court's alleged devotion to empiricism. The jury had seemed unimpressed by that question, and did not appear to have subsequently become more sympathetic.

Perhaps, if worst came to worst, their verdict might be set aside on technical grounds. But the closest thing to a precedent the Defence could unearth was *Dexter v. HerpBGone*, involving a mail-order scheme in which a mixture of sugar and baking soda had been marketed as a cure for herpes at $200/treatment. Although this "cure" had (unsurprisingly) proven ineffective, HerpBGone's council had cited Waber *et al* 2008[1]—which clearly showed that a placebo's efficacy increased with price—arguing that the treatment *could* have worked if Dexter had only paid more for it. As he had refused to do so (the same product was sold under a different name at $4,000), responsibility devolved to the plaintiff. The case had been dismissed.

It would have been a risky gambit. The parallels were far from exact. Instead, the Defence recalled Grace Balfour to the stand and asked whether she believed the Bible to be the revealed Word of God. Mrs. Balfour readily conceded as much. It was her faith, she maintained, that allowed her to stay strong when that horrible man at the Creation display had mocked her with his talk of monkeymen and radioisotopes. She had seen fossils for what they *truly* were, the tests of faith described in Deuteronomy 13.

Asked then why her sister evidently did not share her strength of belief, Mrs. Balfour allowed—somewhat reluctantly—that "that horrid little Russian" had shattered her sister's faith with his "lies and deceit."

But did not the Bible itself arm the faithful against such wickedness? Did not Matthew warn that "false prophets shall rise, and deceive many"? Could Second Peter have *been* any more explicit than "There shall be false teachers among you, who shall bring in damnable heresies"?

Well, yes, Mrs. Balfour allowed. Certainly, Velikovsky was a False Prophet. Sadly, as the Defence reminded her, false prophecy was not a criminal offence.

---

[1] Waber, R. L., Shiv, B., Carmon, Z. & Ariely, D. *J. Am. Med. Assoc.* 299, 1016-1017 (2008).

Ultimately there was no need to resort to technical exemptions. The jury, having been presented with the facts of the case, was unanimous: Lacey Hillcrest had not shown the courage for their conviction.

Whose fault was it, after all, that her faith had been so much smaller than a mustard seed?

REPEATING THE PAST

What you did to your uncle's grave was unforgivable.

Your mother blamed herself, as always. You didn't know what you were doing, she said. I could accept that when you traded the shofar I gave you for that *eMotiv* headset, perhaps, or even when you befriended those young toughs with the shaved heads and the filthy mouths. I would *never* have forgiven the swastika on your game pod but you are my daughter's son, not mine. Maybe it *was* only adolescent rebellion. How could you know, after all? How could any child really *know*, here in 2017? Genocide is far too monstrous a thing for history books and grainy old photographs to convey. You were not there; you could never understand.

We told ourselves you were a good boy at heart, that it was ancient history to you, abstract and unreal. Both of us doctors, all too familiar with the sad stereotype of the self-loathing Jew, we talked ourselves into treating you like some kind of *victim*. And then the police brought you back from the cemetery and you looked at us with those dull, indifferent eyes, and I stopped making excuses. It wasn't just your uncle's grave. You were spitting on six million others, and you *knew*, and it meant nothing.

Your mother cried for hours. Hadn't she shown you the old albums, the online archives, the family tree with so many branches hacked off mid-century? Hadn't we both tried to tell you the stories? I tried to comfort her. An impossible task, I said, explaining *Never Again* to

someone whose only knowledge of murder is the score he racks up
playing *Zombie Hunter* all day...

And that was when I knew what to do.

I waited. A week, two, long enough to let you think I'd excused and
forgiven as I always have. But I knew your weak spot. Nothing happens
fast enough for you. These miraculous toys of yours—electrodes that
read the emotions, take orders directly from the subconscious—they
bore you now. You've seen the ads for *Improved Reality™*: sensation
planted directly into the brain! Throw away the goggles and earphones
and the gloves, throw away the keys! *Feel* the breezes of fantasy worlds
against your skin, *smell* the smoke of battle, *taste* the blood of your
toy monsters, so easily killed! Immerse all your senses in the slaughter!

You were tired of playing with cartoons, and the new model wouldn't
be out for so very long. You jumped at my suggestion: *You know, your
mother's working on something like that. It's medical, of course, but it
works the same way. She might even have some sensory samplers loaded
for testing purposes.*

Maybe, if you promise not to tell, we could sneak you in...

Retired, yes, but I never gave up my privileges. Almost two decades
since I closed my practice but I still spend time in your mother's lab,
lend a hand now and then. I still marvel at her passion to know how
the mind works, how it keeps *breaking*. She got that from me. *I* got it
from Treblinka, when I was only half your age. I, too, grew up driven
to fix broken souls—but the psychiatrist's tools were such blunt things
back then. Scalpels to open flesh, words and drugs to open minds. Our
techniques had all the precision of a drunkard stomping on the floor,
trying to move glasses on the bar with the vibrations of his boot.

These machines your mother has, though! Transcranial supercon-
ductors, deep-focus microwave emitters, Szpindel resonators! Specific
pathways targeted, rewritten, erased completely! Their very names
sound like incantations!

I cannot use them as she can. I only know the basics. I can't implant
sights or sounds, can't create actual memories. Not declarative ones,
anyway.

But *procedural* memory? That I can do. The right frontal lobe, the
hippocampus, basic fear and anxiety responses. The reptile is easily

awakened. And you didn't need the details. No need to remember my baby sister face-down like a pile of sticks in the mud. No need for the colour of the sky that day, as I stood frozen and fearful of some *real* monster's notice should I go to her. You didn't need the actual lesson.

The moral would do.

Afterwards you sat up, confused, then disappointed, then resentful. "That was *nothing*! It didn't even *work*!" I needed no machines to see into your head then. *Senile old fart, doesn't know half as much as he thinks.* And as one day went by, and another, I began to fear you were right.

But then came the retching sounds from behind the bathroom door. All those hours hidden away in your room, your game pod abandoned on the living room floor. And then your mother came to me, eyes brimming with worry: never seen you like this, she said. Jumping at shadows. Not sleeping at night. This morning she found you throwing clothes into your backpack—*they're coming, they're coming, we gotta* run—and when she asked who *they* were, you couldn't tell her.

So here we are. You huddle in the corner, your eyes black begging holes that can't stop moving, that see horrors in every shadow. Your fists bleed, nails gouging the palms. I remember, when I was your age. I cut myself to feel alive. Sometimes I still do. It never really stops.

Some day, your mother says, her machines will exorcise my demons. Doesn't she understand what a terrible mistake that would be? Doesn't history, once forgotten, repeat? Didn't even the worst president in history admit that memories belong to *everyone*?

I say nothing to you. We know each other now, so much deeper than words.

I have made you wise, grandson. I have shown you the world.

Now I will help you to live with it.

A NICHE

When the lights go out in Beebe Station, you can hear the metal groan.

Lenie Clarke lies on her bunk, listening. Overhead, past pipes and wires and eggshell plating, three kilometres of black ocean try to crush her. She feels the rift underneath, tearing open the seabed with strength enough to move a continent. She lies there in that fragile refuge and she hears Beebe's armor shifting by microns, hears its seams creak not quite below the threshold of human hearing. God is a sadist on the Juan de Fuca Rift, and His name is Physics.

How did they talk me into this? she wonders. *Why did I come down here?* But she already knows the answer.

She hears Ballard moving out in the corridor. Clarke envies Ballard. Ballard never screws up, always seems to have her life under control. She almost seems *happy* down here.

Clarke rolls off her bunk and fumbles for a switch. Her cubby floods with dismal light. Pipes and access panels crowd the wall beside her; aesthetics run a distant second to functionality when you're three thousand meters down. She turns and catches sight of a slick black amphibian in the bulkhead mirror.

It still happens, occasionally. She can sometimes forget what they've done to her.

It takes a conscious effort to feel the machines lurking where her left lung used to be. She's so acclimated to the chronic ache in her chest, to that subtle inertia of plastic and metal as she moves, that she's scarcely aware of them any more. She can still feel the memory of what it was to be fully human, and mistake that ghost for honest sensation.

Such respites never last. There are mirrors everywhere in Beebe; they're supposed to increase the apparent size of one's personal space. Sometimes Clarke shuts her eyes to hide from the reflections forever being thrown back at her. It doesn't help. She clenches her lids and feels the corneal caps beneath them, covering her eyes like smooth white cataracts.

She climbs out of her cubby and moves along the corridor to the lounge. Ballard is waiting there, dressed in a diveskin and the usual air of confidence.

Ballard stands up. "Ready to go?"

"You're in charge," Clarke says.

"Only on paper." Ballard smiles. "No pecking order down here, Lenie. As far as I'm concerned, we're equals." After two days on the rift Clarke is still surprised by the frequency with which Ballard smiles. Ballard smiles at the slightest provocation. It doesn't always seem real.

Something hits Beebe from the outside.

Ballard's smile falters. They hear it again; a wet, muffled thud through the station's titanium skin.

"It takes a while to get used to," Ballard says, "doesn't it?"

And again.

"I mean, that sounds *big*—"

"Maybe we should turn the lights off," Clarke suggests. She knows they won't. Beebe's exterior floodlights burn around the clock, an electric campfire pushing back the darkness. They can't see it from inside—Beebe has no windows—but somehow they draw comfort from the knowledge of that unseen fire—

Thud!

—most of the time.

"Remember back in training?" Ballard says over the sound, "When they told us that the fish were usually so—small..."

Her voice trails off. Beebe creaks slightly. They listen for a while. There's no other sound.

"It must've gotten tired," Ballard says. "You'd think they'd figure it out." She moves to the ladder and climbs downstairs.

Clarke follows her, a bit impatiently. There are sounds in Beebe that worry her far more than the futile attack of some misguided fish. Clarke can hear tired alloys negotiating surrender. She can feel the ocean looking for a way in. What if it finds one? The whole weight of the Pacific could drop down and turn her into jelly. Any time.

Better to face it outside, where she knows what's coming. All she can do in here is wait for it to happen.

Going outside is like drowning, once a day.

Clarke stands facing Ballard, diveskin sealed, in an airlock that barely holds both of them. She has learned to tolerate the forced proximity; the glassy armor on her eyes helps a bit. *Fuse seals, check headlamp, test injector*; the ritual takes her, step by reflexive step, to that horrible moment when she awakens the machines sleeping within her, and *changes*.

When she catches her breath, and loses it.

When a vacuum opens, somewhere in her chest, that swallows the air she holds. When her remaining lung shrivels in its cage, and her guts collapse; when myoelectric demons flood her sinuses and middle ears with isotonic saline. When every pocket of internal gas disappears in the time it takes to draw a breath.

It always feels the same. The sudden, overwhelming nausea; the narrow confines of the airlock holding her erect when she tries to fall; seawater churning on all sides. Her face goes under; vision blurs, then clears as her corneal caps adjust.

She collapses against the walls and wishes she could scream. The floor of the airlock drops away like a gallows. Lenie Clarke falls writhing into the abyss.

They come out of the freezing darkness, headlights blazing, into an oasis of sodium luminosity. Machines grow everywhere at the Throat, like metal weeds. Cables and conduits spiderweb across the seabed in a dozen directions. The main pumps stand over twenty meters high, a regiment of submarine monoliths fading from sight on either side. Overhead floodlights bathe the jumbled structures in perpetual twilight.

They stop for a moment, hands resting on the line that guided them here.

"I'll never get used to it," Ballard grates in a caricature of her usual voice.

Clarke glances at her wrist thermistor. "Thirty-four Centigrade." The words buzz, metallic, from her larynx. It feels so *wrong* to talk without breathing.

Ballard lets go of the rope and launches herself into the light. After a moment, breathless, Clarke follows.

There's so much power here, so much wasted strength. Here the continents themselves do ponderous battle. Magma freezes; seawater boils; the very floor of the ocean is born by painful centimeters each year. Human machinery does not *make* energy, here at Dragon's Throat; it merely hangs on and steals some insignificant fraction of it back to the mainland.

Clarke flies through canyons of metal and rock, and knows what it is to be a parasite. She looks down. Shellfish the size of boulders, crimson worms three meters long crowd the seabed between the machines. Legions of bacteria, hungry for sulfur, lace the water with milky veils.

The water fills with a sudden terrible cry.

It doesn't sound like a scream. It sounds as though a great harp string is vibrating in slow motion. But Ballard is screaming, through some reluctant interface of flesh and metal:

"LENIE—"

Clarke turns in time to see her own arm disappear into a mouth that seems impossibly huge.

Teeth like scimitars clamp down on her shoulder. Clarke stares into a scaly black face half a meter across. Some tiny dispassionate part of her searches for eyes in that monstrous fusion of spines and teeth and gnarled flesh, and fails. *How can it see me?* she wonders.

Then the pain reaches her.

She feels her arm being wrenched from its socket. The creature thrashes, shaking its head back and forth, trying to tear her into chunks. Every tug sets her nerves screaming.

She goes limp. *Please get it over with if you're going to kill me just please God make it quick*—She feels the urge to vomit, but the 'skin over her mouth and her own collapsed insides won't let her.

She shuts out the pain. She's had plenty of practice. She pulls inside, abandoning her body to ravenous vivisection; and from far away she feels the twisting of her attacker grow suddenly erratic. There's another creature at her side, with arms and legs and a knife—*you know, a knife, like the one you've got strapped to your leg and completely forgot about*—and suddenly the monster is gone, its grip broken.

Clarke tells her neck muscles to work. It's like operating a marionette. Her head turns. She sees Ballard locked in combat with something as big as she is. Only—Ballard is tearing it to pieces, with her bare hands. Its icicle teeth splinter and snap. Dark icewater courses from its wounds, tracing mortal convulsions with smoke-trails of suspended gore.

The creature spasms weakly. Ballard pushes it away. A dozen smaller fish dart into the light and begin tearing at the carcass. Photophores along their sides flash like frantic rainbows.

Clarke watches from the other side of the world. The pain in her side keeps its distance, a steady, pulsing ache. She looks; her arm is still there. She can even move her fingers without any trouble. *I've had worse*, she thinks.

Then: *Why am I still alive?*

Ballard appears at her side; her lens-covered eyes shine like photophores themselves.

"Jesus Christ," Ballard says in a distorted whisper. "Lenie? You okay?"

Clarke dwells on the inanity of the question for a moment. But surprisingly, she feels intact. "Yeah."

And if not, she knows, it's her own damn fault. She just lay there. She just waited to die. She was asking for it.

She's always asking for it.

Back in the airlock, the water recedes around them. And within them; Clarke's stolen breath, released at last, races back along visceral channels, reinflating lung and gut and spirit.

Ballard splits the face seal on her 'skin and her words tumble into the wetroom. "Jesus. Jesus! I don't believe it! My God, did you see that thing! They get so huge around here!" She passes her hands across her face; her corneal caps come off, milky hemispheres dropping from enormous hazel eyes. "And to think they're usually just a few centimeters long..."

She starts to strip down, unzipping her 'skin along the forearms, talking the whole time. "And yet it was almost fragile, you know? Hit it hard enough and it just came apart! Jesus!" Ballard always removes her uniform indoors. Clarke suspects she'd rip the recycler out of her own thorax if she could, throw it in a corner with the 'skin and the eyecaps until the next time it was needed.

Maybe she's got her other lung in her cabin, Clarke muses. *Maybe she keeps it in a jar, and she stuffs it back into her chest at night...* She feels a bit dopey; probably just an aftereffect of the neuroinhibitors her implants put out whenever she's outside. *Small price to pay to keep my brain from shorting out—I really shouldn't mind...*

Ballard peels her 'skin down to the waist. Just under her left breast, the electrolyser intake pokes out through her ribcage.

Clarke stares vaguely at that perforated disk in Ballard's flesh. *The ocean goes into us there,* she thinks. The old knowledge seems newly significant, somehow. *We suck it into us and steal its oxygen and spit it out again.*

Prickly numbness leaks through her shoulder into her chest and neck. Clarke shakes her head, once, to clear it.

She sags suddenly, against the hatchway.

Am I in shock? Am I fainting?

"I mean—" Ballard stops, looks at Clarke with an expression of sudden concern. "Jesus, Lenie. You look terrible. You shouldn't have told me you were okay if—"

The tingling reaches the base of Clarke's skull. "I'm—okay," she says. "Nothing broke. I'm just bruised."

"Garbage. Take off your 'skin."

Clarke straightens, with effort. The numbness recedes a bit. "It's nothing I can't take care of myself."

Don't touch me. Please don't touch me.

Ballard steps forward without a word and unseals the 'skin around Clarke's forearm. She peels back the material and exposes an ugly purple bruise. She looks at Clarke with one raised eyebrow.

"Just a bruise," Clarke says. "I'll take care of it, really. Thanks anyway." She pulls her hand away from Ballard's ministrations.

Ballard looks at her for a moment. She smiles ever so slightly.

"Lenie," she says, "there's no need to feel embarrassed."

"About what?"

"You know. Me having to rescue you. You going to pieces when that thing attacked. It was perfectly understandable. Most people have a rough time adjusting. I'm just one of the lucky ones."

Right. You've always been one of the lucky ones, haven't you? I know your kind, Ballard, you've never failed at anything...

"You don't have to feel ashamed about it," Ballard reassures her.

"I don't," Clarke says, honestly. She doesn't feel much of anything any more. Just the tingling. And the tension. And a vague sort of wonder that she's even alive.

The bulkhead is sweating.

The deep sea lays icy hands on the metal and, inside, Clarke watches the humid atmosphere bead and run down the wall. She sits rigid on her bunk under dim fluorescent light, every wall of the cubby within easy reach. The ceiling is too low. The room is too narrow. She feels the ocean compressing the station around her.

And all I can do is wait...

The anabolic salve on her injuries is warm and soothing. Clarke probes the purple flesh of her arm with practiced fingers. The diagnostic tools in the Med cubby have vindicated her. She's lucky, this time; bones intact, epidermis unbroken. She seals up her 'skin, hiding the damage.

She shifts on the pallet, turns to face the inside wall. Her reflection stares back at her through eyes like frosted glass. She watches the image, admires its perfect mimicry of each movement. Flesh and phantom move together, bodies masked, faces neutral.

That's me, she thinks. *That's what I look like now.* She tries to read what lies behind that glacial facade. *Am I bored, horny, upset?* How to tell, with her eyes hidden behind those corneal opacities? She sees no trace of the tension she always feels. *I could be terrified. I could be pissing in my 'skin and no one would know.*

She leans forward. The reflection comes to meet her. They stare at each other, white to white, ice to ice. For a moment, they almost forget Beebe's ongoing war against pressure. For a moment, they don't mind the claustrophobic solitude that grips them.

How many times, Clarke wonders, *have I wanted eyes as dead as these?*

Beebe's metal viscera crowd the corridor beyond her cubby. Clarke can barely stand erect. A few steps bring her into the lounge.

Ballard, back in shirtsleeves, is at one of the library terminals. "Rickets," she says.

"What?"

"Fish down here don't get enough trace elements. They're rotten with deficiency diseases. Doesn't matter how fierce they are. They bite too hard, they break their teeth on us."

Clarke stabs buttons on the food processor; the machine grumbles at her touch. "I thought there was all sorts of food at the rift. That's why things got so big."

"There's a lot of food. Just not very good quality."

A vaguely edible lozenge of sludge oozes from the processor onto Clarke's plate. She eyes it for a moment. *I can relate.*

"You're going to eat in your gear?" Ballard asks, as Clarke sits down at the lounge table.

Clarke blinks at her. "Yeah. Why?"

"Oh, nothing. It would just be nice to talk to someone with pupils in their eyes, you know?"

"Sorry. I can take them off if you—"

"No, it's no big thing. I can live with it." Ballard turns off the library and sits down across from Clarke. "So, how do you like the place so far?"

Clarke shrugs and keeps eating.

"I'm glad we're only down here for a year," Ballard says. "This place could get to you after a while."

"It could be worse."

"Oh, I'm not complaining. I was looking for a challenge, after all. What about you?"

"Me?"

"What brings you down here? What are you looking for?"

Clarke doesn't answer for a moment. "I don't know, really," she says at last. "Privacy, I guess."

Ballard looks up. Clarke stares back, her face neutral.

"Well, I'll leave you to it, then," Ballard says pleasantly.

Clarke watches her disappear down the corridor. She hears the sound of a cubby hatch hissing shut.

Give it up, Ballard, she thinks. *I'm not the sort of person you really want to know.*

Almost start of the morning shift. The food processor disgorges Clarke's breakfast with its usual reluctance. Ballard, in Communications, is just getting off the phone. A moment later she appears in the hatchway.

"Management says—" She stops. "You've got blue eyes."

Clarke smiles faintly. "You've seen them before."

"I know. It's just kind of surprising, it's been a while since I've seen you without your caps in."

Clarke sits down with her breakfast. "So, what does Management say?"

"We're on schedule. Rest of the crew comes down in three weeks, we go online in four." Ballard sits down across from Clarke. "I wonder sometimes why we're not online right now."

"I guess they just want to be sure everything works."

"Still, it seems like a long time for a dry run. And you'd think that— well, they'd want to get the geothermal program up and running as fast as possible, after all that's happened."

After Lepreau and Winshire melted down, you mean.

"And there's something else," Ballard says. "I can't get through to Piccard."

Clarke looks up. Piccard Station is anchored on the Galapagos Rift; it is not a particularly stable mooring.

"You ever meet the couple there?" Ballard asks. "Ken Lubin, Lana Cheung?"

Clarke shakes her head. "They went through before me. I never met any of the other Rifters except you."

"Nice people. I thought I'd call them up, see how things were going at Piccard, but nobody can get through."

"Line down?"

"They say it's probably something like that. Nothing serious. They're sending a 'scaphe down to check it out."

Maybe the seabed opened up and swallowed them whole, Clarke thinks. *Maybe the hull had a weak plate—one's all it would take—*

Something creaks, deep in Beebe's superstructure. Clarke looks around. The walls seem to have moved closer while she wasn't looking.

"Sometimes," she says, "I wish we didn't keep Beebe at surface pressure. Sometimes I wish we were pumped up to ambient. To take the strain off the hull." She knows it's an impossible dream; most gases kill outright when breathed at three hundred atmospheres. Even oxygen would do you in if it got above one or two percent.

Ballard shivers dramatically. "If *you* want to risk breathing ninety-nine percent hydrogen, you're welcome to it. I'm happy the way things are." She smiles. "Besides, you have any idea how long it would take to decompress afterwards?"

In the Systems cubby, something bleats for attention.

"Seismic. Wonderful." Ballard disappears into Comm. Clarke follows.

An amber line writhes across one of the displays. It looks like the EEG of someone caught in a nightmare.

"Get your eyes back in," Ballard says. "The Throat's acting up."

They can hear it all the way to Beebe: a malign, almost electrical hiss from the direction of the Throat. Clarke follows Ballard towards it, one hand running lightly along the guide rope. The distant smudge of light that marks their destination seems wrong, somehow. The color is different. It *ripples*.

They swim into its glowing nimbus and see why. The Throat is on fire.

Sapphire auroras slide flickering across the generators. At the far end of the array, almost invisible with distance, a pillar of smoke swirls up into the darkness like a great tornado.

The sound it makes fills the abyss. Clarke closes her eyes for a moment, and hears rattlesnakes.

"Jesus!" Ballard shouts over the noise. "It's not supposed to *do* that!"

Clarke checks her thermistor. It won't settle; water temperature goes from four degrees to thirty-eight and back again, within seconds. A myriad ephemeral currents tug at them as they watch.

"Why the light show?" Clarke calls back.

"I don't know!" Ballard answers. "Bioluminescence, I guess! Heat-sensitive bacteria!"

Without warning, the tumult dies.

The ocean empties of sound. Phosphorescent spiderwebs wriggle dimly on the metal and vanish. In the distance, the tornado sighs and fragments into a few transient dust devils.

A gentle rain of black soot begins to fall in the copper light.

"Smoker," Ballard says into the sudden stillness. "A *big* one."

They swim to the place where the geyser erupted. There's a fresh wound in the seabed, a gash several meters long, between two of the generators.

"This wasn't supposed to happen," Ballard says. "That's why they built here, for crying out loud! It was supposed to be stable!"

"The rift's never stable," Clarke replies. *Not much point in being here if it was.*

Ballard swims up through the fallout and pops an access plate on one of the generators. "Well, according to this there's no damage," she calls down, after looking inside. "Hang on, let me switch channels here—"

Clarke touches one of the cylindrical sensors strapped to her waist, and stares into the fissure. *I should be able to fit through there,* she decides.

And does.

"We were lucky," Ballard is saying above her. "The other generators are okay too. Oh, wait a second; number two has a clogged cooling duct, but it's not serious. Backups can handle it until—*get out of there!*"

Clarke looks up, one hand on the sensor she's planting. Ballard stares down at her through a chimney of fresh rock.

"Are you *crazy*?" Ballard shouts. "That's an active smoker!"

Clarke looks down again, deeper into the shaft. It twists out of sight in the mineral haze. "We need temperature readings," she says, "from inside the mouth."

"Get out of there! It could go off again and fry you!"

I suppose it could at that, Clarke thinks. "It already blew," she calls back. "It'll take a while to build up a fresh head." She twists a knob on the sensor; tiny explosive bolts blast into the rock, anchoring the device.

"Get out of there, *now*!"

"Just a second." Clarke turns the sensor on and kicks up out of the seabed. Ballard grabs her arm as she emerges, starts to drag her away from the smoker.

Clarke stiffens and pulls free. *"Don't—" touch me!* She catches herself. "I'm out, okay? You don't have to—"

"Further." Ballard keeps swimming. "Over here."

They're near the edge of the light now, the floodlit Throat on one side, blackness on the other. Ballard faces Clarke. "Are you out of your *mind*? We could have gone back to Beebe for a drone! We could have planted it on remote!"

Clarke doesn't answer. She sees something moving in the distance behind Ballard. "Watch your back," she says.

Ballard turns, and sees the gulper sliding toward them. It undulates through the water like brown smoke, silent and endless; Clarke can't see the creature's tail, although several meters of serpentine flesh have come out of the darkness.

Ballard goes for her knife. After a moment, Clarke does too.

The gulper's jaw drops open like a great jagged scoop.

Ballard begins to launch herself at the thing, knife upraised.

Clarke puts her hand out. "Wait a minute. It's not coming at us."

The front end of the gulper is about ten meters distant now. Its tail pulls free of the murk.

"Are you crazy?" Ballard moves clear of Clarke's hand, still watching the monster.

"Maybe it isn't hungry," Clarke says. She can see its eyes, two tiny unwinking spots glaring at them from the tip of the snout.

"They're *always* hungry. Did you sleep through the briefings?"

The gulper closes its mouth and passes. It extends around them now, in a great meandering arc. The head turns back to look at them. It opens its mouth.

"Fuck this," Ballard says, and charges.

Her first stroke opens a meter-long gash in the creature's side. The gulper stares at Ballard for a moment, as if astonished. Then, ponderously, it thrashes.

Clarke watches without moving. *Why can't she just let it go? Why does she always have to prove she's better than everything?*

Ballard strikes again; this time she slashes into a great tumorous swelling that has to be the stomach.

She frees the things inside.

They spill out through the wound; two huge giganturids and some misshapen creature Clarke doesn't recognize. One of the giganturids is still alive, and in a foul mood. It locks its teeth around the first thing it encounters.

Ballard. From behind.

"*Lenie!*" Ballard's knife hand is swinging in staccato arcs. The giganturid begins to come apart. Its jaws remain locked. The convulsing gulper crashes into Ballard and sends her spinning to the bottom.

Finally, Clarke begins to move.

The gulper collides with Ballard again. Clarke moves in low, hugging the bottom, and pulls the other woman clear.

Ballard's knife continues to dip and twist. The giganturid is a mutilated wreck behind the gills, but its grip remains unbroken. Ballard can't twist around far enough to reach the skull. Clarke comes in from behind and takes the creature's head in her hands.

It stares at her, malevolent and unthinking.

"Kill it!" Ballard shouts. "Jesus, what are you waiting for?"

Clarke closes her eyes, and clenches. The skull in her hand splinters like cheap plastic.

There is a silence.

After a while, she opens her eyes. The gulper is gone, fled back into darkness to heal or die. But Ballard's still there, and Ballard is angry.

"What's *wrong* with you?" she says.

Clarke unclenches her fists. Bits of bone and jellied flesh float about her fingers.

"You're supposed to back me up! Why are you so damned—*passive* all the time?"

"Sorry." *Sometimes it works.*

Ballard reaches behind her back. "I'm cold. I think it punctured my diveskin—"

Clarke swims behind her and looks. "A couple of holes. How are you otherwise? Anything feel broken?"

"It broke through the diveskin," Ballard says, as if to herself. "And when that gulper hit me, it could have—" She turns to Clarke and her voice, even distorted, carries a shocked uncertainty. "—I could have been killed. I could have been *killed*!"

For an instant, it's as though Ballard's 'skin and eyes and self-assurance have all been stripped away. For the first time Clarke can see through to the weakness beneath, growing like a delicate tracery of hairline cracks.

You can screw up too, Ballard. It isn't all fun and games. You know that now.

It hurts, doesn't it?

Somewhere inside, the slightest touch of sympathy. "It's okay," Clarke says. "Jeanette, it's—"

"You *idiot*!" Ballard hisses. She stares at Clarke like some malign and sightless old woman. "You just floated there! You just let it happen to me!"

Clarke feels her guard snap up again, just in time. *This isn't just anger,* she realizes. *This isn't just the heat of the moment. She doesn't like me. She doesn't like me at all.*

And then, dully surprised that she hasn't seen it before:

She never did.

Beebe Station floats tethered above the seabed, a gunmetal-gray planet ringed by a belt of equatorial floodlights. There's an airlock for divers at the south pole and a docking hatch for 'scaphes at the north. In between there are girders and anchor lines, conduits and cables, metal armor and Lenie Clarke.

She's doing a routine visual check on the hull; standard procedure, once a week. Ballard is inside, testing some equipment in the Communications cubby. This is not entirely within the spirit of the buddy system. Clarke prefers it this way. Relations have been civil over the past couple of days—Ballard even resurrects her patented chumminess on occasion—but the more time they spend together, the more forced things get. Eventually, Clarke knows, something is going to break.

Besides, out here it seems only natural to be alone.

She's examining a cable clamp when a razormouth charges into the light. It's about two meters long, and hungry. It rams directly into the nearest of Beebe's floodlamps, mouth agape. Several teeth shatter against the crystal lens. The razormouth twists to one side, knocking the hull with its tail, and swims off until barely visible against the dark.

Clarke watches, fascinated. The razormouth swims back and forth, back and forth, then charges again.

The flood weathers the impact easily, doing more damage to its attacker. Over and over again the fish batters itself against the light. Finally, exhausted, it sinks twitching down to the muddy bottom.

"Lenie? Are you okay?"

Clarke feels the words buzzing in her lower jaw. She trips the sender in her diveskin: "I'm okay."

"I heard something out there," Ballard says. "I just wanted to make sure you were—"

"I'm fine," Clarke says. "Just a fish."

"They never learn, do they?"

"No. I guess not. See you later."

"See—"

Clarke switches off her receiver.

Poor stupid fish. How many millennia did it take for them to learn that bioluminescence equals food? How long will Beebe have to sit here before they learn that electric light doesn't?

We could keep our headlights off. Maybe they'd leave us alone—

She stares out past Beebe's electric halo. There is so much blackness there. It almost hurts to look at it. Without lights, without sonar, how far could she go into that viscous shroud and still return?

Clarke kills her headlight. Night edges a bit closer, but Beebe's lights keep it at bay. Clarke turns until she's face to face with the darkness. She crouches like a spider against Beebe's hull.

She pushes off.

The darkness embraces her. She swims, not looking back, until her legs grow tired. She doesn't know how far she's come.

But it must be lightyears. The ocean is full of stars.

Behind her, the station shines brightest, with coarse yellow rays. In the opposite direction, she can barely make out the Throat, an insignificant sunrise on the horizon.

Everywhere else, living constellations punctuate the dark. Here, a string of pearls blink sexual advertisements at two-second intervals. Here, a sudden flash leaves diversionary afterimages swarming across Clarke's field of view; something flees under cover of her momentary blindness. There, a counterfeit worm twists lazily in the current, invisibly tied to the roof of some predatory mouth.

There are so many of them.

She feels a sudden surge in the water, as if something big has just passed very close. A delicious thrill dances through her body.

It nearly touched me, she thinks. *I wonder what it was.* The rift is full of monsters who don't know when to quit. It doesn't matter how much they eat. Their voracity is as much a part of them as their elastic bellies, their unhinging jaws. Ravenous dwarves attack giants twice their own size, and sometimes win. The abyss is a desert; no one can afford the luxury of waiting for better odds.

But even a desert has oases, and sometimes the deep hunters find them. They come upon the malnourishing abundance of the rift and gorge themselves; their descendants grow huge and bloated over such delicate bones—

My light was off, and it left me alone. I wonder—

She turns it back on. Her vision clouds in the sudden glare, then clears. The ocean reverts to unrelieved black. No nightmares accost her. The beam lights empty water wherever she points it.

She switches it off. There's a moment of absolute darkness while her eyecaps adjust to the reduced light. Then the stars come out again.

They are so beautiful. Lenie Clarke rests on the bottom of the ocean and watches the abyss sparkle around her. And she almost laughs as she realizes, three thousand meters from the nearest sunlight, that it's only dark when the lights are on.

"What the hell is wrong with you? You've been gone for over three hours, did you know that? Why didn't you answer me?"

Clarke bends over and removes her fins. "I guess I turned my receiver off," she says. "I was—wait a second, did you say—"

"You *guess*? Have you forgotten every safety reg they drilled into us? You're supposed to have your receiver on from the moment you leave Beebe until you get back!"

"Did you say *three hours*?"

"I couldn't even come out after you, I couldn't find you on sonar! I just had to sit here and hope you'd show up!"

It only seems a few minutes since she pushed off into the darkness. Clarke climbs up into the lounge, suddenly chilled.

"Where *were* you, Lenie?" Ballard demands, coming up behind her. Clarke hears the slightest plaintive tone in her voice.

"I—I must've been on the bottom," Clarke says. "That's why sonar didn't get me. I didn't go far."

Was I asleep? What was I doing for three hours?

"I was just—wandering around. I lost track of the time. I'm sorry."

"Not good enough. Don't do it again."

There's a brief silence. It's ended by the sudden, familiar impact of flesh on metal.

"Christ!" Ballard snaps. "I'm turning the externals off right now!"

Whatever it is gets in two more hits by the time Ballard reaches Comm. Clarke hears her punch a couple of buttons.

Ballard comes back into the lounge. "There. Now we're invisible."

Something hits them again. And again.

"Or maybe not," Clarke says.

Ballard stands in the lounge, listening to the rhythm of the assault. "They don't show up on sonar," she says, almost whispering. "Sometimes, when I hear them coming at us, I tune it down to extreme close range. But it looks right through them."

"No gas bladders. Nothing to bounce an echo off of."

"We show up just fine out there, most of the time. But not those things. You can't find them, no matter how high you turn the gain. They're like ghosts."

"They're not ghosts." Almost unconsciously, Clarke has been counting the beats: *eight—nine—*

Ballard turns to face her. "They've shut down Piccard," she says, and her voice is small and tight.

"What?"

"The grid office says it's just some technical problem. But I've got a friend in Personnel. I phoned him when you were outside. He says Lana's in the hospital. And I get the feeling—" Ballard shakes her head. "It sounded like Ken Lubin did something down there. I think maybe he attacked her."

Three thumps from outside, in rapid succession. Clarke can feel Ballard's eyes on her. The silence stretches.

"Or maybe not," Ballard says. "We got all those personality tests. If he was violent, they would've picked it up before they sent him down."

Clarke watches her, listens to the pounding of an intermittent fist.

"Or maybe—maybe the rift *changed* him somehow. Maybe they misjudged the pressure we'd all be under. So to speak." Ballard musters a feeble smile. "Not the physical danger so much as the emotional stress, you know? Everyday things. Just being outside could get to you after a while. Seawater sluicing through your chest. Not breathing for hours at a time. It's like—living without a heartbeat—"

She looks up at the ceiling; the sounds from outside are a bit more erratic, now.

"Outside's not so bad," Clarke says. *At least you're incompressible. At least you don't have to worry about the plates giving in.*

"I don't think you'd change suddenly. It would just sort of sneak up on you, little by little. And then one day you'd just wake up changed, you'd be different somehow, only you'd never have noticed the transition. Like Ken Lubin."

She looks at Clarke, and her voice drops a bit.

"And you."

"Me." Clarke turns Ballard's words over in her mind, waits for the onset of some reaction. She feels nothing but her own indifference. "I don't think you have much to worry about. I'm not the violent type."

"I know. I'm not worried about my own safety, Lenie. I'm worried about yours."

Clarke looks at her from behind the impervious safety of her lenses, and doesn't answer.

"You've changed since you came down here," Ballard says. "You're withdrawing from me, you're exposing yourself to unnecessary risks. I don't know exactly what's happening to you. It's almost like you're trying to kill yourself."

"I'm not," Clarke says. She tries to change the subject. "Is Lana Cheung all right?"

Ballard studies her for a moment. She takes the hint. "I don't know. I couldn't get any details."

Clarke feels something knotting up inside her.

"I wonder what she did to set him off?" she murmurs.

Ballard stares at her, openmouthed. "What *she* did? I can't believe you said that!"

"I only meant—"

"I know what you meant."

The outside pounding has stopped. Ballard does not relax. She stands hunched over in those strange, loose-fitting clothes that Dry-backs wear, and stares at the ceiling as though she doesn't believe in the silence. She looks back at Clarke.

"Lenie, you know I don't like to pull rank, but your attitude is putting both of us at risk. I think this place is really getting to you. I hope you can get back online here, I really do. Otherwise I may have to recommend you for a transfer."

Clarke watches Ballard leave the lounge. *You're lying,* she realizes. *You're scared to death, and it's not just because I'm changing.*

It's because you are.

Clarke finds out five hours after the fact: something has changed on the ocean floor.

We sleep and the earth moves, she thinks, studying the topographic display. *And next time, or the time after, maybe it'll move right out from under us.*

I wonder if I'll have time to feel anything.

She turns at a sound behind her. Ballard is standing in the lounge, swaying slightly. Her face seems somehow disfigured by the concentric rings in her eyes, by the dark hollows around them. Naked eyes are beginning to look alien to Clarke.

"The seabed shifted," Clarke says. "There's a new outcropping about two hundred meters west of us."

"That's odd. I didn't feel anything."

"It happened about five hours ago. You were asleep."

Ballard glances up sharply. Clarke studies the haggard lines of her face. *On second thought...*

"I—would've woken up," Ballard says. She squeezes past Clarke into the cubby and checks the topographic display.

"Two meters high, twelve long," Clarke recites.

Ballard doesn't answer. She punches some commands into a keyboard; the topographic image dissolves, reforms into a column of numbers.

"Just as I thought," she says. "No heavy seismic activity for over forty-two hours."

"Sonar doesn't lie," Clarke says calmly.

"Neither does seismo," Ballard answers.

There's a brief silence. There's a standard procedure for such things, and they both know what it is.

"We have to check it out," Clarke says.

But Ballard only nods. "Give me a moment to change."

They call it a squid: a jet-propelled cylinder about a meter long, with a headlight at the front end and a towbar at the back. Clarke, floating between Beebe and the seabed, checks it over with one hand. Her other hand grips a sonar pistol. She points the pistol into blackness; ultrasonic clicks sweep the night, give her a bearing.

"That way," she says, pointing.

Ballard squeezes down on her own squid's towbar. The machine pulls her away. After a moment Clarke follows. Bringing up the rear, a third squid carries an assortment of sensors in a nylon bag.

Ballard's traveling at nearly full throttle. The lamps on her helmet and squid stab the water like twin lighthouse beacons. Clarke, her own lights doused, catches up about halfway to their destination. They cruise along a couple of meters over the muddy substrate.

"Your lights," Ballard says.

"We don't need them. Sonar works in the dark."

"Are you breaking regs for the sheer thrill of it, now?"

"The fish down here, they key on things that glow—"

"Turn your lights on. That's an order."

Clarke doesn't answer. She watches the beams beside her, Ballard's squid shining steady and unwavering, Ballard's headlamp slicing the water in erratic arcs as she moves her head—

"I told you," Ballard says, "turn your—*Christ!*"

It was just a glimpse, caught for a moment in the sweep of Ballard's headlight. She jerks her head around and it slides back out of sight. Then it looms up in the squid's beam, huge and terrible.

The abyss is grinning at them, teeth bared.

A mouth stretches across the width of the beam, extends into darkness on either side. It is crammed with conical teeth the size of human hands, and they do not look the least bit fragile.

Ballard makes a strangled sound and dives into the mud. The benthic ooze boils up around her in a seething cloud; she disappears in a torrent of planktonic corpses.

Lenie Clarke stops and waits, unmoving. She stares transfixed at that threatening smile. Her whole body feels electrified, she's never been so explicitly aware of herself. Every nerve fires and freezes at the same time. She is terrified.

But she's also, somehow, completely in control of herself. She reflects on this paradox as Ballard's abandoned squid slows and stops itself, scant meters from that endless row of teeth. She wonders at her own analytical clarity as the third squid, with its burden of sensors, decelerates past and takes up position beside Ballard's.

There in the light, the grin does not change.

Clarke raises her sonar pistol and fires. *We're here,* she realizes, checking the readout. *That's the outcropping.*

She swims closer. The smile hangs there, enigmatic and enticing. Now she can see bits of bone at the roots of the teeth, and tatters of decomposed flesh trailing from the gums.

She turns and backtracks. The cloud on the seabed is starting to settle.

"Ballard," she says in her synthetic voice.

Nobody answers.

Clarke reaches down through the mud, feeling blind, until she touches something warm and trembling.

The seabed explodes in her face.

Ballard erupts from the substrate, trailing a muddy comet's tail. Her hand rises from that sudden cloud, clasped around something glinting in the transient light. Clarke sees the knife, twists almost too late; the blade glances off her 'skin, igniting nerves along her ribcage. Ballard lashes out again. This time Clarke catches the knife-hand as it shoots past, twists it, pushes. Ballard tumbles away.

"It's me!" Clarke shouts; the vocoder turns her voice into a tinny vibrato.

Ballard rises up again, white eyes unseeing, knife still in hand.

Clarke holds up her hands. "It's okay! There's nothing here! It's dead!"

Ballard stops. She stares at Clarke. She looks over to the squids, to the smile they illuminate. She stiffens.

"It's some kind of whale," Clarke says. "It's been dead a long time."

"A—a whale?" Ballard rasps. She begins to shake.

There's no need to feel embarrassed, Clarke almost says, but doesn't.

Instead, she reaches out and touches Ballard lightly on the arm. *Is this how you do it?* she wonders.

Ballard jerks back as if scalded.

I guess not—

"Um, Jeanette—" Clarke begins.

Ballard raises a trembling hand, cutting Clarke off. "I'm okay. I want to g—I think we should get back now, don't you?"

"Okay," Clarke says. But she doesn't really mean it.

She could stay out here all day.

Ballard is at the library again. She turns, passing a casual hand over the brightness control as Clarke comes up behind her; the display darkens before Clarke can see what it is. Clarke glances at the eyephones hanging from the terminal, puzzled. If Ballard doesn't want her to see what she's reading, she could just use those.

But then she wouldn't see me coming...

"I think maybe it was a ziphiid," Ballard's saying. "A beaked whale. Except it had too many teeth. Very rare. They don't dive this deep."

Clarke listens, not really interested.

"It must have died and rotted further up, and then sank." Ballard's voice is slightly raised. She looks almost furtively at something on the other side of the lounge. "I wonder what the chances are of that happening."

"What?"

"I mean, in all the ocean, something that big just happening to drop out of the sky a few hundred meters away. The odds of that must be pretty low."

"Yeah. I guess so." Clarke reaches over and brightens the display. One-half of the screen glows softly with luminous text. The other holds the rotating image of a complex molecule.

"What's this?" Clarke asks.

Ballard steals another glance across the lounge. "Just an old bio-psych text the library had on file. I was browsing through it. Used to be an interest of mine."

Clarke looks at her. "Uh huh." She bends over and studies the display.

Some sort of technical chemistry. The only thing she really understands is the caption beneath the graphic.

She reads it aloud: "True Happiness."

"Yeah. A tricyclic with four side chains." Ballard points at the screen. "Whenever you're happy, really happy, that's what does it to you."

"When did they find *that* out?"

"I don't know. It's an old book."

Clarke stares at the revolving simulacrum. It disturbs her, somehow. It floats there over that smug stupid caption, and it says something she doesn't want to hear.

You've been solved, it says. *You're mechanical. Chemicals and electricity. Everything you are, every dream, every action, it all comes down to a change of voltage somewhere, or a—what did she say—a tricyclic with four side chains—*

"It's wrong," Clarke murmurs. *Or they'd be able to fix us, when we broke down—*

"Sorry?" Ballard says.

"It's saying we're just these—soft computers. With faces."

Ballard shuts off the terminal.

"That's right," she says. "And some of us may even be losing those."

The jibe registers, but it doesn't hurt. Clarke straightens and moves towards the ladder.

"Where you going? You going outside again?" Ballard asks.

"The shift isn't over. I thought I'd clean out the duct on number two."

"It's a bit late to start on that, Lenie. The shift will be over before we're even half done." Ballard's eyes dart away again. This time Clarke follows the glance to the full-length mirror on the far wall.

She sees nothing of particular interest there.

"I'll work late." Clarke grabs the railing, swings her foot onto the top rung.

"Lenie," Ballard says, and Clarke swears she hears a tremor in that voice. She looks back, but the other woman is moving to Comm. "Well, I'm afraid I can't go with you," she's saying. "I'm in the middle of debugging one of the telemetry routines."

"That's fine," Clarke says. She feels the tension starting to rise. Beebe is shrinking again. She starts down the ladder.

"Are you sure you're okay going out alone? Maybe you should wait until tomorrow."

"No. I'm okay."

"Well, remember to keep your receiver open. I don't want you getting lost on me again—"

Clarke is in the wetroom. She climbs into the airlock and runs through the ritual. It no longer feels like drowning. It feels like being born again.

She awakens into darkness, and the sound of weeping.

She lies there for a few minutes, confused and uncertain. The sobs come from all sides, soft but omnipresent in Beebe's resonant shell. She hears nothing else except her own heartbeat.

She's afraid. She's not sure why. She wishes the sounds would go away.

Clarke rolls off her bunk and fumbles at the hatch. It opens into a semi-darkened corridor; meager light escapes from the lounge at one end. The sounds come from the other direction, from deepening darkness. She follows them through an infestation of pipes and conduits.

Ballard's quarters. The hatch is open. An emerald readout sparkles in the darkness, bestowing no detail upon the hunched figure on the pallet.

"Ballard," Clarke says softly. She doesn't want to go in.

The shadow moves, seems to look up at her. "Why won't you show it?" it says, its voice pleading.

Clarke frowns in the darkness. "Show what?"

"You know what! How—afraid you are!"

"Afraid?"

"Of being here, of being stuck at the bottom of this horrible dark ocean—"

"I don't understand," Clarke whispers. Claustrophobia begins to stir in her, restless again.

Ballard snorts, but the derision seems forced. "Oh, you understand all right. You think this is some sort of competition, you think if you can just keep it all inside you'll win somehow—but it isn't like that at all, Lenie, it isn't helping to keep it hidden like this, we've got to be able to trust each other down here or we're lost—"

She shifts slightly on the bunk. Clarke's eyes, enhanced by the caps, can pick out some details now; rough edges embroider Ballard's silhouette, the folds and creases of normal clothing, unbuttoned to the waist. She thinks of a cadaver, half-dissected, rising on the table to mourn its own mutilation.

"I don't know what you mean," Clarke says.

"I've tried to be friendly," Ballard says. "I've tried to get along with you, but you're so *cold*, you won't even admit—I mean, you *couldn't* like it down here, nobody could, why can't you just admit—"

"But I don't, I—I *hate* it in here. It's like Beebe's going to—to clench around me. And all I can do is wait for it to happen."

Ballard nods in the darkness. "Yes, yes, I know what you mean." She seems somehow encouraged by Clarke's admission. "And no matter how much you tell yourself—" She stops. "You hate it *in here?*"

Did I say something wrong? Clarke wonders.

"Outside is hardly any better, you know," Ballard says. "Outside is even worse! There's mudslides and smokers and giant fish trying to eat you all the time, you can't possibly—but—you don't mind all that, do you?"

Somehow, her tone has turned accusing. Clarke shrugs.

"No, you don't," Ballard is speaking slowly now. Her voice drops to a whisper: "You actually *like* it out there. Don't you?"

Reluctantly, Clarke nods. "Yeah. I guess so."

"But it's so—the rift can kill you, Lenie. It can kill *us*. A hundred different ways. Doesn't that scare you?"

"I don't know. I don't think about it much. I guess it does, sort of."

"Then why are you so happy out there?" Ballard cries. "It doesn't make any sense..."

I'm not exactly "happy," Clarke thinks. "I don't know. It's not that weird, lots of people do dangerous things. What about free-fallers? What about mountain climbers?"

But Ballard doesn't answer. Her silhouette has grown rigid on the bed. Suddenly, she reaches over and turns on the cubby light.

Lenie Clarke blinks against the sudden brightness. Then the room dims as her eyecaps darken.

"Jesus Christ!" Ballard shouts at her. "You *sleep* in that fucking costume now?"

It's something else Clarke hasn't thought about. It just seems easier.

"All this time I've been pouring my heart out to you and you've been wearing that *machine* face! You don't even have the decency to show me your goddamned *eyes!*"

Clarke steps back, startled. Ballard rises from the bed and takes a single step forward. "To think you could actually pass for human before they gave you that suit! Why don't you go find something to play with out in your fucking ocean!"

And slams the hatch in Clarke's face.

Lenie Clarke stares at the sealed bulkhead for a few moments. Her face, she knows, is calm. Her face is usually calm. But she stands there, unmoving, until the cringing thing inside of her unfolds a little.

"Okay," she says at last, very softly. "I guess I will."

Ballard is waiting for her as she emerges from the airlock. "Lenie," she says quietly, "we have to talk. It's important."

Clarke bends over and removes her fins. "Go ahead."

"Not here. In my cubby."

Clarke looks at her.

"Please."

Clarke starts up the ladder.

"Aren't you going to take—" Ballard stops as Clarke looks down. "Never mind. It's okay."

They ascend into the lounge. Ballard takes the lead. Clarke follows her down the corridor and into her cabin. Ballard dogs the hatch and sits on her bunk, leaving room for Clarke.

Clarke looks around the cramped space. Ballard has curtained over the mirrored bulkhead with a spare sheet.

Ballard pats the bed beside her. "Come on, Lenie. Sit down."

Reluctantly, Clarke sits. Ballard's sudden kindness confuses her. Ballard hasn't acted this way since...

...Since she had the upper hand.

"—might not be easy for you to hear," Ballard is saying, "but we have to get you off the rift. They shouldn't have put you down here in the first place."

Clarke doesn't reply.

"Remember the tests they gave us?" Ballard continues. "They measured our tolerance to stress; confinement, prolonged isolation, chronic physical danger, that sort of thing."

Clarke nods slightly. "So?"

"So," says Ballard, "did you think for a moment they'd test for those qualities without knowing what sort of person would have them? Or how they got to be that way?"

Inside, Clarke goes very still. Outside, nothing changes.

Ballard leans forward a bit. "Remember what you said? About mountain climbers, and free-fallers, and why people deliberately do dangerous things? I've been reading up, Lenie. Ever since I got to know you I've been reading up—"

Got to know me?

"—and do you know what thrillseekers have in common? They all say that you haven't lived until you've nearly died. They need the danger. It gives them a rush."

You don't know me at all—

"Some of them are combat veterans, some were hostages for long periods, some just spent a lot of time in dead zones for one reason or another. And a lot of the really compulsive ones—"

Nobody knows me.

"—the ones who can't be happy unless they're on the edge, all the time—a lot of them got started early, Lenie. When they were just children. And you, I bet—you don't even like being touched—"

Go away. Go away.

Ballard puts her hand on Clarke's shoulder. "How long were you abused, Lenie?" she asks gently. "How many years?"

Clarke shrugs off the hand and does not answer. *He didn't mean any harm.* She shifts on the bunk, turning away slightly.

"That's it, isn't it? You don't just have a tolerance to trauma, Lenie. You've got an *addiction* to it. Don't you?"

It only takes Clarke a moment to recover. The 'skin, the eyecaps make it easier. She turns calmly back to Ballard. She even smiles a little.

"*Abused*," she says. "Now *there's* a quaint term. Thought it died out after the Saskatchewan witch-hunts. You some sort of history buff, Jeanette?"

"There's a mechanism," Ballard tells her. "I've been reading about it. Do you know how the brain handles stress, Lenie? It dumps all sorts of addictive stimulants into the bloodstream. Beta-endorphins, opioids. If it happens often enough, for long enough, you get hooked. You can't help it."

Clarke feels a sound in her throat, a jagged coughing noise a bit like tearing metal. After a moment, she recognizes it as laughter.

"I'm not making it up!" Ballard insists. "You can look it up yourself if you don't believe me! Don't you know how many abused children spend their whole lives hooked on wife beaters or self-mutilation or free-fall—"

"And it makes them happy, is that it?" Clarke says, still smiling. "They *enjoy* getting raped, or punched out, or—"

"No, of course you're not happy! But what *you* feel, that's probably the closest you've ever come. So you confuse the two, you look for stress anywhere you can find it. It's physiological addiction, Lenie. You ask for it. You always asked for it."

I ask for it. Ballard's been reading, and Ballard knows: Life is pure electrochemistry. No use explaining how it *feels*. No use explaining that there are far worse things than being beaten up. There are even worse things than being held down and raped by your own father. There are the times between, when nothing happens at all. When he leaves you alone, and you don't know for how long. You sit across the table from him, forcing yourself to eat while your bruised insides try to knit themselves back together; and he pats you on the head and smiles at you, and you know the reprieve's already lasted too long, he's going to come for you tonight, or tomorrow, or maybe the next day.

Of course I asked for it. How else could I get it over with?

"Listen." Clarke shakes her head. "I—" But it's hard to talk, suddenly. She knows what she wants to say; Ballard's not the only one who reads. Ballard can't see it through a lifetime of fulfilled expectations, but there's nothing special about what happened to Lenie Clarke. Baboons and lions kill their own young. Male sticklebacks beat up their mates. Even *insects* rape. It's not abuse, really, it's just—biology.

But she can't say it aloud, for some reason. She tries, and she tries, but in the end all that comes out is a challenge that sounds almost childish:

"Don't you know *anything*?"

"Sure I do, Lenie. I know you're hooked on your own pain, and so you go out there and keep daring the rift to kill you, and eventually it will, don't you see? That's why you shouldn't be here. That's why we have to get you back."

Clarke stands up. "I'm not going back." She turns to the hatch.

Ballard reaches out toward her. "Listen, you've got to stay and hear me out. There's more."

Clarke looks down at her with complete indifference. "Thanks for your concern. But I don't have to stay. I can leave any time I want to."

"You go out there now and you'll give everything away, they're watching us! Haven't you figured it out *yet*?" Ballard's voice is rising. "Listen, they *knew* about you! They were *looking* for someone like you! They've been testing us, they don't know yet what kind of person works out better down here, so they're watching and waiting to see who cracks first! This whole program is still experimental, can't you see that? Everyone they've sent down—you, me, Ken Lubin and Lana Cheung, it's all part of some cold-blooded test—"

"And you're failing it," Clarke says softly. "I see."

"They're *using* us, Lenie—*don't go out there!*"

Ballard's fingers grasp at Clarke like the suckers of an octopus. Clarke pushes them away. She undogs the hatch and pushes it open. She hears Ballard rising behind her.

"*You're sick!*" Ballard screams. Something smashes into the back of Clarke's head. She goes sprawling out into the corridor. One arm smacks painfully against a cluster of pipes as she falls.

She rolls to one side and raises her arms to protect herself. But Ballard just steps over her and stalks into the lounge.

I'm not afraid, Clarke notes, getting to her feet. *She hit me, and I'm not afraid. Isn't that odd—*

From somewhere nearby, the sound of shattering glass.

Ballard's shouting in the lounge. "The experiment's over! Come on out, you fucking ghouls!"

Clarke follows the corridor, steps out of it. Pieces of the lounge mirror hang like great jagged stalactites in their frame. Splashes of glass litter the floor.

On the wall, behind the broken mirror, a fisheye lens takes in every corner of the room.

Ballard is staring into it. "Did you hear me? I'm not playing your stupid games any more! I'm through performing!"

The quartzite lens stares back impassively.

So you were right, Clarke muses. She remembers the sheet in Ballard's cubby. *You figured it out, you found the pickups in your own cubby, and Ballard, my dear friend, you didn't tell me.*

How long have you known?

Ballard looks around, sees Clarke. "You've got *her* fooled, all right," she snarls at the fisheye, "but *she's* a goddamned basket case! She's not even sane! Your little tests don't impress *me* one fucking bit!"

Clarke steps toward her.

"Don't call me a basket case," she says, her voice absolutely level.

"That's what you *are*!" Ballard shouts. "You're sick! That's why you're down here! They *need* you sick, they depend on it, and you're so far gone you can't see it! You hide everything behind that—that *mask* of yours, and you sit there like some masochistic jellyfish and just take anything anyone dishes out—you *ask* for it—"

That used to be true, Clarke realizes as her hands ball into fists. *That's the strange thing.* Ballard begins to back away; Clarke advances, step by step. *It wasn't until I came down here that I learned that I could fight back. That I could win. The rift taught me that, and now Ballard has too—*

"Thank you," Clarke whispers, and hits Ballard hard in the face.

Ballard goes over backwards, collides with a table. Clarke calmly steps forward. She catches a glimpse of herself in a glass icicle; her capped eyes seem almost luminous.

"Oh Jesus," Ballard whimpers. "Lenie, I'm *sorry*."

Clarke stands over her. "Don't be," she says. She sees herself as some sort of exploding schematic, each piece neatly labeled. *So much anger in here*, she thinks. *So much hate. So much to take out on someone.*

She looks at Ballard, cowering on the floor.

"I think," Clarke says, "I'll start with you."

But her therapy ends before she can even get properly warmed up. A sudden noise fills the lounge, shrill, periodic, vaguely familiar. It takes a moment for Clarke to remember what it is. She lowers her foot.

Over in the Communications cubby, the telephone is ringing.

Jeanette Ballard is going home today.

For half an hour the 'scaphe has been dropping deeper into midnight. Now the Comm monitor shows it settling like a great bloated tadpole onto Beebe's docking assembly. Sounds of mechanical copulation reverberate and die. The overhead hatch drops open.

Ballard's replacement climbs down, already mostly 'skinned, staring impenetrably from eyes without pupils. His gloves are off; his 'skin is open to the forearms. Clarke sees the faint scars running along his wrists, and smiles a bit inside.

Was there another Ballard up there, waiting, she wonders, *in case I was the one who didn't work out?*

Out of sight down the corridor, a hatch hisses open. Ballard appears in shirtsleeves, one eye swollen shut, carrying a single suitcase. She seems about to say something, but stops when she sees the newcomer. She looks at him for a moment. She nods briefly. She climbs into the belly of the 'scaphe without a word.

Nobody calls down to them. There are no salutations, no morale-boosting small talk. Perhaps the crew have been briefed. Perhaps they've figured it out on their own. The docking hatch swings shut. With a final clank, the 'scaphe disengages.

Clarke walks across the lounge and looks into the camera. She reaches between mirror fragments and rips its power line from the wall.

We don't need this any more, she thinks, and she knows that somewhere far away, someone agrees.

She and the newcomer appraise each other with dead white eyes.

"I'm Lubin," he says at last.

Ballard was right again, she realizes. *Untwisted, we'd be of no use at all...*

But she doesn't really mind. She won't be going back.

OUTTRO:
EN ROUTE TO DYSTOPIA
WITH THE ANGRY OPTIMIST

I'm quite a cheerful guy in person. Apparently people are surprised by this.

I don't know what they were expecting: Some aging goth in eyeliner and black leather, maybe. A wannabe hipster born a generation out of synch. But insofar as I'm known at all, I seem to be known as The Guy Who Writes The Depressing Stories. My favorite thumbnail of that sentiment comes from James Nicoll—"Whenever I find my will to live becoming too strong, I read Peter Watts"—but the dude's hardly alone in his opinion. While mulling over what to put in this essay I did a quick Google search for the descriptors commonly applied to my writing. I list a few for illustrative purposes:

Brutal
Dark (frequently "unrelentingly" so)
Paranoid
Nightmarish
Relentless
The blackest depths of the human psyche
Ugly
Savage
Misanthropic
Dystopian

Those last two get used a *lot*. Googling my name in conjunction with misanthropy and its variants nets around ten thousand hits; "Peter Watts AND dystopian OR dystopic" returns almost 150,000 (although presumably, not all of them can be about me).

I submit that this is a serious mischaracterization.

Harlan Ellison opened one of his collections[1] with a hyperbolic Author's Warning about the emotional distress you risked if you read the whole book in a single sitting. That is not me. I would not pull that shit on you—because quite honestly, I don't think my stuff *is* especially depressing.

Look at the stories in this volume. "The Things" is fan fiction, an homage to one of my favorite movies and also—to my own surprise—a rumination on the missionary impulse. "Nimbus" is pure unresearched brain fart: an off-the-cuff fantasy seeded by a former girlfriend who looked out the window one day and said, *Wow, those thunderclouds almost look alive*. "The Eyes of God" asks whether we should define a monster by its impulses, or its actions. And "The Island" started out as a raspberry blown at all those lazy-ass writers who fall back on stargates to deal with the distance issue. None of these stories focuses on dystopia in the sense that, say, John Brunner's *The Sheep Look Up* does.

There's wonder here, too. A diaphanous life-form big enough to envelop a star; mermaids soaring through luminous nightscapes on the ocean floor; a misguided Thing whose evolutionary biology redeems Lamarck. Even the idea of a vast, slow intelligence in the clouds has a certain Old Testament beauty to it. Whether the stories themselves succeed is for you to judge—but the things they attempt to describe verge, to my mind at least, on the sublime.

(It must also be admitted that there's some pretty crappy writing in these pages as well. In particular, the emo and overwrought "Flesh Made Word" has not aged well. I'm a bit mystified that the good folks at Tachyon chose to include it in a collection presumably intended to be read for pleasure. Still. Everyone's got to start somewhere.)

The worldview that supports these stories may not be to every-

---

[1] *Deathbird Stories*, if you must know.

one's taste. People aren't used to seeing their noblest dreams and aspirations reduced to the deterministic sparking of chemicals in a bone bowl, for example. Some might resist the thought that our brain stems continue to call the shots, no matter what that spoiled petulant neocortex keeps insisting. The most fundamental underpinnings of human biology—that evolution tinkered us into existence using the same hit-and-miss processes that shaped every other life-form on the planet—are downright offensive to some. But these are not especially dark thoughts where I come from. It's just biology: neutral, empirical, *useful*. I've grown up with these ideas; I think they're *neat*. I've never felt like opening my wrists when I write the stuff. If you feel that way when reading it, well, that's your problem.

I'll grant that you may not want to live in some of these worlds. I wouldn't want to bunk up with Walter White, either; that doesn't make *Breaking Bad* a piece of dystopian story-telling. Backdrop isn't story; it's not even theme. I'm a dystopian writer? Might as well insist that *CSI* is a show about automotive engineering because cars figure so prominently in every episode.

And it's just as well, because truth be told, I'm not very *good* at writing dystopias. For one thing, my worlds embody an almost Pollyannaesque view of human nature.

Consider: We live in a world where planet-spanning financial institutions screen job applicants for symptoms of sociopathy— not to weed out the sociopaths, but to *recruit* them. Even after those institutions ran the global economy off a cliff—knowingly, as it turns out—the bodies ostensibly set up to regulate them have stated explicitly that no matter what laws were broken, no matter what damage was done, nobody's going to jail. In terms of despots running the asylum, you can't get much more explicit than that—and these are the *good* guys, the leaders of the so-called "free world."

But you won't find any Goldman Sachses in my work. No Dick Cheneys or Osama bin Ladens either. Nobody starts wars under false pretences to enrich their buddies in the oil industry; nobody justifies mass murder by invoking the divine. The pope rates a brief mention near the end of the Rifters trilogy, but only to establish that he's fled into exile, reviled and hunted for his corporation's traditional abuse of the helpless; another instance of sunny naivety in my world-building, perhaps.

Bad things do happen in Wattsworld, of course, but generally to avert worse ones. Jasmine Fitzgerald guts her husband like a fish, but only to save his life. The nameless narrator of "Repeating the Past" deliberately induces PTSD in his grandson, but only to save his soul. Patricia Rowan (from the Rifters books again) may authorize the destruction of the Pacific Northwest and enough human collateral to put the Iraq war to shame, but she's not doing it to pad her bank account; she's trying to save the goddamn *world*. Any of the half-dozen people who read *βehemoth*—alert for classic cardboard villainy— might point to the unleashed sexual sadism of Achilles Desjardins, but even he wasn't to blame for what he did. He was a profoundly moral individual whose conscience was neurochemically excised by someone who (again, with the best of intentions) only wanted to set him free.

I can't write real villains. I tried, once. I based one of *Starfish*'s characters on someone I knew in real life. No one too extreme of course, no rapist or murderer: just a slimy little opportunist who made a career out of taking credit for other people's work and customizing his scientific opinions to suit the highest bidder. But I wasn't up to capturing even that penny-ante level of perfidy; writing the character as I saw him, he came across as a mustache-twirling cutout. The only way I could sell him to myself was to give the character more depth, make him more sympathetic, than his inspiration was in real life.

I can't do fundamentalists very well either. I try to describe a biblical creationist and end up with a condescending cartoon scribbled by a smug elitist. So characters who *do* survive to publication all come across as products of some parallel timeline where even the garbage collectors have BScs. Lenie Clarke may be a glorified pipe-fitter, but she'd never deny the existence of climate change. Kim and Andrew Goravec are pretty crappy parents, but not so crappy that you'd ever catch them at an anti-vaccine rally. Even Jess's nameless widowed dad—hunkered down against vast forces he can only dimly comprehend—regards sex in curiously erudite terms: "just another pair of mammals, trying to maximize our fitness before the other shoe dropped."

And yet, the world is in the mess it's in largely because real people *do* deny climate change and evolution, because 85 percent of the North American population believes in an invisible sky fairy who sends you to Space Disneyland after you die, so who gives a shit about the eastern beach tiger beetle? Here in reality those folks make up the majority; they're nowhere to be found in Wattsworld.[2] You could argue that I don't write about real people at all. For all their personal demons, for all the squalor of their surroundings, my characters are more like some kind of human Platonic ideals.

You could also argue that, having spent most of my adult life hanging out with scientists and academics, my range is just too limited to craft any other kind of character. Fair enough.

I'm not claiming that I don't tell my stories against a dystopian backdrop. Take the Rifters trilogy, for example. The desperate rearguard against ongoing environmental collapse, the neurochemically enslaved bureaucrats deciding which part of the world they'll incinerate today to hold back the latest plague, the exploitation of abuse victims to run power plants on the deep-ocean floor—none of this is the stuff of Hallmark Theatre. But in a very real sense, these are not *my* inventions; they are essential features of any plausible vision of the future. The thing that distinguishes science fiction, after all—what sets it apart from magic realism and horror and the rest of speculative horde—is that it is *fiction* based on *science*. It has to be at least semiplausible in its extrapolations from *here* to *there*.

Where can we go, from *here*? Where can we go, starting with seven billion hominids who can't control their appetites, who wipe out thirty species a day with the weight of their bootprints, who are too busy rejecting evolution and building killer drones to notice that the icecaps are melting? How do you write a plausible near-future in which we somehow stopped the flooding and the water wars, in

---

[2] Actually, that's not quite true; my next novel centers around the existence of an omnipotent, miracle-performing god, and the very smart folks who study it. But I can assure you that the god of *Echopraxia* is far removed from your run-of-the-mill scripture-based deity.

which we *didn't* wipe out entire ecosystems and turn millions into environmental refugees?

You can't. That ship—that massive, lumbering, world-sized ship—has already sailed, and it turns so very slowly. The only way you can head off those consequences by 2050 is by telling a tale in which we got serious about climate change back in the nineteen-seventies—and then you're not talking science fiction any more, you're talking fantasy.

So if my writing tends toward the dystopic it's not because I'm in love with dystopias; it's because reality has forced dystopia upon me. A ravaged environment is no longer optional when writing about the near future. All I can do now is imagine how my characters might react to the hand they've been dealt. The fact that they resort to implanting false memories and neurological shackles in their employees, that they may order the immolation of ten thousand innocent refugees—that's not what makes dystopia. What makes dystopia is an inheritance in which these awful actions are the *best ones available*, where every other alternative is even worse; a world where people commit mass murder not because they are sadists or sociopaths, but because they are trying to do the least harm. It is not a world my characters built. It is only the world we left them.

There are no real villains in Wattsworld. If you want villains, you know where to look.

Dystopia is not always an unhappy place. There are, as it happens, certain dystopias in which it's perfectly possible to be happy as a clam. Vast numbers of people go through life never even realizing that they're in one, might live through the real-time decay from freedom to tyranny and never notice the change.

It basically comes down to wanderlust.

Imagine your life as a path extending through time and society. To either side are fences festooned with signs: *No Trespassing, Keep Off the Grass, Thou Shalt Not Kill*. These are the constraints on your behavior, the legal limits of acceptable conduct. You are free to wander anywhere between these barriers—but cross one and you risk the weight of the law.

Now imagine that someone starts moving those fences closer together.

How you react—whether you even notice—depends entirely on how much you wandered beforehand. A lot of people never deviate from the center of the path their whole lives, wouldn't deviate even if there *were* no fences. They're the ones who can never understand what all those fringe radicals are whining about; after all, *their* lives haven't changed any. It makes no difference to them whether the fences are right on the shoulder or out past the horizon.

For the rest of us, though, it's only a matter of time before you wander back to a point you've always been free to visit in the past, only to find a fence suddenly blocking your way.

When that happens, you might be surprised at how close those things have crept when you weren't looking. I know I was. I'm not what you'd call a hardened criminal. I've found myself in the little white room at US Customs somewhat more often than might be expected from a "random" selection process, but I suspect that's just because your average customs agent doesn't quite know what to make of the self-employed ("Biostatistical consultant and writer? What the hell is that supposed to be?")[3] I may have once been guilty of associating with tewwowists, back when my dad was still alive—a retired preacher and the General Secretary of the Baptist Convention of Ontario and Quebec, I'm told he earned a CSIS[4] file for his efforts on behalf of unpatriotic groups like Amnesty International—but none of Obama's flying terminators were likely to get all twinkly-eyed when they ran me through facial recognition.

Which is not to say that I was *intellectually* unaware of the ongoing erosion of civil rights on this continent. Only that, as a well-educated

[3] In more recent years—back before I was banned outright from entering your fine country—I just decided to have fun with it and list "masturbation" as one of my Professional Activities. In such cases it's generally a good idea to show up at least four hours before departure.
[4] Canada's equivalent of the CIA, albeit with an annual budget of about $43.26. Known primarily for pulling into traffic after forgetting the briefcase full of national secrets they'd just parked on the roof of their shiny black sedan while unlocking the driver's door.

white dude with a relatively sheltered life, my awareness was more academic than visceral, more second- than first-hand. So while returning to Toronto with a friend after a trip to Nebraska, I expected to be stopped at the Canadian border, by Canadian Customs. I expected that if they decided to search the vehicle, they'd inform me first, and ask me to pop the trunk.[5]

And when none of this happened—when I was pulled over by US border guards two kilometres from the Canadian border, and looked over my shoulder to find eager guards already going through our luggage like a swarm of army ants—I expected no real trouble when I got out of the car to ask what was going on.

I imagine a number of readers rolling their eyes at this point. *Well, of* course. *You* never *get out of a vehicle unless ordered. You* never *make eye contact. You* never *ask questions; if you do, you deserve what you get.* I have nothing to say to these people. To the rest of you I say: see what we've come to. We have criminalized the expectation of reasonable communication with those who are supposed to protect us. *And people approve.*

(One of the things we tend to forget about Ray Bradbury's classic *Fahrenheit 451* is that the banning of books was not imposed against the will of the people by some tyrannical authority. The grass roots in that dystopian novel didn't *want* to read.)

I learned more than I wanted to about Michigan's legal system in the months that followed. I learned of a miraculous little statute—750.81(d) by name—which bundles everything from murder down to "failure to comply with a lawful command" into one felonious little package. It spends almost half a page defining what constitutes a "person"; nowhere does it define what makes a command "lawful." If you happen to be crossing the border and a "person" tells you to get down on all fours and bark like a dog, you might want to keep that in mind. (Fun fact: according to US law, "the border" is actually a *zone* extending a hundred miles from the actual line on the map. The rights-free atmosphere one encounters at Customs—warrantless searches, detention without

---

[5] Yes, this is the official protocol. It was confirmed on the record by a spokesperson for US Customs who was being interviewed about this very case.

cause, the whole shebang—extends throughout that band. If the Border Patrol decides on a whim to kick in the door of some poor sap living in Potsdam, there's not a lot anyone can do about it; it's a "border search," exempt from the usual checks and balances.)

In the end, of course, I was convicted. Not of assault, despite what you may have heard. The trial established that there was no aggression on my part, not so much as an expletive or a raised voice, despite prosecutorial allegations that I "resisted," that I "choked an officer."[6] What the prosecution fell back on, ultimately, was that just after I'd been repeatedly punched in the face and just before I got maced, I'd been ordered to get on the ground—and instead of immediately complying, I'd said, "What is the *problem*?" It didn't matter that I *had* been punched in the face, or that the guards themselves had lied under oath. (The jury threw out their testimony wholesale because—as one of them stated on the record—"they couldn't keep their stories straight.") It didn't matter that DHS itself, called up from Detroit in hopes of boosting the charges (my arrest sheet originally accused me of "Assaulting a Federal Officer") refused to participate in the case once they'd interviewed those involved. It didn't even matter that jury members publicly opined that the *guards* should have been the ones on trial. 750.81(d) forced them to convict regardless.

It's important to note that what happened to me was *not* an abuse of the law. The law functioned exactly as it was supposed to; it gave carte blanche to authority, while criminalizing any act—even asking a question—short of immediate and unthinking compliance. We live in a society where laws are designed to protect not the populace, but the right to *abuse* the populace under almost any circumstance.

I'm focusing on the US here because that's where I encountered my own personal fence; it's also where most of you happen to live. But lest you think I'm just another smug Canuck taking a fashionable dump on the Ugly American, let me emphasize that I hold my own country in no greater esteem. The Canadian government routinely muzzles its

---

[6] To this day I remain puzzled as to why they'd even make those allegations in the first place; they must have known that my passenger saw the whole thing, and would call bullshit. Which is exactly what happened.

own scientists and is currently busy dismantling even the rudimentary environmental protections with which we once made do. My home town of Toronto was the site of Canada's largest violations of civil rights, during the G20 protests in 2010: over a thousand people arrested and detained, the vast majority of them without charge.[7] Hundreds kettled for hours in a freezing downpour: ordered to leave, prevented from leaving, arrested for noncompliance. Preemptive gunpoint roustings in private bedrooms, 4 a.m. arrests on the chance that some activist might otherwise commit a crime later in the day. And what kind of party would it have been without the traditional beating of unarmed, unresisting protestors by officers with obscured badge numbers, who then leveled charges of "assaulting police" on their victims? Thank the gods for cell-phone cameras. Thank the gods for YouTube.

Should you be tempted to suggest that North America—with all its authoritarian abuses—is still a paragon of liberty next to the likes of Iran or communist China or North Korea, I will not argue the point. In fact, I will emphasize it. From the saturation surveillance of central London to the Toronto PD arresting people for failure to obey search-and-seizure laws that don't actually exist, the systemic abuse of civil rights seems to be a feature of freedom-loving democracies everywhere. This, apparently, is the best we can do.

I'm still quite a cheerful guy in person. Apparently people are surprised by this.

Especially now.

I've been asked if recent experience has altered my worldview, if my tango with the US justice system might birth even darker visions to come. I don't think so. After all, it's not as if I was unaware of this stuff before it happened to me; one or two journalists have even highlighted parallels between my real-life experiences and the things I've inflicted on fictional protagonists, as though my imaginings of police brutality were somehow prescient because they happened to occur in the future.

---

[7] 1,118 arrested; 231 charged; 24 guilty pleas; 0 convictions after trial.

If anything, though, my perspective has *brightened*. I came out of it relatively unscathed, after all; I was convicted, but despite the prosecution's best efforts I didn't go to jail. I'm not welcome back in the US any time soon—maybe not ever—but at this point that's more of a badge of honor than a professional impediment.

In a very real way, I *won*.

Most would not have. Most people, up against an enemy bureaucracy with deep pockets and only the most token accountability, would have been swallowed whole. There would have been surrender regardless of guilt; desperate plea-bargains to avoid crippling court costs. If the accused did somehow summon the audacity to fight back there would have been a lopsided battle and captivity and years of debt. Michigan bills you for your time behind bars: thirty bucks a day, as if you were staying at a fucking Motel 6, as though you'd chosen to bunk up for the room service and free cable. The longer you're incarcerated, the higher the bill they shove in your face when you get out.

I've stopped getting those little yellow cards in the mail. Maybe they gave up, maybe they lost track of me when I moved, maybe the fact that I'm on the far side of an international boundary makes me not worth going after for the price of one measly night in the clink.[8] Those poor bastards I shared beans and Kool-Aid with, though: no protective borders, no sanctuary, no breaks for *them*. A year in jail and they walk out ten thousand dollars in debt. And even *they* have it pretty damn easy next to a family friend whose activist husband was disappeared in Latin America, who was gang-raped and gave birth in jail. Conversations with such folk leave you a bit less inclined to whinge about the injustice of Michigan's legal leg-hold traps.

I had so much help. Half the internet woke up on my behalf. Thanks to Dave Nickle and Cory Doctorow and Patrick Nielson Hayden and John Scalzi—thanks to all the myriad folk who boosted the signal and

---

[8] From the Dept. of Small Worlds: there were books in my cell. Most had been picked over for use as pillows (which aren't allowed in the St. Clair County Jail), but amongst the remaining dregs—*Good News for Modern Man!* and *Mr. God, This Is Anna*—I did make one anomalous finding: an ARC from Tor. Some kind of Benchleyesque thriller about the Loch Ness Monster. If anyone can remember the title, drop me a line.

chipped in to my defense fund[9]—I walked away no poorer than when it all began. I walked away *heartened*: look at all those friends I didn't know I had. See how obviously corrupt the authorities were shown to be in the court of public opinion. See what outrage and anger can accomplish, when the rocks are kicked over and their undersides exposed to the light (Port Huron now posts signs warning travelers of upcoming exit searches; that's something, at least). So many reasons for a white middle-class guy with influential friends to have hope.

And a lot of folks in this privileged demographic *do* seem to have hope. I once attended an event in which Cory Doctorow and China Miéville chatted about the inherent goodness of humanity, about their shared belief that the vast majority of people are decent and honorable. Another time I was the one on stage, debating Minister Faust on the subject of whether science fiction could be "a happy place," and the same sentiment resurfaced: Minister attested that the vast majority of people *he'd* encountered were *good* folks. The problems we face as a species, he said—the intolerance, the short-sighted greed, the accelerating threats of climate change and strip-mined ecosystems and floating islands of immortal plastic garbage the size of the fucking Sargasso—are thanks to those few despots and sociopaths who sit atop the world's power structures, shitting on the world for their own profit.

I concede the point, to some extent at least; even in the depths of the system arrayed against me, bright spots ignited where I least expected them. That one border guard who refused to fall in line with her fellows, who testified that she didn't see me committing the acts of which I stood accused. The jurors who, having voted to convict, spoke out publicly on my behalf (one of them stood at my side during sentencing, in a show of support that netted her an extended ordeal of police harassment and home invasion). A judge who set me free with a small fine, admitting that I was the kind of guy he'd like to sit down and have a beer with.

Reasons to hope. The anger remains, though, even if all those other folks are right about the goodness of grassroots humanity. *Especially* if they're right; because what do you call a world of decent folks ground

---

[9] Some of whom are *still* owed thank you e-mails, three years later.

beneath the boot-heels of despots and sociopaths if *not* dystopia? You can trot out your folksy tales of good hearts and personal redemption, your small hopeful candles flickering down at street level; I can't help noticing the darkness pressing down from overhead, the global dysfunction that throws the world on its side despite the angels of our better natures. I don't even entirely believe in those angels, not really, not even down here in the happy realm of the little people. Zimbardo and Milgram didn't create thugs and torturers with their infamous experiments; they merely uncovered them. And it's not just psychos and sickos who level the forests and flush their shit into the ocean and fire up their dinosaur-burning SUVs for a two-block drive to the local Target. Those plastic islands in the Pacific have grass roots all over them.

Down in the basement, my anger never goes away; and that's informative in a way you might not expect, because I don't believe true misanthropes generally feel that way. Bitter, sure. Cynical, deeply. But angry?

You may not think much of tapeworms, but you don't generally get mad at them. You might wipe cancer off the face of the earth if you could, but not because the thought of cancer leaves you spluttering with rage. You don't blame something for doing what it does, what it's always done, what you *expect* it to do.

You only get mad if you expected better.

Apparently my writing spells *misanthrope* to a fair number of readers. It's my anger, I think, that puts the lie to that label. It winds through so much of my fiction: in the collapsing civilization of the Rifters trilogy, in the Island's betrayal of Sunday's faith, in an anonymous ambassador's paradigm-shifting realization that back-stabbing is just the way we do things out here. You wouldn't find it in the work of a true misanthrope; such a person would just wrinkle his nose, shrug, turn away with contemptuous indifference. *Well, of course. What did you expect?*

It's why I can't pull off convincing villains. It's why I got out of that car back in 2009 even though everyone knows the rules, even though we've all heard the stories: *Don't fuck with those assholes at the border, don't even make eye contact with them. You should hear what happened to me last year...*

It's because down in my gut, I still can't quite believe that villains do exist. No matter what I've read and heard, I just can't believe that you could get shit-kicked for asking a simple, reasonable question.

Most of the time, of course, I'm dead wrong. And so I get angry, because I expected better. I *still* expect better, even now. And in what might be charitably characterized as an ongoing act of noblest stupidity, I continue to act as if people *were* better, in worlds both fictional and real.

You know what that makes me, by definition?

An optimist.